RUN
FOR HER
LIFE

BOOKS BY RUHI CHOUDHARY

RUHI CHOUDHARY

RUN FOR HER LIFE

bookouture

Published by Bookouture in 2025

An imprint of Storyfire Ltd.
Carmelite House
50 Victoria Embankment
London EC4Y 0DZ

www.bookouture.com

The authorised representative in the EEA is Hachette Ireland
8 Castlecourt Centre
Dublin 15 D15 XTP3
Ireland
(email: info@hbgi.ie)

ISBN: 978-1-80550-069-8
eBook ISBN: 978-1-80550-068-1

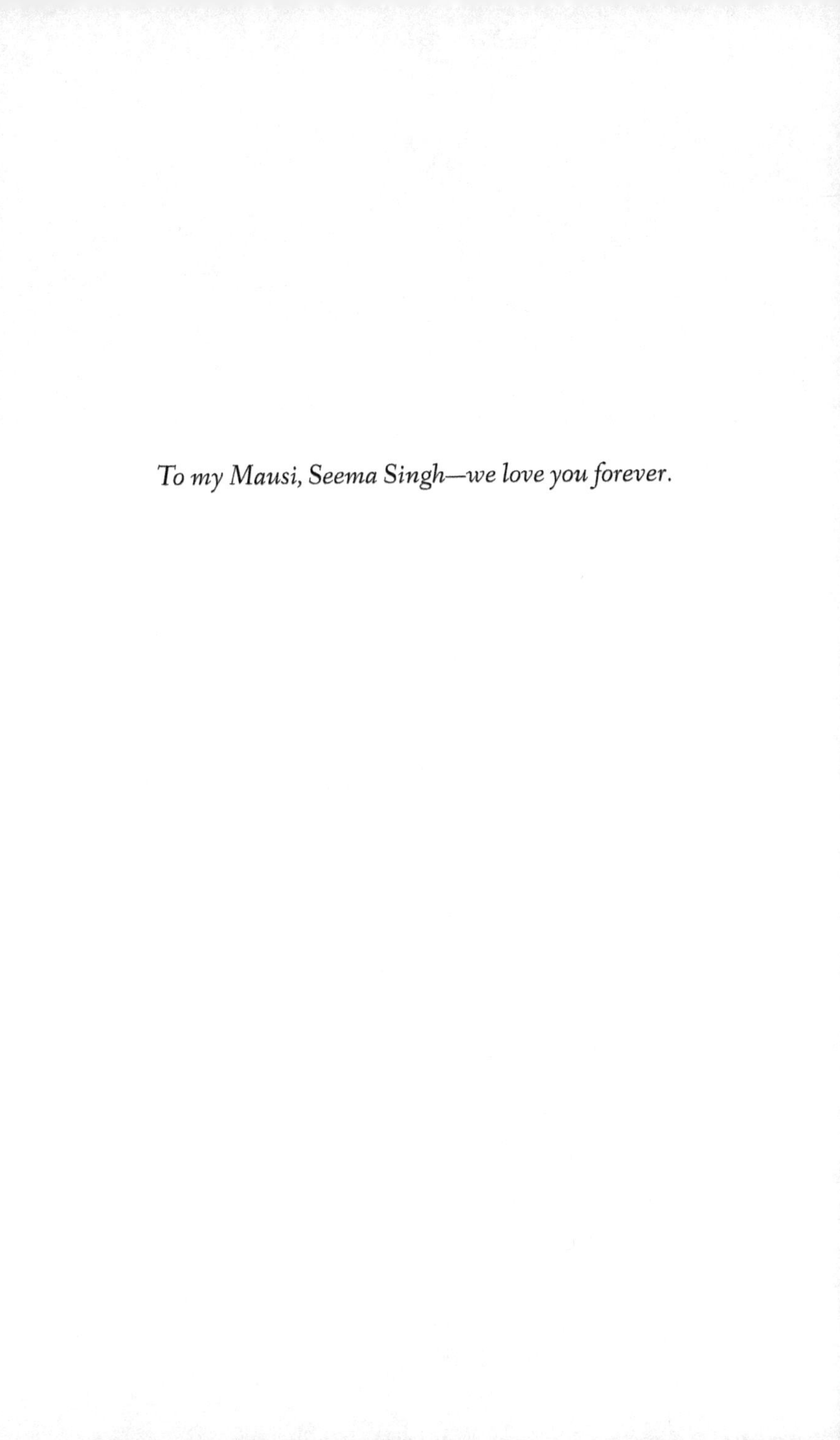

To my Mausi, Seema Singh—we love you forever.

PROLOGUE

Zoe's fingers were covered in something sticky. She slumped down the wall, landing on the ground with a thud. A metallic whiff clogged her nose. She lifted her trembling hand to inspect it.

It was covered in blood.

Her thumping heart had slowed into a sluggish rhythm. A chill enveloped her. She traced her hand down her abdomen until she found it. The hole in her stomach. It was tiny but it emitted a steady stream of blood, which gushed out with every disjointed breath she took.

She stared up into the sky. The gold light was fading quickly. A wall of trees surrounded her. Its shadow encroached closer, threatening to engulf her. There was no one around—not anymore. No one to hear her whimper, no one to watch her bleed.

The gunshot was the last booming sound that had echoed in this remote part of the woods. Now only birds chirped. The cold seeped into her bones and darkness lingered at the periphery.

She felt like she was sinking. She was shivering and thought she would throw up at any moment.

"Storm!" Someone materialized from the woods. A voice she recognized. Her vision sharpened as he drew closer. "Oh my God." Aiden's usual stoic face was frantic and alarmed. He hovered over her, his hand shooting out to put pressure on her bleeding stomach. "Just stay with me."

"I'm... I want to sleep," she whispered, her eyes beginning to close.

"No! Eyes on me, Storm," he roared, pressing his phone to his ear. "I need an ambulance. My partner has been shot in the stomach."

He was losing her. And then Aiden's head whipped up as he looked behind her.

"Who's there?" he called out, his free hand searching for Zoe's gun. A twig snapped. Footsteps pounded. Aiden frowned and raised his hands in the air in surrender. "Who are you?"

A familiar voice replied, "Who the hell are *you* and why did you shoot her?"

ONE

PAST

The woman took out a tube of lipstick from her pocket and uncapped it. She smeared it across her lips and smacked them together. The bus station was a lonesome, glass structure standing in the middle of the winding road lined with pine trees on either side; their tips resembled spikes piercing into the night sky dotted with glittering stars.

She was the only one sitting on the bench. Her sharp eyes gazing around the darkness, always searching for danger, always plotting a way out. From the corner of her eye, she spotted a bedraggled man with worn shoes, clumps of dirty hair, and stained, tattered clothes approach her. The stench of urine and cigarettes wafted up her nose. He collapsed onto the end of the bench and stared at her. She ignored him, avoiding eye contact, pretended that this homeless man didn't exist, just like the rest of society did every day.

They were alone on a spooky night. Halloween. But it didn't scare her. Nothing scared her.

Bright lights appeared at the end of the road, growing larger.

The outline of a bus crystallized against the darkness and the engine coughed as it arrived at the stop. The doors swung open with a creak, and a gangly boy with a long neck and acid-washed jeans and an oversized sweatshirt got off.

"Michael!" The woman beamed. "For a minute I thought you wouldn't come."

"It was hard to get away from my folks," he said, his Adam's apple bobbing as he swallowed hard. The woman realized just how young he was.

"Well, let's have some fun." She draped her arm over his shoulder. "Hope you did your math homework. I'll be checking tomorrow."

He grinned, his braces gleaming. "I wouldn't have showed up if I hadn't. I know how strict you are."

"Work and fun go hand in hand."

"Don't you ever get scared?" he asked, looking over his shoulder at the homeless man, who was still sitting on the bench. "Alone at night like this."

He was so innocent and caring. Just sixteen years old. A tiny tremor of guilt disturbed her calm demeanor for a fleeting second. "Nothing scares me, Michael."

"You're so cool." Then his eyes darted ahead to the glimmering lights in the distance.

She followed his gaze to the pocket of magic—the Ferris wheel, like a luminous circle, towering lights flashing green, red, and blue, a swirl of neon and golden lights blinking in hypnotic patterns. A burst of fireworks flared in the sky, casting a glow on their faces.

"This is going to be the best night ever!" Michael exclaimed.

"Yes, it will be." The woman's voice softened around the edges.

Her pulse quickened as she shoved a hand in her pocket and wrapped it around the cold, unyielding metal grip of a gun.

TWO

NOW

Zoe peered into the dark pit of the well, into a tunnel of pitch blackness with no end in sight. Vines and tendrils extended into the lip of the well, filling the cracks running along the glistening, weathered stones.

"Help!" a young girl's voice called out from the darkness. "Help me, please!"

Zoe wanted to jump in. But fear had her body locked. She swallowed hard and braced herself. But before she could take the plunge, her mother, Rachel, breezed past her.

"Emily!" Rachel shrieked, panic-stricken. "Emily! Honey!"

Zoe was standing inches away from her mother, but she hadn't noticed her. Rachel's face was streaked with tears, her hair was in disarray, and her breaths a tangled mess. She found a rope coiled by her feet and threw it down the well. "Grab the rope, Emily!"

Silence fell as Zoe watched her mother desperately shake the rope and pull at it with all her strength. Rachel was a muscular woman—not merely toned from Pilates or yoga. There was a dexterity with which she handled the rope. In hindsight, Zoe tried to spot the smallest things about Rachel that had been cloaked over the years. There was something about her mother she didn't know—something that had forced her to go into witness protection for ten years, something that had got her murdered.

Zoe raised her hand to touch her mother. A touch that had been fading for twenty years but hadn't entirely disappeared. Before her fingers made contact, she slipped and toppled over the edge of the well, hurtling through the darkness.

"Ah!" Zoe shot up from the bed, her back as taut and straight as an arrow. She blinked profusely as fractured pieces of her nightmare dissolved and reality closed in.

She was in her bedroom. Early morning light seeped in through the curtains, bathing the room in a soft, golden hue. Her alarm was set to go off in exactly one minute but once again she woke up just before. She pinched the bridge of her nose, pain blossoming behind her eyelids.

Same nightmare every single night. Rachel and Emily.

Filing it away, she grabbed her hand wraps and headed to the living room where a punchbag hung from the ceiling.

Smack.

Smack.

Smack.

Rage burned through her as she struck the bag over and over until her knuckles ached. She didn't want to think about the nightmare, Rachel, Emily, Keith.

For one damn moment, she just wanted to forget what she carried around with her all the time.

Her phone kept pinging. She ignored it and focused on thrashing the bag until the hinge loosened. There was no technique or skill to her punches anymore. It was pure emotion— reckless and uninhibited. When she could no longer ignore the pings, she let out a frustrated breath and checked her phone.

Aiden. Again.

A: Storm, what's going on?

A: Why haven't you reported it yet?

A: I can help.

Ever since Aiden had found her in the motel room attacked and injured a month ago, he was constantly pressing her to find out what exactly had transpired. But she had no intention of involving him in this. She ignored his messages and fired up her laptop.

A four-week witch-hunt and she had finally tracked down the man she was after. A picture and a name came into focus on the screen.

Viktor Axenov. The man who had beaten her black and blue and threatened to kill her if she didn't stop looking into her mother's murder.

THREE

"I want a seat on the board," David said in a tight voice.

Dawn ground her teeth, her grip on the shears unwavering as she trimmed the hedges in the garden. Leaves fluttered at her feet in an uneven pile before dancing in the air. It was another gloomy day in Pineview Falls. A gray sky with spinning clouds and whooshing wind. "Getting a seat on the board isn't like floating in on a breeze, David."

"I've worked hard, Mother. You know it."

Dawn continued shaping the hedge. "The problem with your generation is your sense of entitlement." She dropped the shears on the ground and removed her gloves with a huff. "Working hard doesn't mean you are deserving. You have to be good at what you do." She turned around to find his face flushing red and his thick eyebrows knitted in a frown. "When I was your age, I was busy busting my ass trying to make ends meet because your father had dragged us into debt. And you know what I got in return? His infidelity."

"Yes, yes, I know, Mother. I don't know why we go over this every—"

"Because you are yet to learn that life is unfair," Dawn snapped. "Accept your failures. You aren't ready."

He blanched at her words. "How can I become ready? I care about this company."

Her eyes narrowed as she scrutinized her forty-four-year-old son with a receding hairline, thick round glasses, and unkind eyes, wild with desperation. A longing to prove himself. "There's a board meeting at the end of the week. I need to focus on that first." She had barely slept these past few weeks. It wasn't that long ago when she had woken to the news that had shattered her peace like a smashed mirror. And the last thing Dawn needed right now was her son demanding a share of the pie, only to make the situation worse by his inadequacy. She breezed past him to head back to the office when his voice came again.

"Will you ever forgive me?" His voice cracked.

Dawn's eyes flitted to the secluded alcove on her left with a wrought-iron bench under the dappled shade of a centuries-old oak. A lone wooden swing swayed from a willow branch. The unfurling cobblestone path was bordered by rosebushes. The only sounds were bees humming and water trickling down a tiered fountain. The little corner that Dawn had designed and constructed all by herself. An oasis in the otherwise dreary town of Pineview Falls. The part of the garden that breathed a story.

The story of the child she had lost. Her eyes landed on the grave.

Dawn didn't have the heart to say no. It seemed cruel. So she replied with silence and walked away, feeling lost like an untethered shadow.

* * *

Sheriff Lisa Gray stared at the pamphlet on her desk.

Enter if you're brave. Survive if you can.
Pineview Falls Carnival.

The glossy paper was a splash of colors displaying roller coasters, bumper cars, food stalls of cotton candy and funnel cakes, game stands from ring toss to dunk tanks, and the main attraction dominating the pamphlet: Fun House, a haunted house experience.

Lisa felt shards of glass clog her throat as she swallowed hard. "What has the world come to?" She stared at Fun House, a rusty structure with cracked windows, peeling paint, rotting wooden siding, and cobwebs in corners. The front porch consisted of a caved-in railing, and broken steps that led to a torn screen door.

"I swear, Lisa, she makes me feel like a weekend subscription." The deputy sheriff, Toby, sat across from her, his shoulders tense, his fat fingers interlaced over his beer belly. "Enjoy your limited time as a father. Expires on Sunday at 6 p.m."

She smirked, putting the pamphlet away. "You should check if there's an auto-renew option."

"Very funny," he said flatly.

"You want more time with your kid, go talk to a lawyer."

"Lawyers are snakes in fancy suits," he grumbled, chewing a toothpick. "The last two I spoke with burned a hole in my wallet and used fancy words that went over my head."

"I'll give you a dictionary bonus at Christmas."

"You're in a mood today."

Lisa flipped through the reports piling up on her desk. Delinquent teenagers getting into trouble around town. This wasn't how she had imagined her life would be the day she decided to get into law enforcement. The sparkling glamour surrounding the job had dried up after her first week busting crackheads around town.

Because Pineview Falls was only known for two things: the fire of 1995, and drugs.

"I don't even know if my kid knows that I want to spend more time with him," Toby continued. "The worry you carry constantly when you have a kid... You're lucky you don't have any."

Lisa froze, her breath imprisoned in her chest. Her eyes drifted to Toby who blankly stared out the window that looked onto the back alley of a Chinese restaurant. Little did he know how "lucky" she felt when this morning she got her period—again.

They were interrupted when a deputy waltzed in with a report. "Remember that 911 call yesterday from the man saying his wife hadn't come home after work?"

"Yeah." Lisa uncapped a bottle of painkillers. "What about it?"

"He called again asking if we're looking into it."

Before Lisa could reply, Toby rolled his eyes. "Tell him to stay put and let us do our jobs. Jesus Christ."

Lisa pursed her lips in disapproval, but she didn't chide him. She felt it too—the mundaneness of this colorless brick building blunting her thoughts and curiosity. Sometimes she wondered if she was living the same day over and over again. It was locking up one sallow-skinned, scab-covered man with greasy, patchy hair and arms covered in clusters of dark dots after another. She knew them by name, knew more about them than their pillaged brains did.

But this deputy was young and hungry. He was yet to learn that life only got worse as time went by.

"She's an adult and there is no evidence of foul play. We will wait out the standard twenty-four-hour period since her last sighting," she explained gently. "Just tell him that."

The deputy looked disappointed as he left the office.

"Ah, young blood," Toby said. "The only form of entertainment around here."

Lisa swallowed her pills. "We should bring back hazing. Just to kill some time." She flipped open the dispatcher's report on the call.

The woman's name popped out—Annabelle Stevens. Lisa liked the name and added it to her list. When her phone buzzed with a notification, she saw it was an email from the clinic.

Dear Mrs. Gray,

We hope this email finds you well. Your recent fertility test results from Horizon Fertility Clinic are now available. At this time, we would like to discuss your results with you. Please use the link below to schedule an appointment…

Her vision blurred as she was unable to read the following words. They wanted her to call, which probably meant that the results were bad. A prickle formed in her heart.

How was she going to break the news to her husband?

* * *

Zoe opened a box of donuts lathered in chocolate sauce and icing and brandished it under Simon's nose, which was buried in a file.

He took a deep whiff and looked up. His eyes gleamed with a lazy debauchery. "What do you want?"

She knew Simon's biggest weakness, as it was hers too. Sugar. It was the reason the two had bonded at Quantico when she was training and he was a guest lecturer.

"A favor."

"I figured." He reached for the box, but she whipped it

away and planted herself on the chair across from him. "You're never just nice to me for no reason."

She flashed him an exaggerated smile. "I am, but a bribe goes a long way. Surely, you've learned that as the special agent in charge here."

He chuckled. "Okay, give it to me."

"Viktor Axenov. Do you know the name?" She kept her expression passive. Simon didn't know what had transpired a month ago at Harborwood and she had no intention of telling him. He liked her—a little too much—something that turned her stomach since he was married.

He thought about it. "No. Should I?"

"Can you look into him?" She had tracked down his name from a bus ticket in Harborwood but there was no record of him in the FBI database. "I need anything on him. And I know you have access to a lot more resources than I do."

"Okay..." Simon's eyes narrowed as he twisted on his chair. "This is the part where you tell me why."

"This is the part where I tell you it's personal."

"Come on, Z."

Warmth trickled down her spine when he called her by her nickname, like he did when they were together many years ago. "Please. It's for Gina. My sister. Something's going on. Nothing super serious. But I can't find anything on him. Anything would do. Other than his name, of course."

He blinked and shifted in his seat. "All right. I'll do it." He scribbled the name on a notepad. "Sounds like the name of a Russian mobster. Is Gina's bakery a front for the KGB?"

"The KGB dissolved in 1991."

"Or did it?" His eyes widened.

She snickered. Simon appeared more relaxed to her. She tried not to think too much about why he was in a good mood even though his wife, Nancy, had asked to spend some time apart. Deep down she knew the answer. She knew why Nancy had left. She knew how Simon looked at Zoe and it left her brimming with both shame and pity.

"Thanks, Simon." She stood up and headed back to her desk.

Simon would find something, and she would go from there. She eyed the bustling office of FBI Seattle with suspicion. Like she was waiting for someone to jump out at her. Or someone watching her. She scanned the room for any hint of deception or even the slightest crack in normalcy. She knew she was being watched. That's how that man—Viktor—had forced his way into her motel room, beaten her up, stolen a key to the safety deposit box in Chicago, and warned her to stop trying to find out the truth about what happened to Rachel.

Was she being watched *now*? She must be. Her eyes flitted across the room. Everyone was familiar to her. Her colleagues. Agents and admin staff—all vetted thoroughly. Then why could she sense a hostile gaze on her? Why were the hairs on the back of her neck standing up? Why was her blood bubbling under her skin and making her toes curl?

It was the natural response of a prey sensing a predator. A harsh and heavy presence right over her shoulder.

When she reached her desk, she stopped at the sight of an envelope addressed to her. She tore it open without thinking, spilling the contents onto the desk, and gasped, stepping back.

A lock of blonde hair, neatly tied with a red ribbon. And a note.

Like the snap of an elastic, her mind switched gears. She grabbed the first person walking past and instructed him to find Simon. She didn't see or wait for a response. Her vision tunneled on the lock of hair drizzled with what looked like flecks of dried blood.

Her heart skittered in her chest and her lips quivered. Slowly, she picked up a pen and used it to open the folded piece of paper.

Ticktock goes the clock

Annabelle lies beneath the rock

Weeping roots will not betray.

Once she begged, now she sleeps,

Locked in silence, six feet deep.

Last breath stolen, fingers curled,

Ever rotting, beneath this world.

Marrow blackens, flesh turns stone,

If you find her, you're not alone.

FOUR

Thump.

"Did you touch it?" Simon asked, standing next to her with his hands in his pocket.

Thump.

"No."

Thump.

A small crowd had gathered around Zoe's desk. All eyes glued to the lock of hair and the note. Zoe chewed on her painted nail as she tried to make sense of the contents of the envelope. Her heart thumped in her chest slowly—too slowly. It almost made her lightheaded. There was something very off about this and it wasn't just the spine-tingling note or the bloodied hair.

"Why was it sent to *her?*" she heard someone say behind her.

The words reverberated through Zoe like an electric current. That's what was bothering her. Why *her?*

"All right. Show's over. Back to work. Now," Simon snapped, shepherding the crowd away. "You, stay," he said to one of the junior agents. A muscle in his jaw ticked. "Bag this. It's evidence. Get the lab to test the hair."

Zoe continued to stare at the envelope as a gloved hand picked it up, scooped the contents back inside and took it away. Her eyes zoomed in on a dried fleck of blood that had come away from the hair and lay gleaming on the white desk. "Do you think it's a prank?"

"Could be someone chopped off their hair," Simon said. "Wouldn't be the first time some asshole is trying to screw with us."

"But what if it's not some sick joke?" She looked up at Simon.

His face was grim. "In that case, we're looking at someone dangerous. Sending a lock of hair and a riddle to the FBI... this is a game to them."

She cleared her throat. "I'll check if there's anyone called Annabelle missing in Seattle."

He nodded. "Check at the state level."

Three hours later, Zoe was hunched over her desk with her hands tangled in her curly hair. She had combed through all the databases from Washington State Identification System to the Washington State Patrol Missing and Unidentified Persons Unit. But no one named Annabelle had been reported missing.

Perhaps this was a sick joke. A deranged person with too much free time on their hands had decided to yank Zoe's chain. But who? Who would do this? From the corner of her eye, she saw a colleague sipping on a hot chocolate. Her mouth flooded with saliva. Only sugar could help her think straight.

"Agent Storm!" Simon stuck his head out of his office and beckoned her over.

She took a steadying breath, got up, and walked to his office, closing the door behind her. "I couldn't find anything. Did you?"

"I did." He straightened his tie before sitting. "I made some calls to a few counties. Heard of Pineview Falls?"

"No, I'm from Chicago." She glanced at the lush green view from Simon's office and winced, muttering under her breath, "I have no idea what I'm doing here."

"It's in Lewis County. They didn't file a report as Annabelle has been missing for less than twenty-four hours and no foul play was suspected."

Damn it. "So this is real."

Before Simon could reply, there was a knock on the door. "Come in."

Zoe felt it first—a familiar woodsy scent and a looming, grating presence. And then his voice, which made her nerves sizzle.

"Storm."

She sighed. "Simon, what is he doing here?"

"Nice to see you, too." Dr. Aiden Wesley appeared at her side in his crisply tailored suit, gelled black hair that swooped over his head, and thick glasses concealing eyes that twinkled at her oddities.

"He's the best profiler in the country," Simon muttered. "And the only one who was available to take the case."

"You've got to be kidding me." Zoe crossed her arms.

"Is there a problem?" Simon's eyes bounced between them. "You worked well on the last case."

"*I* have no problem." Aiden shrugged.

"Z?" Simon raised his eyebrows. "I mean... Agent Storm?"

From the corner of her eye, Zoe saw Aiden's jaw clench and unclench at Simon's slip. After her long, deep undercover mission, Zoe had been dispatched to Aiden so that he could help her process her experience, unspool her thoughts, and decide whether she was fit to return to duty. That was the first time Aiden had gotten dangerously close to what Zoe was hiding. The second time was when they worked a case together and Aiden sensed that Simon had lingering feelings for Zoe—and she was aware of them.

"Fine by me." She plastered on her best professional smile. "Is this our case though? What did the sheriff say?"

"Lisa Gray. She's out of her depth on this one. It's a small town and a small county. They're more used to dealing with farm disputes and meth labs. Either way, this evidence was sent to us. This is our jurisdiction now."

"To this office?" Aiden craned his head.

"To Zoe specifically," Simon said.

Zoe felt Aiden's curious gaze and wanted to wilt. If there was anyone who could unravel her meticulously crafted cheerful mood, it was Aiden Wesley.

"Hot chocolate?" Aiden offered Zoe a cup when she climbed into his car. She narrowed her eyes at it. "It's not poisoned."

"When did you get so funny?" She huffed and reluctantly accepted the hot chocolate. Aiden's car was exactly as she thought it would be—slick, well-proportioned, and spotless. She scoured for some imperfection. A wrapper or a parking ticket or a coffee stain. But the car looked and smelled brand-new. It irked her. "I should get my car back in a week or so."

"What's wrong with it?" he asked as he backed out of the parking spot.

"Something about the gasket."

"Blown head gasket, huh? Yeah, that'll do it. Probably noticed white smoke coming out the exhaust or your engine temp spiking before it died."

She frowned as they got on the I-5 South. "How the hell do you know that?"

"I fix up vintage cars in my spare time. 1969 Mustangs don't exactly repair themselves."

Zoe choked on the hot chocolate as the liquid snaked down the wrong pipe, unleashing a series of coughs that raked through her body.

"You okay?"

"Yeah." She patted her chest and settled down. The thought of Aiden in a garage fixing cars made her head hurt. "Sorry, you just don't look like someone who has hobbies."

"What do you think I do on weekends?"

"Volunteer at mental asylums?" she said playfully.

The corner of his lips twitched but he didn't reply. Zoe rested her head against the cool window, watching the Seattle skyline being slowly swallowed by the low-hanging clouds. The rain was sparse now, but the air still smelled of wet mud and exhaust. Wheels barreled through puddles, sending arcs of water spraying on the sides. She stared into the streaks of green blurring past—Douglas firs and farmlands, which soon dissolved into gas stations and restaurants. Her mind wandered to the letter—the threat, the *game*.

But every time she blinked, something else transpired in her mind. Viktor Axenov. And the key to the safety deposit box that he'd stolen. She checked her phone. She had been trying to get in touch with Keith—an old friend of her mother's—who had given her the key and told her how Rachel had been afraid of someone powerful and was hiding something in that safety deposit box as leverage.

More than twenty years later, someone wanted that *leverage*.

"Are you thinking about that note?" Aiden's voice cut through her spiraling thoughts.

She jerked and blinked. "Yeah... I... I don't know what to think."

"I don't know yet either. What connection do you have to Pineview Falls?"

Zoe's mind got stuck again. She and Aiden traded a glance. The question hung between them. Why had the note been sent to *Zoe?*

FIVE

As the car glided through Pineview Falls, Zoe shuddered involuntarily. The town sat low in the valley with thick forests pressing down on both sides. The trees reached up like skeletal fingers brushing the gray skies. Fog clung to roads that were cracked and had been patched up too many times. The buildings looked worn out, and the gas stations had neon lights that flickered too brightly. A stagnant vibe hung over Pineview Falls.

It looked like a town stuck in the past. A town where every day was exactly the same. The only thing about it that was alive was the wind. It roared through the streets, whipping dried leaves and litter into the air.

"Have you been here before?" she asked Aiden, scrunching her nose in distaste. Something clung to this town. Something beyond the rotten fence posts and rusty doors.

It had a secret. They all did.

"Nope." He killed the engine. They'd reached a low, bricked building with a faded sign indicating *Lewis County Sheriff's Office—Pineview Falls Substation.* "We are meeting Lisa Gray here. She knows about the letter to you, right?"

"Simon sent over a scanned copy." She spotted a sturdy

woman in uniform standing next to a patrol SUV, its tires caked in dirt. The woman was thick around the middle and towering in height. Her dark, silky hair was tied in a loose ponytail; wisps flicked in her face that had dark, piercing eyes, an upturned nose, and a double chin. "There she is."

As soon as Zoe opened the door, a gust of wind slammed it shut in her face. She recoiled and pushed the door open again despite the mounting resistance. It was the town's way of telling her she wasn't welcome. But she was from Chicago—she was used to arctic cold wind scouring her face and nipping at her skin.

"Sheriff Gray?" Zoe flashed her badge. "Special Agent Zoe Storm. This is Dr. Aiden Wesley, a profiler with the bureau."

"Nice to meet you." Lisa's eyes slid over them and beyond to Aiden's shiny BMW. Zoe knew the drill. They were the *suits* who had arrived in a small town where roots mattered more than ambition, where preservation mattered more than exploration. While the rest of the world took flight and evolved, a small town took pride in staying staunchly in the past. Like holding on to an old heirloom no matter how useless and faded it got with time.

It was everything Zoe despised because it reminded her of what she was doing. She was still stuck in the past. Still trying to pry it open. Still refusing to let go.

"What do we know about Annabelle?" Zoe asked.

"Thirty-three-year-old with no priors. I just ran her through the system. She's a scientist. An educated woman, making good money. I made some initial inquiries today. She was last seen two days ago leaving work but never came home, according to the husband," Lisa said. "Oh, this is Ethan. He's the deputy here."

A long-limbed man with a thick neck and a bushy mustache stepped forward and tipped his hat, extending his pudgy hand.

"Did you know Annabelle? It's a small town," Aiden said.

"Just by sight. Stayed out of trouble. She was bright." He spoke in a monotone, the cords in his neck jutting out like cables. "Our kids go to the same day care, so we crossed paths."

"She has a kid?" Zoe's eyes widened.

Ethan pressed his lips in a hard line. "Two boys. A nine-month-old and an eleven-year-old."

"A new mother doesn't come home to her infant and husband, and her name isn't entered in any missing person database?" she asked incredulously.

"Some wires got crossed." Lisa avoided meeting her blazing eyes. "The report we received didn't mention any kids, so we just followed procedure."

"But *you* knew?" Aiden said, pointing at Ethan.

"I did but I figured she's a new mom working a full-time job, she probably just wanted to blow off some steam. Catch a break. I know my wife and I wanted to when our first baby was born."

Zoe grimaced at the callousness of his justification. But it wasn't something she could deem unreasonable after years of coming across one bad day causing good people to spiral.

"This poem." Lisa switched gears. "I've read it many times but I don't know what it means. Her body could be anywhere. If there is a body."

Once she begged, now she sleeps. Marrow blackens; flesh turns stone.

The words had jangled Zoe's nerves. They swam in her head, making it bulky. A small part of her still wanted to believe that this was a hoax. Perhaps Annabelle was in on it. Maybe this was a ploy to get attention. Maybe she was having problems with her husband. Zoe had stumbled across all kinds of people with too many screws loose in their heads.

Aiden was studying the picture of the poem on his phone. His thick eyebrows dipped low and his forehead creased.

"What is it?" Zoe asked.

He shook his head. "There's something here."

"What?" Lisa's interest piqued. The three of them leaned closer around Aiden as he focused on the poem.

Internally, Zoe reluctantly admitted that Aiden was actually very helpful. The last thing his cockiness required was encouragement. But she couldn't have cracked the last case without him. She also wouldn't have felt naked and porous under his scrutinizing glare. His words and his eyes were determined to pop open her jovial, happy façade. To him, she was an anomaly, a thing of academic curiosity, an object to poke and study. It would satiate the psychologist in him. But it would force Zoe to something—or someone—she had locked away and stifled inside her.

Emily.

Aiden's head snapped up. She could see a plan forming in his dark eyes. "Does the word 'Wollemi' mean anything to you?"

Lisa turned to Ethan. "Not to me. Ethan, you know this area better than I do. Ring a bell?"

"Yeah. It's a tree. It's not found naturally in this part of the state but a botanist imported a few and planted them many decades ago. Only one has survived. Why?"

"If you take the first letter of every sentence in the note, starting from the third line, it spells out W-O-L-L-E-M-I. This person wrote a long poem. He was saying a lot without really saying much. There has to be some clue here."

Zoe nodded. "The poem insinuates she's buried. Maybe under this tree. Can you take us there, Ethan?"

Zoe's fingers and toes were cold as she plunged her way through the mossy trees dotting the squishy ground carpeted with pine needles and twigs. The sky had bled into a shade somewhere between brown and underbelly black that tightened her stomach. Cedars and firs stood like ancient guardians with gnarly roots that swelled above the ground like traps waiting to trip intruders.

It was nature growing uninhibited, untouched. The wilderness of Washington that enjoyed its isolation.

Zoe followed Ethan and Lisa, who were completely at ease in the woods. The beam from their flashlights swung haphazardly, illuminating the path. The wind had softened but the trees whispered and leaves rustled.

An owl hooted and Zoe jumped, bumping into Aiden. "Sorry."

"Not a fan of the woods?" he guessed, hopping over a log strewn in their path.

"I like cities and buildings with bright lights and people. You can't trust a place with more animals than humans—isn't reliable." She tried to squint through the growing darkness almost waiting for something to jump out at her.

"There it is!" Ethan pointed at a tree rising up between evergreens and maples, its bark fractured like reptile scales. Its stiff branches cast shadows on the ground. "The only one in the county."

Zoe scanned the area around the tree. There was patch of disturbed soil, more speckled than the area around it. "Look."

"Could just be an animal." Lisa stepped forward and lightly brushed over the patch with her boot. A squeak escaped her throat and she sprang back. Ethan shone his flashlight at her feet.

Zoe's face fell. The world changed—darkened and stilled.

A pale, waxy hand protruded from the soil. The fingers were slightly curled and dirt was lodged under the intact nails, now crawling with small insects. On one of the fingers, a diamond ring flanked with two sapphire gems glittered under the dirt. The sour and sweet smell of decay flooded Zoe's nostrils.

"I think we just found Annabelle," Zoe whispered to Aiden who was silent and rigid next to her.

Lisa was already on the radio, calling for backup. But Zoe couldn't stop staring at the hand sticking out of the shallow grave. It wasn't a hoax after all. That lock of hair and that note addressed specifically to Zoe.

And then there was another sound. A sharp snap of the twigs, a wave of rustling leaves and receding steps. It wasn't the wind.

Someone was in the woods with them.

SIX

Zoe shot out of there like a bullet. Her legs moved like a machine, leaping over the bulging roots and thorny shrubs. Leaves scraped her face and hair as she weaved her way through the choking woods. She felt a sharp stitch under her ribs. She saw her target—a shadowy silhouette moving a few feet ahead, visible due to the silvery moonlight and the faint glow from a phone.

With another surge of adrenaline, she pushed off a fallen log, catapulting in the air before crashing into him.

"Ah!"

Zoe landed on top of the man on the ground with a thud. Pain shot through her as her head slammed into his but she kept her weight on him. "FBI."

"Son of a bitch. Get off me!" he hissed through gritted teeth.

Zoe couldn't see anything in the dark. His phone had flown in the air when she landed on him. He writhed under her, trying to break free. He was of medium build and she was short. But she had rage—renewable, infinite, replenishable rage that injected her with strength. "Fleeing a crime scene. I ought to arrest you."

Footsteps neared and Aiden and Lisa appeared, standing over them.

Zoe grabbed the man by the back of his collar and pulled him up harshly. Lisa pointed a flashlight at him, revealing his curly mop of hair and thick glasses. "Adam? What the hell are you doing here?"

"You know this guy?" Zoe panted in disbelief.

"He's a reporter." Lisa sighed. "An annoying one at that."

"What are you doing in the middle of the woods at this time?" Aiden asked.

"Okay, you can let me go now." Adam scowled and yanked away from Zoe's grip. She let him go, deciding he wasn't stupid enough to flee now that he had been identified. "I followed you," he said to Lisa.

"Followed me? From where?"

"I was at Bernie's across the street from the station when I saw two suits pull up and talk to you. I know a story when I see one. And when I saw your car heading into the woods, I figured something was up. You found a body?" His eyebrows waggled.

Zoe and Aiden looked at each other.

"For God's sake, Adam, it wouldn't kill you to be more sensitive." Lisa rolled her eyes. "Agent Storm, he's as harmless as a puppy. He just likes to sniff around."

"Why did you run away?" Aiden asked.

"It was a reflex! Besides, I know how pissed Lisa here would be with me. We go way back."

"By 'way back,' he means he tries to poke his nose into every case," Lisa explained. "Adam, get out of here. We got work to do."

"No. He's not going anywhere," Zoe said. "He was fleeing a crime scene. We are holding him for questioning."

"I know him. I can vouch for him."

"I hate to pull rank here but this is FBI jurisdiction now. We have to follow protocol."

Lisa pursed her lips and gave her a curt nod. "Ethan will secure the scene. The CSI is on their way to dig her up and collect samples."

"*Her?*" Adam's eyes sparkled with intent. "The victim is a woman?"

"Jesus Christ," Aiden muttered under his breath.

"We should head back," Zoe said to Aiden. "They can stay here and supervise."

She sensed that Lisa wasn't entirely on board with the plan as she made her way back to Ethan.

"I'm innocent," Adam said. "And I can help you catch the killer. I know things. And I know everyone in town."

Zoe's gut twisted. She'd found herself navigating an unknown terrain and already managed to piss people off.

Zoe could feel the pressure building behind her eyelids the longer she stared at the laptop screen. She was busy scouring the Internet for anything she could find on Annabelle Stevens. But the woman wasn't on any social media, which Zoe found odd given that everybody was on social media these days. She peered out the window into the cinching darkness of the woods that lay behind the station. Not a single flicker of light. Idly, she wondered how many bodies could be buried in such places. No light, no surveillance, no witnesses.

That was why she preferred cities.

She chewed on the pad of her thumb. Restlessness brewed in her chest like a swarm of bees trapped in there, desperate to get out. She needed something. An outlet. There was too much going on. Too many unknowns. She took out her phone and texted Benny.

Z: When can you pencil me in?

His reply was instantaneous.

B: Never. You didn't tell me you were a suit.

She ground her teeth. She wasn't FBI Agent Zoe Storm when she went to Benny's club of underground fighting. She transformed into an animal, operating on pure instincts and emotions. Without that outlet, she could feel herself hardening into stone.

Emily! Her mother's voice rang in her ears.

"Lisa just texted us." Aiden waltzed into the room where Zoe had set up camp. "Storm?" Zoe blinked. "What are you thinking?"

"Nothing." She rubbed her temple. "What were you saying?"

Aiden stared at her and she stared back evenly, defiantly. She knew he wanted her to open up and he knew she wanted him to back off. He conceded and sat across from her. "They dug up the body. It's Annabelle Stevens. They found ID on her."

"Great. We got a killer who likes a game."

"There will be more," Aiden warned darkly. "Sending a poem to you means it's a cat-and-mouse game. Look at the baseline behavioral markers. The offender presents with a high-functioning cognitive profile—linguistic complexity in the riddle suggests premeditation, possibly compulsive tendencies. This isn't impulsive violence; we're looking at someone who derives gratification from intellectual engagement with their own crime scene. This individual is asserting control over both the victim and the investigative process."

"Yeah."

He leaned forward and placed his elbows on the table. "You have enemies. Is what's happening related to what went down a month ago?"

Zoe stiffened. "This feels like an interrogation."

"We're on this case together. I need to know if there's a link."

She scoffed, irritated that he wouldn't let it go. "That was my personal business. *This* is unrelated."

"What kind of personal business would lead to someone attacking you and you won't even file a police report?"

"Move on, Aiden." Steel crept into Zoe's tone. "Focus on the case. Where's Adam?"

Aiden's jaw hardened but he relented. "Still in holding. Insisting that he can help. You seem... irritable, which is rare for you."

Zoe's smile didn't reach her eyes. "The hot chocolate you got for me wasn't sweet enough." Her phone rang. Simon's name flashed on the screen. "Hello."

"Z, everything okay there?" he asked.

"Yeah. We found Annabelle's body." Her voice came out small and shaky. She could sense Aiden watching her. She felt like she was being strip-searched at an airport by the TSA. "Anyway, what's up?"

"That name you gave me? Viktor Axenov?"

"Yes..."

"I checked with Criminal Enterprises Branch. He's linked to Red Trigger. A ghost organization. Like a criminal think tank. They sell intelligence, logistics, and strategies to criminals... How the hell do you know this guy?"

Zoe's mind exploded into a million frantic thoughts. But one blasted through her mind—what had Rachel been involved in?

SEVEN

Jim peered into the scope of his bolt-action rifle. The animal was in sight—a deer, small and stocky with fur glistening from the misty rain that was inborn in the state of Washington. He prepared for the kill.

It was what he'd been taught since he was a child. The first time his father had sauntered with him into a store and bought a gun, he was only twelve. All he had to do was exert pressure with a forefinger to take a life, of an animal who breathed, cried, fed, protected its loved ones, and fought to be born into this world only for its life to be cut short.

His finger hovered. His breath grew ragged. The towering western hemlocks and cedars with gnarly roots and ancient bark roughened over time appeared to lean closer. The distant hum of a bubbling stream grew louder. The low light knifing through the thick canopy darkened.

He could do this. It was just one click. One muscle that had to twitch. But he was frozen, trying to straddle the mind and the heart.

A booming sound punched through the air. A strangled

mewling sound. The deer dropped, its body disappearing in the underbrush with a thud.

Jim spun round. Behind him, Lisa stood with her rifle still pointing at the deer and smoke curling out of it. "I was going to take that shot!"

Lisa smirked. "You say that every time. Why do you force it if it isn't your thing?" Her boots swished through the moss-draped ground and decaying leaves.

"It used to be," he muttered under his breath. He swung the rifle over his shoulder, feeling the heavier weight of yet another weapon he couldn't fire. He followed Lisa to the fallen animal. She quickly reported the kill using an app online as he stared around at the crowded woods. A familiar terrain with unpredictable dangers. He felt her gaze on him. "Jim, what is it? This hunting trip was your idea."

"Yeah, I know." He kicked at the rocks with his foot. "I just need to dip my toe in the water again. Get used to this feeling." He grazed the cold rifle that felt like an alien strapped to him. Unlike Lisa, who carried everything on her like an extension, how seamlessly she blended into each role.

And then there was Jim. Never able to fully embrace anything.

"Can you help?" she asked him as she laid the animal on its back. Jim spread its hind legs open and propped them in place. She fished out a knife and too soon the blade was cutting across the sternum in an upward motion.

Blood oozed from its body as an earthy smell filled the air. Steam rose from its cavity. Warm organs meeting a cold morning. "No internal bleeding," Lisa observed. "The shot was clean. This shouldn't be that dirty... Are you okay?"

Jim winced. "Yeah."

"You're as white as a ghost."

He gulped. "No... I'm fine." He could do this. He was the man in this marriage. The husband. He had gone hunting with his father since he was a child. In fact, *he* had taught Lisa how to hunt.

Then what had gone wrong?

A sudden movement. One of the deer's legs kicked and its muscles twitched. Jim fell back on his hands, startled, his heart hammering against his ribcage. He should have anticipated that. It was only a reflex—the deer's body shutting down.

Lisa was immediately all over him, making sure he was all right. He didn't know what had shaken him more—his wife's concern or his inadequacy.

* * *

The next morning Zoe brushed her teeth vigorously as she stared at her reflection in the mirror.

Another motel with a squeaky bed and the walls reeking of cigarettes. Another window with a view of a throng of trees too thick and leafy for sunlight to penetrate. But it was the same reflection that stared back at her. Her long dark hair, soft features, upturned nose, and eyes filled with chaos.

She could see the million thoughts in her eyes that were busy twisting her brain into all kinds of shapes. She kept brushing her teeth over and over, until foam trickled out of her mouth and dripped down her chin. Is that how everyone saw her? Not as a happy woman but a woman whose emotions were always bubbling and frothing and itching to explode.

No—only Aiden saw that. No wonder he stared at her with a curiosity that was less friendly and more clinical. And now she was stuck with him again.

She bent down over the sink to rinse her mouth, wiping away her concerns about working with him. She could deal with Dr. Aiden Wesley. She had dealt with men twice her size at her underground fight club. When she stood upright, there was a girl standing behind her.

Zoe screamed and whirled around, her heart in her knees. The girl was gone.

As Zoe caught her breath, she leaned against the sink. Emily had been an echo buried deep inside her. But now that echo was fighting to make itself heard.

Zoe recoiled from the waves of unease rolling off Lisa. The sheriff stomped across a yard littered with stagnant pools of rainwater toward a colonial-style house with blue-trimmed windows. A house Zoe didn't expect to see in Pineview Falls.

"She's pissed," Aiden whispered from Zoe's side. She fixed her collar. "Does that bother you?"

She narrowed her eyes at him. "I have more important things to worry about."

Lisa knocked on the door and looped her thumbs through her belt. She shifted from foot to foot. Zoe was chewing her lip, bracing herself for the difficult conversation while Aiden stood stoic like a statue. But then she saw his knee bobbing.

A weak smile curled up her lip. He was human after all.

The door opened with a jerk. Annabelle's husband, Trevor, appeared with a scruffy jaw, flannel shirt, and eyes rimmed with dark circles. He hadn't slept in days. It took him exactly one second to look at their faces before his knees gave out. A scream escaped him like his soul was trying to leave his body.

Aiden and Lisa swooped down to help him while Zoe remained rooted to the spot. As she watched Annabelle's husband fall apart and weep on the floor, she recalled her reaction to finding her mother dead in the bathtub. An image she would never forget. How brave she was to shed no tears, to sit on the floor in absolute silence, staring at Rachel's body before spurring into action to clean up the crime scene.

"I'm sorry..." Trevor slowly got to his feet, leaning against the door and wiping his nose. "Shit. I... oh God." A baby's cry came from inside the house. "Come inside. Damn it. It's Markus..." Zoe followed him inside with Aiden and Lisa.

Zoe instantly sensed a woman's touch in the house—from the plush rugs and matching throw pillows to the wall-mounted coat hook and decorative organizer bins. And she noticed her glaring absence. Dirty diapers overflowing in the bin, tissue boxes strewn around, and moldy takeout boxes.

"I'm sorry. I have to feed him." Trevor picked up a crying baby from the crib and handed him to Lisa. "Hold him for a second."

Lisa held the baby like a football, blinking at him. A sadness crossed her face.

"We have questions, Mr. Stevens," Zoe said as Trevor quickly moved around the kitchen with jerky, unsure movements. "When was the last time you spoke to your wife?"

"I don't know. When did I make the call? Three days ago? Yeah, yeah. I called her end of the day and she said she was running late." He rubbed his temples. "And then she didn't come back."

"What was her behavior like in the last few days? Was she stressed or distracted?" Aiden prodded.

The baby's cries grated against Zoe's ears. "May I take him?"

"Sure."

Zoe took the baby from Lisa and held him close to her chest, feeling his drool and fat tears staining her shirt. From the corner of her eye, she saw Lisa's unsure but eager hand reach out before curling back into her pocket.

His eyes darted as he chased a memory. "She was stressed about work. More than usual."

"Did she talk to you about it? Mention anyone in particular from work?" Aiden asked.

He shrugged. "Not really. She was working on some big project for the company. It was a high-pressure situation. But that was it. She didn't mention anything. To be honest, we didn't talk much about work."

Rain pattered on the window, rivulets racing down the glass. The view of the cars in the parking lot was distorted. Clarity and boundaries dissolving and colors bleeding away.

Claustrophobic and incessant. The damned rainy weather of Washington.

Aiden's shoulder brushed against hers, sending a jolt of energy through her body.

"How did you know where to find her?" Trevor asked. "You found her in the woods?"

A whisper of breath caught inside Zoe's throat as she thought of the envelope that had found its way to her desk. "We're not able to share much at the moment," she said softly. "Did Annabelle have other friends? Anyone she was close to?"

"No, she was too busy working."

"And what did she do?" Aiden asked.

"She was a data scientist for Harrington Group." He took the crying baby from Zoe and balanced him in the crook of his elbow to feed him the bottle. "Shit. Where's his burp cloth?"

Zoe exchanged a helpless look with Aiden, who seemed more at ease than her. She wandered around the house while Lisa pressed Trevor for more details. The fridge had a series of photographs stuck to it—Annabelle and Trevor at different wonders of the world from Petra to the Colosseum.

There were only six photographs. They never visited the last one—the Taj Mahal.

She walked through the rest of the house, seemingly looking for the baby's burp cloth but actually focused on finding a clue and a connection. What was it about this victim that the killer sent Zoe a riddle? It didn't make any sense. Her mind stretched in all directions as she trailed the hallways with yellow walls, reaching a doorway with markings on it. A child growing up.

The master bedroom was a mess, like it had been turned

upside down. Zoe didn't know where to start as she waded through the crumpled bedsheets on the floor. Her eyes fixed on a wall with pictures of all kinds of birds.

"She was into birds." A voice said. "She learned it from my grandpa."

Zoe reeled back at the young boy standing next to her. She wouldn't have expected a calm voice to come out of such a small boy. He was the mirror image of Annabelle. His brown hair was silky. A slightly crooked nose with a bulbous tip and too thin lips crowning a long chin. There was a sharp awareness in his teary eyes—a rarity, and another inheritance from his mother.

"One time Mom told me she saw the marbled murrelet but she was too late to take the camera out. It was our thing. Watching birds."

"I'm Zoe."

"Kevin."

"How old are you, Kevin?"

"Twelve." His mouth twisted. "My dad says she's lost. Did you find her?"

Zoe didn't know what to say. She could see the boy was holding back tears—his lips quivered and his eyes fluttered. Zoe wanted to say something reassuring him but she was silent for too long. His face turned red and he scampered away.

As they left the house, Zoe felt like a rock was sitting on her chest. A small family now decimated. She couldn't get Kevin's haunted eyes out of her mind. "Aiden, what do you think?"

He adjusted his thick glasses. "Well, I was thinking about why Annabelle. It's a small town. Everyone knows each other. They're lifers. Rooted. Small-town cycles, same faces, same routines. but she wasn't part of that. She was more ambitious and educated than the average resident here, I would say."

"Someone was jealous?"

"The current portfolio points to a stranger. Someone who exists on the fringes of society decides to exert some control and even get attention by targeting a high-achieving woman. But with just one data point, I won't draw any conclusions." He shrugged, his eyes boring into hers. "All I know for certain is that a killer who sends riddles to the FBI doesn't just stop at one body."

EIGHT

Pineview Falls reminded Zoe of an abandoned theme park. One where rust ate through the beams of roller coasters, a skeletal Ferris wheel sat frozen with the cars creaking in the occasional wind, and the carousal had cracked horses with missing glass eyes. The air was heavy and the silence was deafening except for the occasional screeching of metal and creaking of rides.

Zoe could imagine stories being spun about this town. Legends and myths about how it was haunted. She could see herself spreading those lies.

The lashing wind slammed a stray newspaper right on the windshield, blocking Aiden's view, causing him to hit the brakes.

"Ouch!" Zoe moaned, her head banging back against the headrest.

"Sorry." He turned on the wiper to clear the view of the spiraling road ahead, weaving through the forested patches of land on either side. The green tips of the trees tickled the strip of gray, cloudless sky. Zoe could feel the strength of the wind as it pushed against the car. It felt like it was gathering for a tornado.

"Is it always like this here?" Zoe said, without meaning to ask out loud.

"Shouldn't you be used to the wind, being from Chicago?"

She sniffed. "The wind here feels... stale."

"Did Simon send that lock of hair for testing?" Aiden's voice carried an edge when he said Simon's name. She wondered if they had history.

"Yeah, the lab will coordinate with the county lab to match the DNA. It's sad..." She looked at the crime scene pictures in her lap. "Her youngest son won't remember her at all."

Aiden swallowed hard and Zoe felt the weight of her words settle on them. She cleared her throat and sipped on the strawberry milkshake she had picked up for the ride. She checked her phone. In his last text, Benny refused to accommodate her. She stifled a rough breath and squirmed in her seat. She could feel a solid heat building up within. The rage that she kept buried deep inside her chest was threatening to claw out.

"Promise me. You will move on with your life if anything happens to me. You will forget about me. Promise me, Zoe."

"I promise."

Why had she made that promise? Why had she cleaned up the scene after discovering her mother dead in the bathtub?

Why had someone sent *her* Annabelle's hair and location?

"What's on your mind?" Aiden asked.

"Questions. So many questions," she mumbled, faintly rubbing her elbow, which Viktor Axenov had dislocated when he'd stolen the key to a safety deposit box.

The car halted in front of a concrete, squat, single-story building with a parking lot littered with potholes filled with rainwater. A back alley ran along one side, leading to a set of heavy metal double doors—no windows, just a security keypad and a dented *AUTHORIZED PERSONNEL ONLY* sign.

There was a glass door at the front, blinds pulled halfway down. A gnarled tree stood in a corner with an owl perched on it.

The sharp scent of bleach hit Zoe as they entered the building. The sterile, white-tiled hallways hummed with fluorescence as Zoe and Aiden walked down the labyrinth in the basement. A cold draft whizzed past her. She tried searching for *something* positive, anything about this place that didn't scream like it used to be a tuberculosis hospital where ghosts of dead patients still floated in the sickening, grimy hallways.

"Agent Storm and Dr. Wesley." A tall, bony man with clumps of thinning hair scattered on his scalp came out of a metal door. "I'm Rodney Doyle. The county coroner. The sheriff told me to expect you."

"She's not coming?" Zoe asked.

"She's meeting with the mayor. I'll send her everything I have. Come on in."

"Skittles?" Zoe offered him a packet with a bright smile.

He stared at them as if they were poisoned. "Uhm... no, thank you."

"Okay." She shrugged.

They followed him into a cold room lined with metal shelves stacked with solutions and instruments. A sanitization station and a wall-mounted dissection bench ran along the left wall. Two post-mortem tables situated with fridges in the back. It wasn't as rudimentary as Zoe had been expecting in a small county.

As Zoe approached the table where Annabelle's body lay, she noticed Aiden turn ashen. He retrieved a handkerchief and pressed it against his nose. "You don't have to be here, you know."

"I'm fine," he croaked stubbornly.

A part of Zoe relished the sight of the mighty Aiden Wesley crumbling—it was usually him sniffing for weaknesses.

"The cause of death is stress-induced myocardial infarction," Rodney read out from a file.

"A heart attack?" Zoe's eyebrows shot up.

She looked down at the body and her stomach flipped. Annabelle's skin was grayish blue and slightly sunken, her lips parted and cracked, and a brutal Y-shaped scar ran down her chest. Her hallowed body had been cut open and stitched back with thick black sutures. She had been reduced to a bag of bones, her skin stretched taut. Zoe's eyes trailed over Annabelle's arms and legs covered in bruises and lacerations, all the way down to the soles of the feet, which were torn.

"Was she tortured?" Zoe whispered.

"Essentially, yes," Rodney replied. "Blood tests show high levels of myoglobin and creatine kinase—markers of extreme muscle fatigue and stress. She was dehydrated. Her kidneys were in early stages of acute failure and her lips, mucous membranes, and tongue are all dried up. Evidence of blunt force trauma, as you can see." His pen hovered over her arm. "Excessive bruising across the arms, legs, and torso could have resulted from falls, collisions, or defensive wounds. There are abrasions and scratches consistent with running through brush or crawling away. The calves, thighs, and shoulders have micro tears. Deep-tissue bruising and cracked ribs. Hairline fractures on joints... She was under *extreme* physical duress."

"What are these?" Aiden looked uneasy, pointing out the clusters of small, circular, purple bruises on the arms and chest.

"There's deep hemorrhaging beneath the tissue. High-velocity impact, sharp entry, but no exit. My guess is a modified hunting dart."

"Hunting dart?" Zoe repeated. "She was... chased before she had a heart attack?"

"Her heart was enlarged from a massive surge of adrenaline that triggered her heart failure. There were also micro tears on her heart, which means it was under extreme stress. This wasn't a slow death." Rodney's eyes were hollow and blank. Years of cutting people open and patching them up like puppets had dulled him to the horrors. "Her own body killed her before he could."

Zoe didn't like this at all. She imagined how it had played out—Annabelle running through the woods manically while being hunted like an animal, hiding in bushes, crawling and dragging herself through foliage, twisting ankle, crashing into the bulging roots. Her blood ran cold. A killer who was a hunter, who enjoyed torturing and breaking someone down.

"Were the darts laced with any drug?" Zoe asked.

"I'll need more time. Still waiting on some tests."

"What do you think?" She turned to Aiden.

"This is a process-focused killer, not a product-focused one. He's not killing for disposal; he's killing for experience. That makes him harder to predict because his gratification isn't bound to a single act, but the sequence itself. That coupled with the trophy behavior—sending us her hair—he's reinforcing—"

"Sorry, what did you say about the hair?" Rodney said.

"The killer sent us a lock of her hair," Zoe explained. "We're clearly dealing with someone methodical, controlling, and straight-up evil."

"Oh, that's interesting. What color was the hair?"

"It was black and straight..." And then Zoe's eyes shifted to Annabelle's hair spread out on the table. With a gloved hand, she felt the strands between her fingertips. Brown and curly. "Did she color her hair?"

His tone was unsure. "Highly doubt it. This is her real hair."

Zoe was startled. Could the killer have gotten her lock of hair before snatching her? At a time when she had colored her hair? Not plausible. Before she could sift through the possibilities, her phone buzzed. It was a message from Simon. When she read the words, her heart came to a racing halt.

> *S: Got back the results from the lab. The DNA from the hair and from Annabelle did not match.*

Then who did the hair belong to?

NINE

Lisa twisted the rusty knob to turn on the shower. The hot water ejected from the showerhead like pellets striking her skin. It was probably too hot—she could feel the skin on her back turning red and angry. But she closed her eyes and absorbed the pain. This was nothing.

Months of injections and treatments had made her immune. She stared at the water pooling around her swollen feet. A lingering reminder of the ringer she had been through for nothing. The memory of getting another negative pregnancy test played on a loop in her tired brain. She wanted to cry but she had run out of tears as well. All that was left was bone-melting exhaustion.

"Hey, Lisa!" The door to the bathroom burst open and Jim, all beady eyes, thin mustache, and bushy hair, popped his head in. "Did we get any new packages? I didn't see any in the hallway."

"I don't know. I'll have to check the email for the tracking information." She wiped the glass wall fogged from the steam.

"I guess I can check that too. Damn it, I really wanted to try out that new console tonight." Jim breezed in the washroom and began fixing his hair in the mirror. "Have been waiting for it for weeks."

A lump formed in the base of her throat. "Don't you have a job interview tomorrow?"

"Yeah, it will be fine. I'm overqualified for that one anyway." He gave a careless shrug despite claiming to be overqualified for the two other job interviews he'd been rejected after.

"That guy had it out for me, Lisa. He was biased."

"The commute would have killed me, so I didn't give it my best shot."

She searched his handsome face as he began to shave, remembering how butterflies had filled her stomach when she first met him in college. Years ago, she'd fallen in love with his boyish charm and the ease with which he floated through life. But ten years later, Jim was still floating. And Lisa had found herself unmoored and disenchanted.

Jim washed his face and wiped it with a towel, his eyes darting to Lisa. "What are you thinking?"

"Huh?" She blinked. "Nothing..."

He ran his hands through his hair. "I know you're stressed about the email. Lisa, I... I don't think this is worth it. Let's not force it. Maybe it isn't meant to be, you know? It just doesn't seem worth it." His face was pinched like this conversation was making him awkward. "Think about it." With that he left.

She felt her body go cold despite the scalding hot water. She stepped out of the shower in a daze, wrapped a towel around her body, and waited for the anger to subside. But all she felt was numbness.

Her phone trilled. She unplugged it from the outlet by the sink and checked it. It was time to meet the mayor.

Annabelle Stevens had been murdered, buried, and exploited in a twisted game. It wasn't the first tragedy to strike Pineview Falls and Lisa knew that it wouldn't be the last.

* * *

Once upon a time, Dawn Harrington used to be a different woman. A young woman who chased vibrancy. Back in the day, she would find rooftops to soak in the skylines. She would find silhouettes and contours in city lights instead of the stars. She would look down to the streets and relish the feeling of people being small like ants. It was then she decided that she always wanted to feel that way—closer to the stars. She was always drowning in that hunger for *more*.

And now she was drowning in grief.

She pulled down the visor and looked at her eyes in the mirror. The corners were wrinkled and the icy blue irises somehow looked a faded powdery blue. She tightened her grip on the steering wheel, glancing around at the empty street behind the gas station.

A knock came on the passenger side window, startling her.

She whirled her head and unlocked the door. Adam climbed inside, his frail body disappearing in a lumpy coat and a blotchy beard dotting his jaw. "Don't you own a mirror? You look disheveled."

Adam's smile was forced. "It's nice to see you too, Dawn."

"Well, why did you want to meet me?" She huffed. "I'm very busy. It's not a good time."

"A source told me you might have to delay your pivotal announcement. A data company deciding to venture into a new market," he prodded. "Any truth in that?"

She ground her teeth. "Who have you been talking to?"

This time his smile was genuine. "Sources are my bread and butter. Surely you know that? Any idea how much of a hit your stock price is going to take after your shareholders' false hope that change was coming?"

Dawn had a fair idea. The data storage company she had started from scratch had been fighting to survive for years. It hadn't diversified enough early on and now the world was changing at the speed of light. The ability to write code was at everyone's fingertips and Dawn's company found itself marching toward irrelevancy. It was then that David had had the bold idea to launch into a new space. Gaming. His voice had wavered when he'd first suggested it and his words had eaten into her heart.

"Why don't you get to the point?" Dawn snapped. "Why did you want to meet?"

"To discuss the same. I have it on good intel that there was a company theft."

Dawn stifled a gasp, her throat tightening. "What the hell are you talking about?"

Adam chuckled and drummed his fingers on his lap. "What I'm curious about is what are you doing about it? You can't go to the authorities and have your shareholders get wind of this or you'll go bankrupt. But you can't afford to keep delaying this announcement either as you'll lose money there too."

The vultures were circling, their sharp teeth ready and snapping to pick away at Dawn and her years of hard work. No one wanted to support her when she was starting out. But now that she had built something, everyone wanted a slice of the pie. But she wasn't ready to feed the leeches. Not even her own son.

"Aren't there bigger things happening in this town? I don't know about you but a murder sells more than writing about earnings reports." She flashed him a cruel smile and leaned forward, as she lowered her voice. "Don't make an enemy out of me. You have no idea what I'm willing to do to save what's mine. Now get out of my car."

Adam swallowed hard. "I'll see you around." With that, he opened the door and almost fell out of it.

She watched his toad-like frame grow smaller in the side mirror as he walked away. That was one bug she had squashed —for now. A plan formulated in her mind on how to control the situation before it escalated. The engine revved as she turned the corner and glided the car through the empty streets of Pineview Falls. Overhead the sky was overcast with clouds that hung low and swollen, ready to pop. Her mind was buzzing when she found herself in front of Fun House.

The house that had been decomposing for the last two decades had a sagging roof and was sinking in a thick mass of overgrown grass and weed. Vines crept up the walls and threaded through the cracks. It reeked of must and death and there was only a warped, wooden fence separating it from the outside world. A flimsy barrier that was easy to breach, and some twisted people did every now and then.

She felt salty tears in the back of her throat as her nose turned red. She drove away, willing herself not to cry, but Fun House stood there hulking and casting a looming shadow on her life.

TEN

1995

Sweat made the woman's hands clammy. She rubbed them together. Her breaths fell over each other as if she'd just run a marathon. She eyed the rotary phone next to her. A gust of wind blew, making the open curtains swish.

The woman was never nervous like this. Some would say she was cold-blooded like a reptile. Nothing fazed her—not what was demanded of her, not what she was expected to do. No amount of blood and gore and screams and tears rattled her. She worked like a machine.

Efficient and icy.

But this job was different. There were some lines she didn't cross. Tonight, she did. Tonight, she felt *something*. Raw emotion whipping inside her and twisting her insides. She gazed out the window into the starless night sky. Thunder cracked but rain was still to come. A storm brewed as the wind picked up, sending chills up her arms.

And then the phone rang. Right on time.

She stared at it.

Ring.

Ring.

Ring.

"It's me." She answered the phone like this whenever it was time for this call.

The familiar voice filtered through—throaty with a tinge of eastern European accent. "Is it done?"

"Yes. The target was delivered to the destination." Her finger clutched the fabric of her sweater.

"Good. You will receive the payment in twenty-four hours. You are needed in Philly for the next job."

The woman wasn't supposed to ask questions. She never bothered to. But this time the words tumbled out of her mouth. "He was only a kid. What did you want with him?"

Silence. A deafening silence before the man spoke again. "Do not make the mistake of asking questions. Consider this your final warning. Is that clear?"

Her chest squeezed. There were very few people she feared —and he was one of them. "Y-yes."

"Good. Now prepare for Philly. You'll receive instructions with your payment."

"Understood." She felt weighed down by the memory of the gangly boy and the thrill in his clueless eyes as she walked him to his death.

The realization crystallized inside her with pristine clarity. Without a flicker of doubt, the decision had been made.

It was time for her to quit.

ELEVEN

"The hair doesn't belong to Annabelle," Zoe said, chewing her nail as she paced back and forth in the parking lot.

Aiden emptied his guts in a corner, retching loudly. "Get away from me, Storm."

"And miss this chance of making you uncomfortable? Never," she quipped although her focus was elsewhere.

"It's not that. I think I ate something bad last night." He winced, taking a deep breath. "Shouldn't have had those burgers."

Zoe suddenly became aware of his body, in particular how sculpted his shoulders were, capping a broad back that trimmed into a slim waist. Right now, he looked like the sort of person who would strip and face her in that underground ring she was addicted to, rather than the bookish type she had him down as.

He clearly spent a lot of time perfecting his body. Her mind wandered as she imagined him working out.

"You're staring, Storm." He took out a handkerchief and wiped his mouth, a blush creeping up his cheeks.

She wished the ground would open up and swallow her. She cleared her throat and redirected the conversation.

"The hair isn't Annabelle's. Then why send it to us? Do you think it's the killer's?"

"Sent to *you*. Not to us. To *you*. You need to look at your old cases."

"My old cases?"

"Someone you put away or someone you pissed. This is a challenge for *you* not just the FBI."

"Yeah, it's obvious. Don't need a doctorate to figure that out."

As soon as the words left her mouth, she bit her tongue. She didn't know where the flash of irritation came from. This wasn't like her. She strived to be that ray of sunshine, stubbornly refusing to become too bogged down by the horrors she saw every day. Her unyielding niceness wasn't some moral high ground but a lifeboat. Yet, clinging to the light was treading a thin line—one slight nudge would be all it took to slip into the abyss that lay on either side.

"I can look into any old cases that you worked on." Aiden avoided her eyes. "It should be someone who wasn't involved."

She opened her mouth to say something, *anything*, but he walked past her to the car. A part of her wondered if Aiden truly wanted to help with the case, or was he using this to dig into her past to solve the mystery of the attack on her? As she headed back to the car, a blast of wind blew past her, making the shrubbery surrounding her rustle. She whirled at the sound, her eyes frantically looking for the source of the sound. A caustic feeling rose inside her, bleeding the colors from her surroundings. Someone was after her.

"I didn't expect a house like this in Pineview Falls," Zoe commented, standing in front of a tall house that was a mix of white stone and dark wood accents and guarded by wrought-iron gates. The driveway was a smooth ribbon of dark stone, curving up to the front entrance flanked by two columns. A balcony jutted out above the entrance from the second floor. The front lawn was beautifully landscaped, with manicured hedges and sculpted topiaries.

"They moved here around twenty years ago. I was only a volunteer at the sheriff's office back then," Lisa told her, adjusting her belt buckle.

"So you know the family well?"

Lisa didn't look at her. "It's a small town, Agent Storm." She pressed the bell on the wall and a security camera tilted in their direction. When Lisa announced herself, the gates unlocked and opened slowly.

"This isn't creepy at all," Zoe muttered but Lisa didn't respond and stared straight ahead. Zoe watched her from the corner of her eye as they walked up the driveway. The air between them was thick with simmering tension. Lisa was guarded, only talking when spoken to, her tone curt and impersonal. "Sheriff, I want to apologize."

Lisa paused and frowned. "What do you mean?"

"Yesterday, I crossed a line in the woods. This is your jurisdiction and this case won't be solved without you. I was just stressed."

"Oh." She blinked, surprised. "No, no, you don't have to apologize. I get it. I just had a bad meeting with the mayor... nothing to do with you."

Zoe didn't press further despite her bubbling curiosity. "Do we have Annabelle's phone and computer activity?"

"We pinged the carrier, and the cell tower triangulation puts her phone's last known location fifty or so miles around her place of work."

"We can't narrow it down any further?"

"Not enough cell towers here, unlike big cities." Lisa's face was drawn. "I put out a hit on her credit cards. We'll know if they've been used."

As they waited for the main door to open, Lisa looked at her phone and sighed, her features tightening.

"Everything okay?"

"Yeah, it's just my husband, Jim." She put her phone away. "Never mind."

Lisa looked permanently exhausted. Her skin was dull and sagged under her chin. There were bags under her hollow eyes and her lips were shredded from being chewed on. Her gaze wasn't alert and piercing—it was exasperated. The county didn't have a high crime rate. So what was making Lisa look perpetually worn out?

"Sheriff Gray." A slim man with bushy eyebrows and hair cropped along the sides opened the door. "What brings you here?"

"David." Lisa nodded. "This is Agent Zoe Storm from the FBI."

David's lips parted. "FBI?" He offered his hand. "Is everything okay?"

"Yes, we need to talk. May we come inside?" Zoe said.

"Of course, of course." He led them into the vast foyer with a crystal chandelier hanging from an impossibly high ceiling. A sweeping staircase curved upward, paired with arched windows. Zoe grimaced at her muddy shoes leaving tracks on the polished marble. The house reminded her of the lavish houses in Texas she used to see when she lived there briefly as a child. She would walk back home on sweltering hot summer days through the neighborhood where lawns managed to look like glossy green carpets and people were dignified and careless with money. A little taste of the good life before she returned home to find Rachel struggling to prepare a meal.

"What's g-going on?" David's voice reeled her back from the memory.

"Do you know Annabelle Stevens?" Lisa asked.

David shoved his hands in his pockets. "Yes, yes. She works for us."

"She was killed. The FBI is here to help us out."

His eyes widened and he blinked repeatedly. "Jesus... *killed?* I-I-I don't know what to think."

"She never returned home from work two days ago," Zoe said.

"I'm sorry to hear that but I don't keep tabs on my employees in my position," David scoffed and crossed his arms. "I don't even know if she came into work. I only met her once a week for a meeting."

"So you wouldn't know if she had any problems with anyone at work or anything like that?" Zoe said. There was something about David that was off. Beads of sweat glistened atop his upper lip. His face twitched oddly. And he kept fidgeting. Either he was hiding something or he was nervous about talking to them.

"You should ask HR about that. I have no idea."

"Her husband told me and my partn— colleague that Annabelle was stressed because of work. Some project she was on..."

David licked his lips. "Well, yes. She's very talented, so she was one of the few minds on the project. This project could be big for the company. It's taking a toll on everyone involved."

"And what is the project?" Lisa asked.

"I can't talk about it. We've all signed NDAs. It's top-secret. But it has nothing to do with whatever happened to her."

Zoe didn't think it did. "We couldn't find her laptop at home."

"Oh, that's company property. We are in data storage. Due to the nature of our work, we don't allow employees to take computers home."

"Are they allowed to use it for personal correspondence?" Lisa asked.

"No, but many of them do. It's hard to stop them. Social media websites are blocked but there's always email…"

"Then we'll need to take a look," Zoe said.

He let out a shaky laugh. "That won't be possible. It contains confidential information—our product specs, demos, contracts, everything."

"We aren't interested in that. We are looking for any correspondence that Annabelle may have had."

"I'm sorry but we can't take the risk. Millions are at stake." His eyes were clouded with panic.

"Come on, David," Lisa chimed in with a friendly tone. "You have my word. We don't care about that. We'll just retrieve Annabelle's private communications and give the laptop back to you."

David brushed past them, deeper into the house. "I'm sorry, Lisa. Nothing comes before the company."

Zoe followed while Lisa continued to urge David. "Mr. Harrington, if you don't cooperate, then we'll have to get a court order."

"Then do that." He wiped his lips, his eyes shifty. "Now, please. I'm a busy man."

The temperature in the room suddenly plummeted. Lisa frowned in surprise as David busied himself in the kitchen, his face set hard in stone. But Zoe didn't miss the tremor in his hand as he poured himself a drink. After he gulped it down in one swig, Lisa gestured to Zoe to head out, perturbed by David's lack of cooperation.

But Zoe wasn't. She knew that when the choice was between money and justice, money always prevailed. If proxy wars were still being fought in different corners of this world for money, then no one was going to care about some Annabelle Stevens in a small town like Pineview Falls.

"Court order," Zoe mouthed at Lisa, who nodded grimly.

They turned on their heels to leave when Zoe noticed a

large picture above the fireplace of a young girl in her teens with reddish brown hair falling on her forehead and braces pulling together crowded front teeth.

"Who is that?" Zoe asked.

David followed her gaze and his face fell but his eyes flashed with hatred. "The shadow that follows me everywhere." With that, he disappeared into a den.

Zoe was turning his words over when Lisa's phone chirped again. She checked it and her breath hitched. "We just got a hit on Annabelle's credit card."

TWELVE

Zoe felt the ground shake first. The vibrations reverberated up her body. The tracks clanked against each other and the wheels chomped on them, the sound of metal screeching filling the damp air underground to a crescendo. The loud, disjointed creaks and metallic growls thumped inside her head, matching the drum of the rage that beat inside her like another organ.

Only one thing could control the rage—pain. It had evaded her since Viktor from Red Trigger had left her bruised in a motel room. Now she was scrambling, trying to hunt for that release like a crackhead desperately raking through a dumpster for more drugs.

On the platform, a man stood next to her chuckling on his phone, "Women are like used cars, ride them for a while, and when they start acting up, trade them in for a newer model."

Her head snapped up to look at him. A pudgy, middle-aged man with a face no one would remember.

He checked his watch. "The wife is gonna whine again. She's got two jobs—looking pretty and shutting up. And she's failing at both."

Zoe imagined what it would feel like to drive her fists in his face. She would break his nose first and relish the sound of the bone cracking. Then she would punch him again, this time harder to dislocate his jaw and forever distort his smile.

The man continued his telephone conversation, gleefully making fun of his wife. His voice grated and she zeroed in on his throat, imagining all kinds of creative ways she could injure his voice box. He would scream and shout and beg. Blood would run down his face, covering Zoe's hands. But she wouldn't stop. Because he would deserve it. Because people saying and doing wrong things shouldn't get away with it. Unlike whoever killed her mother and left her in a bathtub.

His blood would be sticky first and then become flaky. He would learn a lesson the hard way—the only way to learn anything.

What was she thinking? When did it get so dark? She rubbed her eyes, as if trying to wipe away the image she had conjured. She didn't recognize this person—she liked sugar and babies and carnivals. But then where did this sinister thread of darkness come from? Sometimes she wondered if it was her fault. If she had suppressed everything that had happened too soon, so it slowly and silently grew inside her, now screaming to be let out.

What if this temptation to inflict pain on those who deserved it became too strong to resist? What if it gnawed at her for the rest of her life? Her thoughts drifted to Aiden. He had offered to help her a long time ago, but she had been too afraid to accept.

With shaking fingers, she shot another message to Benny.

Z: Come on, Benny. If I wanted, your operation would have shut down already.

She knew she shouldn't. But if she didn't release this anger inside her where it was allowed, she was worried it would spill over somewhere else.

"Hey!" Lisa joined her. "We might have caught a break. You okay?"

Zoe felt her cheeks heat. "Yeah… yes. It's just chilly down here in the subway. What were you saying?"

She hitched her thumb over her shoulder to the electronics store. "This is the store where Annabelle's credit card was used. The owner showed me the CCTV footage."

"You checked the timestamp? Who is it?"

She pointed past her. "That guy over there." Zoe turned around to find a short man curled up on the floor at the end of the platform against the brick wall. The coat he wore was too thin and his hair was matted and streaked with dirt. "The owner recognized him, luckily. The guy hangs around the station almost every day. Sleeps most nights here too."

Zoe's eyebrows raised. "What the hell is he doing with Annabelle's purse?"

They approached him slowly, and Lisa nudged him on the leg. "Listen up." The man stirred in his sleep and Lisa nudged him again. "Wake up. Come on now."

His heavy-lidded eyes cracked open and a sneer curled up his lips. "What the hell do you want?"

The scent of urine hit Zoe. Her eyes searched the ripped sleeping bag in which he lay, stuffed with food wrappers, coins, and empty bottles. And then under a stained sweatshirt, she spotted a maroon wallet. "There it is." She swooped down to pick it up but he smacked her hand away.

"It's mine!" he growled.

"Oh yeah? You like Kate Spade?" Zoe said. "So do I. Where did you buy it?" He made a face but didn't protest when Zoe picked it up with her handkerchief and went through it. She flicked it open. Annabelle's license and credit cards. "Where did you find it?"

"Outside the station at the east entrance."

"And it was just lying on the floor?" Lisa arched an eyebrow. "That's convenient."

"That's what happened!" Defiance shone on his face. "This lady was walking by and it fell out of her pocket. Finders keepers."

Zoe gave him a quick glance. His eyes were sunken and his face blotchy. His frame was wispy thin; arms riddled with scabs and movements jittery. Could he have killed Annabelle and sent Zoe that letter? He was too shaky and disorganized, but there was a rabidness in his eyes that could easily transcend into violence.

While Lisa took down the homeless man's information, Zoe rang Aiden.

"Storm." He answered.

"Where are you?"

"At the station. I pulled your old case files. Just going through them. What's up?"

"I got a homeless man over here, obviously a drug addict, caught with Annabelle's wallet. He claims he picked it up after it fell out of her pocket. I don't know... could it be him?"

He sighed. "The profile doesn't fit. Chronic substance use, particularly in homeless populations with severe addiction histories, leads to neurocognitive impairment—executive dysfunction and memory deficits. They are significantly more likely to commit reactive violence rather than premeditated, symbolic offenses. Crafting a coherent, coded message while maintaining trophic behavior? That's not a chaotic mind at work. That's structure. We are looking at a high-functioning individual not someone desperate."

"That's what I thought—" She stopped when she noticed a receipt, peeking out of the pockets in the wallet. "I'll call you back." The receipt was for a latte. "Lisa? What time did Annabelle leave the office?"

"Around five o'clock, according to her coworkers. Why?"

Zoe grazed her finger over the timestamp. "This was issued at thirty-three minutes past five that day."

"Interesting. There's no reason for her to be in this area. It's not on her way home." Lisa frowned. "Why would she have gone there?"

"Maybe she was meeting someone." Zoe's mind raced. "It could be the last person to see her alive."

"Or the person who took her."

Zoe's phone vibrated with a message. When she saw it, delight surged through her.

B: Tonight 8 p.m.

A rushing whoosh of air fanned her face and suddenly, the train zipped past her with a final hiss, and Zoe could have sworn she heard a whisper—*Emily*.

"I would like a hot chocolate." Zoe beamed at the teenager with acne behind the counter. "Large. Extra-large," she added, noting the sulking, gray sky through the window. "Do you want anything, Lisa?"

Lisa shook her head.

Outside, the wind swept the litter up into the air. A billboard flickered in the distance advertising the annual carnival—*Pineview Falls Carnival*. The words *survive if you can* flashed in neon red, making Zoe shiver. The bleakness of Pineview Falls was so strong that she wouldn't be surprised to learn that zombies came out at night.

"That would be three ninety-nine," he said.

Zoe pulled out a five-dollar bill along with a picture of Annabelle. "Have you seen this woman?"

"Uhm..."

She showed her badge. "FBI. She came here two days ago and got a coffee around 5:30 p.m."

It was a stretch. Zoe didn't expect anyone in the service industry to remember customer faces. By the end of a long working day they all looked the same. She was already formulating a plan to charm the manager to let them view the security footage rather than having to get a court order.

"Oh, yeah, I've seen her a couple times here." He scratched his head. "That's Anna, right?"

"Yes, Annabelle." Lisa's voice climbed an octave. "She was here two days ago?"

"Yeah. She often dropped by to hang out with Jackie."

"Who is Jackie?" Zoe scoured her memory for the name but it was unfamiliar.

"She works here. They're always talking intensely in that corner."

"And where is Jackie?" Zoe asked. "We need to talk to her."

The boy shrugged. "No idea. She hasn't shown up to work for two days. It's unlike her. Overheard the manager complain because she hasn't been answering her phone."

Zoe's stomach clenched. A slippery feeling bloomed in her chest. She looked at Lisa, who had turned pale. The possibility hung heavy between them, as dreary as the weather outside.

Could Jackie be in danger?

THIRTEEN

Sweat trickled down Zoe's back. Her clothes stuck to her like a second skin. Her breaths were jerky and her heart careened lazily. She tightened her hands into fists, knuckles cracking and blood pounding. The chorus of people chanting names and hooting dissolved in the background and so did their faces.

All Zoe saw was one face—Viktor Axenov. It was *him* who circled her in the ring and not the brute Benny had arranged her match with. Her vision molded around him until she only saw him. He lunged forward but she moved deftly to one side, delivering a sharp uppercut. Before he had a chance to recover, she looped him and struck him behind the knee.

His legs buckled and down he went with a grunt. This is what she would have done to Viktor. But she had been ambushed. He was strong. Unlike some of the men she fought in these underground fight clubs, that man had a defined, specific skill set that came from training and not just experience. His movements had been sharp and controlled; his blows had been effective.

She wrapped an arm around her opponent's neck and

locked it in place. His body writhed; his arms flailed as he tried to free himself. But Zoe tightened her grip, crushing his windpipe with her arm. She let the rage drive her. It pumped through her body, burning her insides, coating them with a thick layer of ash.

She was so close to finding out who Rachel was hiding from. *Viper.* The man who pulled Viktor's strings. What had Rachel stolen from him? Who was so powerful that he had found Rachel in witness protection? Why had she lied to the police about Rachel's death? Each question burrowed deeper into her skin.

Soon the opponent transformed into the man she saw at the subway station yesterday. Then suddenly his face blurred—the faceless entity who had sent her the lock of hair and buried Annabelle Stevens in the woods. And then his face changed again.

This time she saw her own face.

A sharp thread of shock pulled through her and she let go of her opponent, staggering backward and gasping.

The crowd around her erupted as the man went slack-jawed and dropped unconscious. The referee, Benny, raised her hand in triumph. But Zoe didn't register anything—not the noise, not her body's soreness, not that sweet feeling of victory.

Because she knew deep down that it wasn't Rachel's killer or the other bad people in her life she wanted to inflict pain upon; *she* was the biggest villain of her life.

Back at the station, Zoe's finger grazed the edges of Annabelle's autopsy photographs in the file. Snapshots of her arms, collarbone, and legs sprinkled with distinct purple puncture wounds. The dimensions were measured and noted in the file, along with test results pending for particulate analysis. There wasn't a single part of Annabelle's skin that was devoid of injuries. It was as if someone was determined to systematically inflict pain on her—piece by piece, slowly and steadily pushing her because he wanted to see that first crack in her resolve and then the next, until she broke down completely. Like Annabelle was a lab rat in a twisted individual's experiment.

Unlike Zoe for whom pain was a quick fix like a drug. She chased those blows and punches and kicks to assuage some of the guilt that had a permanent grip on her insides.

"How can someone do that to a person?" she wondered out loud, wincing at another photo of Annabelle's thigh where the imprint of barbed-wire fencing was etched into her skin.

Aiden appeared over her shoulder, startling her. "Dehumanization—" He stopped when he saw her watching him flatly. "Ah, it was a rhetorical question."

Zoe rolled her eyes and closed the file, swiveling on her chair. "We might have another missing woman."

His face fell. "Did you get another riddle?"

"Annabelle was last seen at the café and talking with her friend—Jackie Fink. No one has heard from her since Annabelle went missing."

"Did the husband, Trevor, know Jackie?"

"I got off the phone with him an hour ago. He said the name doesn't ring a bell."

He stroked his jaw and slowly sat down. "*Both* women could be in danger?"

She nodded. "The last sighting of Annabelle was with Jackie. Why? What are you thinking?"

"I'm thinking it's not an easy feat for someone to kidnap two adult women." His voice trailed off as he did some calculations. "We might have to revise our profile."

"How?"

"It's more likely that the killer knew both of them, which is why he was able to lure them at the same time. Maybe they were on their way to meet him."

Her chest constricted. "Do you think Jackie is being tortured as we speak? There's a reason I haven't gotten a riddle yet."

FOURTEEN

Jackie's house was a single-story building in need of a fresh coat of paint. The lawn was patchy and unkempt with weeds creeping up the edges of the driveway. Lisa broke open the door after nobody answered.

The first thing Zoe registered was the dust dancing in the stale air. She waded through the personal space of a woman she'd never met—an occupational hazard. A half-empty coffee mug, a stack of unopened mail and bills, a crumpled blanket on the couch, and overflowing garbage infusing the air with a sour smell. A bouquet of stream violets in a vase—limp and dead.

"She forgot to put the milk back." Lisa pulled a face. "She definitely hasn't been home these last couple of days."

"No one at work reported her missing?" Aiden asked.

"I talked to the manager. It sounds like she's checked out of the job."

Zoe twirled the cord of a charger. "How does Jackie know Annabelle?"

"Maybe they just became friends at the coffee house. She could have been a regular there and they bonded," Lisa suggested.

"Possibly." Zoe looked at Aiden. "What do you think?"

He slipped inside the only bedroom without answering. Zoe followed him, noting the bed hadn't been slept in. It was highly likely that Jackie lived alone, from the single toothbrush in the bathroom, and yet she'd made no attempt to engrave the house with an ounce of her personality. No books, no artwork, no mementos, no pictures that told Zoe anything about who Jackie was.

Except for a bunch of flowers—now wilting—sitting in a vase.

"Are you seeing what I'm seeing?" Zoe asked, wandering back out into the kitchen.

"It's a functional house, nothing more," Aiden remarked, opening the closet and flicking through Jackie's clothes. "Is she new to town, Sheriff?"

Lisa leaned against the doorway. "No. Born and bred here, according to Ethan. No priors. I'll ask deputies to canvass the neighborhood. Maybe someone saw something."

Zoe's eyes landed on the magnetic calendar on the fridge. September 5 was circled with the words "MF birthday" next to it. The only intimate detail in this barren house. "Who is MF?"

Lisa made a note of it. "I'll ask Ethan to look into it. Her last name is Fink so probably some family member."

"Storm! Sheriff!" Aiden's voice came from the bedroom. They rushed back to the bedroom to find Aiden in the walk-in closet. He had swiped the clothes to one side to expose the back wall.

Zoe drew a sharp breath.

A single bulb dangled from the ceiling, oscillating and casting shadows. The entire wall was filled with newspaper clippings, photos, and handwritten notes arranged in a haphazard order. Frantic handwriting in margins, scrawled in different inks. Almost like the words were gushing out to be on the wall. Red thread connecting the notes, and maps dotted with pins. Zoe could feel the obsession spilling from the meticulousness and sheer volume of information. She ran her fingers over the words that popped up the most, words that were scribbled hard enough to leave an indentation in the paper.

Pineview Falls Big Fire.

FIFTEEN

Harrington Group just can't seem to catch a break. As if the company wasn't already drowning in rumors of a buyout, now it has a murder attached to its name.

Annabelle Stevens, a rising star in the company's R&D, was found murdered, buried in the woods, and while police are keeping their lips sealed tighter than a CEO at an SEC hearing, the rumor mill has already begun to churn. Stevens was ambitious, sharp, and, according to sources, knee-deep in the kind of company secrets that don't make it into glossy press releases.

Was Annabelle simply in the wrong place at the wrong time, or was she another loose end in a company desperate to keep its skeletons in the closet? Harrington Group has, of course, issued the standard-issue, legally sanitized statement—thoughts and prayers, deepest condolences, full cooperation with authorities, etc., etc.

What really happened to Annabelle Stevens? Was it personal? Was it professional? Or, in the worst-case scenario for Harrington Group, was it both?

One thing's for sure—this isn't a story that's going away anytime soon. Stay tuned.

The white sheet of paper in front of Zoe was the brightest thing at the station. The walls, upholstery, curtains, and files were all brown. Even the plants were turning brown from lack of sunlight. She tipped her chin to look up at the low ceiling that was pressing down on her. She felt like she was trapped in the 1970s. Even the computer was ancient, with wires extending out of it like vines and pooling at her feet.

Adam's latest article on Annabelle's murder was on the screen. His words echoed in her head. It was the most interesting event to have happened in Pineview Falls in a very long time. Finally, something for people to talk about and Adam sounded like that hungry opportunist who was eager to give them fodder to sink their teeth into at the dinner table.

Her phone rang. It was Simon.

"Hey," she answered with a sigh.

"Sorry, I was in a meeting," he replied, the sound of phones trilling in the background. "Dealing with budget cuts again. Then these assholes will blame me for cutting corners in investigations. How's everything over there?"

She peered out the small window with bars and caught a glimpse of the watery sun barely shining through the haze. "It's a dull afternoon. This town looks abandoned even though I know it's not."

He laughed. "That's just you hating anything that isn't a city. Remember you driving all the way to DC to de-stress when we were at Quantico?"

"They have good bakeries."

"Tell me about it. That bakery on Wisconsin Avenue stayed in business because of me, all the times I got you croissants."

Zoe smiled, remembering those lazy, tender mornings when Simon would arrive with her favorite treats. Then she caught herself. He might be separated but technically he was still married. Was she even interested in him now? "Did you manage to get anything from that envelope and the hair?"

His tone sharpened. "Nothing yet. But I've asked forensics to take a closer look since there were no prints. Do you have any suspects?"

"Not yet. I'm worried that we have another woman missing —Jackie Fink."

"Holy shit," he muttered. "Have you received another letter?"

"No. Not yet." She saw Aiden heading toward her, carrying a coffee tray. "I'll keep you posted."

"Take care, Z."

His tenderness made her pause before she hung up. Aiden fell onto the seat across from her and pushed a coffee toward her. His eyes landed on the piece of paper and narrowed with a twinkle. Zoe looked down and her throat closed. She had been mindlessly scrawling the name *Emily* on it. She screwed up the paper and tossed it away.

"Did you read Adam's article?" Zoe changed the unspoken subject.

"I did." He stroked his jaw. "He loves blood in water—anything that smells like a headline."

"Do you think he's forcing the connection with Harrington Group? Jackie has no connection with the company."

"He's a fabulist. Either way, Ethan told me that the court order for Annabelle's work laptop should come through today."

"Why do you think that lock of hair was sent to me if it isn't Annabelle's?" she asked.

A realization crossed Aiden's face. "Get the hair tested for Jackie's DNA. She has straight, dark hair."

"Jackie's? But the poem that came with it led us to Annabelle's body in the woods."

"What was sent to you might have been a clue to *two* victims, Storm."

Pangs of unease spread through her. How far would this go? Was Jackie already dead after being tortured like Annabelle?

"This is interesting," Aiden said, reading a report.

"What's that?"

"The neighbors reported hearing shouting and loud voices two days before she went missing." He read aloud. "They didn't see who it was but there was a red Prius parked outside."

Zoe was on the computer, looking up Annabelle's and Trevor's cars. "Did they call the cops?"

"Before they thought about it, the car left. What car do the Stevens have?" He tipped his chin.

"Neither of them has a Prius registered to them," she said, disappointed.

A sharp knock on the door startled her.

Adam poked his head into the room, his unruly hair all spiky, wearing a beige suit with a red tie falling too long. "Oh, don't mind me. Just here to ruin the mood."

"Why are you here, Adam?" Zoe asked.

"I enjoy the art of conversation and this place happens to be my favorite canvas." His eyes darted around the room like he was hunting another story. Zoe had met people like Adam before. People like him were anarchists deep down. They were desperate for something to shock or unsettle them. The messier, the better. And in this depraved town, Adam had found the perfect supply.

"There is an empty holding cell here if you want to sit down and chat properly," Zoe joked.

He smirked. "You can dismiss me all you want, Agent Storm, but you won't be able to solve this case without me. I'm resourceful."

"Aiden?" Zoe feigned puzzlement. "Is resourceful a synonym for opportunist?"

"I'm doing this town a service by giving them something to talk about. How much longer can we ride the coattails of the big fire?"

Zoe and Aiden exchanged a quick glance. *Pineview Falls*

Big Fire was written in bold all over the back wall of Jackie's closet. When Zoe had asked Lisa about it, she had brushed it off, saying it had happened almost thirty years ago.

Aiden got to the point. "What is this event that everyone keeps talking about?"

Adam's eyes nearly popped out of his head he was so excited. "You don't know?"

When they shrugged and shook their heads, Adam pulled out a chair, his cocky demeanor shifting to conspiratorial. "You're in for a treat. There is an annual carnival that takes place on Founder's Day in November. One of the attractions is a haunted house called Fun House. It wasn't the most popular attraction but proved very popular with teenagers. Thirty years ago, something happened. Something terrible." A dramatic pause. "The controls in Fun House failed. It was a mechanical failure. A chain reaction that led to props misfiring, exposed wires, overloaded sound system, malfunctioning trapdoor, uncontrolled animatronics, including *total blackout*, you name it. Imagine being trapped in a house like that, running around blindly with sounds loud enough to make you go deaf, tripping over your own feet. No one could hear their screams because of the carnival outside." He weaved a disturbing picture that seemed to delight him. "And the final straw was the fire. A short circuit in the lighting sparked a fire and six teenagers died from smoke inhalation. The biggest tragedy of that has haunted Pineview Falls for decades... until this latest tragedy of a murdered woman, and from what the deputies are talking about outside, another woman has gone missing."

Zoe's pulse quickened as she pondered Adam's words. It was like a piece of a jigsaw puzzle that didn't quite fit. The Pineview Falls Fire was the biggest historic event in this town. Now that she replayed the last three days in this bleak, haunting town—it existed all around her in the form of a weight in the air that never quiet lifted.

Jackie Fink had an unhealthy obsession with the incident. Did the big fire have anything to do with Annabelle's death?

SIXTEEN

Dawn twisted open the cap of the bottle and shook out two red pills. She drew a trembling breath. Pain pulsated behind her eyes. Before she could convince herself otherwise, she swallowed the pills dry.

"Did you read this article?" David strolled into the kitchen, holding an iPad. "It says 'was she another loose end in a company desperate to keep its skeletons in the closet?'" He looked at the bottle of pills Dawn quickly pocketed. "What's that?"

"None of your business." She picked up a knife and began chopping some tomatoes. There wasn't a domestic bone in her body. Growing up, she'd spent more time playing ball with her brothers and trying to prove to them that she could run as fast as them, while her mother lamented the fact she wasn't more "feminine." She had spent years mourning her mother but now there was only person she mourned.

The daughter that now only existed in photographs and her dreams.

"If you're sick, I'd like to know." His eyes softened. "Are you sick?"

She paused, staring at the red juice coating the wooden cutting board. "You want a seat on the board? Find the missing prototype and all our problems go away."

David pressed his lips in a hard line. "I thought you launched an internal investigation. Is that not going anywhere?"

"No." She turned on the stove and spurted extra-virgin olive oil. "I can't involve a lot of people. There are corporate spies everywhere and people ready to jump ship and sell our secrets to the highest bidder. I've made an excuse to the board for now but I'll have to come clean if we are still no further forward in two weeks... maybe this was a mistake."

"Which part?"

She hung her head low, her hands digging into the edge of the counter. "This whole change in direction. It makes me sick to my stomach what we tried to do. We should have destroyed the prototype—never let it get to that level."

"We have to innovate," he said tightly. "We're becoming obsolete in a fast-moving world. If we don't grow, we'll disappear. No one cares about some data storage company with the competition that has come up. Creativity will thrive."

"We could have thought of something else." She hated admitting her concerns to David. But the words tumbled out of her after rattling around in her brain ever since the theft. "It's insensitivity not creativity. And Adam's agenda against us doesn't calm any nerves."

"Why is he linking her murder to us?" David spat, clearly frustrated.

Her focus slid back to him. "You tell me."

They stared at each other as the air between them thickened and swelled with tension. The water boiled in a kettle behind Dawn. But she couldn't look away. There was too much distrust between them ever since her daughter died. It twisted her heart how she was unable to look at David the same way again.

"The cops want Annabelle's laptop. I refused." David broke the silence. "I'm afraid they're going to get a court order."

"Damn it." Were her problems ever going to end? "I'll try to delay that on my end. The lawyers make a fortune being on retainer—they'd better earn it. Meanwhile, get to her laptop and begin deleting all the files and data. We should have done that before."

He frowned. "That'll look suspicious. I'll get into trouble."

"We'll get into more trouble if the prototype leaks," She hissed. "The bad publicity will destroy us."

"I know but—"

"You've picked the wrong time to grow a conscience, boy. You want in on the board? You get your hands dirty. Nothing comes before the company. Absolutely nothing."

He scoffed, bitterness bleaching his tone. "Not even family?"

Tears collected at the back of her throat. She was exhausted. She dropped her voice. "David, this is our legacy. We will die but this will live. Our company, our hard work is the mark we leave behind in this world."

"Your ego really knows no bounds, does it?" he argued hotly. "All these years, you've painted *me* as the bad guy when it's my idea that might save this company. But you'll never give me credit. My brainchild and you will—"

Dawn's palm met his face with a sharp crack. He didn't even flinch.

"I'm doing this for *us*. For *our* family. Our family and the company are one and the same. And don't you even dare question my pain and intent. You have no idea what I've been through and what I'm willing to do. You are one of the many irons I have in the fire. Don't give me a reason to pull you out."

His eyes were blank. "She'll be disappointed in us. This game that we greenlit."

He walked away and the world shrunk around her.

* * *

"No, no, no!" Lisa groaned on the phone and pinched the bridge of her nose. "Of course, the judge didn't sign, Ethan. We don't have probable cause. There's no evidence that Annabelle's laptop contains criminal activity."

"Oh, right," he said. "We should go for exigent circumstances. Imminent risk of evidence destruction."

"Yes. The longer Harrington Group has possession of her laptop, the higher the chances they might be deleting files." She shot up from the chair to unload the dishwasher. The kitchen was in a haywire state, as if a tornado had torn through it—takeout boxes, overfilled trash bag, dirty dishes with crumbs welded to the rim, and spills from food and drinks dried up on the counter.

Now after a long day at the office, Lisa was cleaning up after her husband who stayed home all day. She caught her reflection in the window above the sink. Rain lashed against it. She looked small. She had allowed herself to be made this small.

"Ping the carrier to get a location on Jackie's phones and the records," Lisa said and hung up. She instantly regretted it. Had she sounded too curt? She didn't care. She didn't have the energy. Her hair was in disarray, her clothes smelled, and she hadn't eaten since the morning.

"Tough case?" Jim sauntered in and opened the fridge.

"Yeah." She ground her teeth. She wasn't the only one who hadn't showered or combed her hair. "Busy?"

"I'm just playing this game and can't get to the next level." His bloodshot eyes were wide and possessed. "I have to grind for XP, optimize my loadout, or figure out the exact mechanic—"

"How was your interview?"

"Ah, Lisa..." He rubbed the back of his neck, avoiding her eyes. "I rejected it."

"What?" She dropped the dishcloth from her grasp.

"They weren't paying me enough! I'm a software engineer, Lisa. Not some entry-level analyst. I used to easily pull in six figures and they were paying a measly—"

"So *what*?" she snapped. "You've been sitting at home for months! Isn't something better than nothing?"

He flinched at her outburst and guilt flooded her. Had she gone too far? "Lisa, I asked you to hook me up with a gig at that local cybercrime unit but you didn't help me."

"I told you that I didn't have a solid contact there. People aren't able to line up interviews and this is the fourth offer you've rejected, Jim. In this economy, that's just plain stupid."

"I'm trying."

"You're playing video games all the time! I come home after a long day at work and you haven't even done the laundry or the dishes!"

"You know, that's rich coming from you." He scowled. "Did I ever complain about your fertility issues? Did I ever make you feel inferior? I've always been supportive. I'm even okay with never having children. And you have the audacity to make me feel like some chump just because I want to take it easy for a couple of months and wait for the right opportunity?"

His words pricked her skin. They undid her. All that boiling anger dissipated in an instant. Her tongue weighed heavy and all thoughts scattered.

"Ah, damn it." Jim broke the cloud of tension. "Babe, I didn't mean that. I'm sorry. Come on—" He stepped forward, his arms extended to hug her, but she pushed past him and ran up to the bedroom, letting her tears flow unchecked.

SEVENTEEN

PAST

The woman wasn't supposed to be here. She knew that. If her boss found out, then she'd be in trouble. That was an understatement. She would probably be "taken care of." The way she had taken care of so many people for her boss.

She had accepted that there was something pathological about her. A sensitivity chip that the higher power had forgotten to bestow her with. And then a switch flipped. A burst of energy surged through her, infusing her cells with an emotion she had never experienced before.

Guilt.

With a trembling hand, she knocked on the door. A middle-aged woman with shoulder-length hair and skin sagging from the bones opened the door. Her eyes were dead. It sent chills down her spine.

"Who are you?" she asked.

"I'm Celina," the woman replied. "I knew Michael. May I come in?"

She looked inconvenienced but still let her in. Stepping inside, Celina breathed in the stale air. It was a big house with dark wood paneling, ornate ceiling trims, and crown molding.

An entire wall was covered in pictures of Michael and his mother, tracking his journey from when he was brought home from the hospital to his last birthday—two weeks before he died.

Celina's breath stuck in her throat as she stared at his picture. His face was always in the forefront of her mind. His ghost always in her periphery.

"How did you know Michael?" His mother frowned.

"School. I was a substitute teacher." Another lie.

The silence was suffocating. What was she thinking of, coming here? She never cared to visit the carcass she left behind.

"Thank you for coming." The mother's voice cracked. "Michael was always a lonely boy. He didn't have many friends. I... I was surprised when he decided to go that night to the carnival. But I was so happy." Tears shimmered in her eyes. "I thought he was making friends finally. I w-wish I-I had stopped him."

Words choked inside her. "He was a very kind boy. He didn't deserve this. None of them did."

She nodded faintly. There was a sound, and a young girl, around eight years old, dawdled down the stairs. "Sweetie, why don't you go back to your room?"

"I want pancakes," she said, rubbing the sleep from her eyes.

"I'll make you some in a few minutes, honey." The mother wiped away a stray tear. The little girl looked at the woman. When the woman gave her a little wave, she ran back up the stairs scared. The kid had a better instinct than Michael.

Suddenly, Celina shot up from the chair fighting tears. "I don't want to take up too much of your time. I came because... I wanted to offer my condolences. I will leave you now."

She shouldn't have come. It wasn't just Michael's ghost that would haunt her—now it was also the mother's empty eyes that would keep her awake. His mother kept calling after her but the woman stumbled out of the house, almost wheezing as guilt choked her and Michael's ghost followed her. Some ghosts were real. Some were just memory. And sometimes, there was no difference.

She was quitting. She was done being the exterminator. But the question was—would she be allowed to?

EIGHTEEN

Zoe thumped the microwave that had frozen on her again. When it refused to work, she gave up and decided to eat her chocolate croissant cold. She retrieved it and dug her teeth into it, savoring the sweetness exploding in her mouth.

It was a gloomy morning in Pineview Falls. The drive from the motel to the substation was riddled with water pooling in cracked pavement and mist curling off the wet asphalt. The wind rattled loose power lines, making them sway like tired ghosts. The drizzle had become a steady downpour. Zoe looked out the window into the bleak, blurry landscape. Her heart did a little rattle.

"Jackie's step-sister, Amy, is waiting for us." Aiden appeared next to her, stifling a yawn. His cheeks tinged pink in embarrassment.

Zoe rolled her eyes. "You're human, Aiden. You can yawn. Didn't bring your mattress with you?"

He rolled up his sleeves. "I'm trying to be more flexible. It's a personal project. Do you have one?"

It looked like friendly chatter to anyone else. But Zoe didn't miss the pointed twinkle in his eyes, the little movements he made to conceal that he wasn't curious about her response. She clenched her jaw. Would he ever stop trying to psychoanalyze her?

"Aiden, we can be friends if you learn to just accept me for who I am, as supposed to trying to find someone else in me."

His hand, pouring the coffee, stopped in midair. He took a few seconds to reply, like he was choosing his words. "Maybe I'm just getting to know you. You ever thought about that?" He walked past her.

Her face flushed. When did she become so cynical? She wore the rainbows and unicorns on her face. She brazenly showed the world that she wasn't jaded or dulled by what her profession entailed. It wasn't a façade; it was who she was. At least, *one* of who she was. There was another person that resided inside her, hidden in the folds of her brain and screaming to be free.

"Did you find anything? From my old case files?" she asked, trying to be more professional.

"I have a lead. But I just want to confirm something."

"Oh." She couldn't think of anything else to say. "But you think whoever sent me that riddle has a bone to pick with me?"

He shrugged. "What other reason could there be but to challenge you? The letter was sent to you, Storm. Not the FBI. I'm looking into it."

"Guilt is a shitty feeling." She squared her shoulders and headed to their makeshift office, where a thickset woman with lush, golden curls and doe-like eyes sat, playing with the strap of her purse.

"Amy, I'm Zoe Storm from the FBI and this is Dr. Aiden Wesley."

"What is this regarding?" She shook their hands confidently.

Zoe gestured at Aiden to go ahead.

"Jackie Fink is your sister?"

"*Step*-sister. My father married her mother. Jackie kept her biological father's last name. Is she okay?" She frowned.

"When was the last time you heard from her?"

"I don't know. Last week? What's going on?"

Zoe braced herself to break the news. "She's missing. We have reason to believe she might be in trouble."

"*What?*" Her jaw hung open and then a range of emotions crossed her face, from confusion to shock to concern. "W-why? I don't understand."

"Did she ever mention Annabelle Stevens to you?" Aiden asked.

"No. I don't think so. Isn't that the woman who was murdered?" Her eyes bugged out. "Has Jackie been abducted too?"

"We don't have evidence of anything yet. It's better for the investigation if you keep things to yourself for now," Zoe said, trying to reassure her. "Are you sure she's never mentioned Annabelle?"

"Positive. Though, maybe they met through work?"

"At the café?" Aiden prodded.

"That or Jackie's new gig. She was working freelance as a video game tester."

"Oh." Zoe frowned. "For whom?"

"Harrington Group." Amy's gaze slid back and forth between them. "They are apparently making some video game, or they were, I don't know. But Jackie was working part-time for them."

Zoe and Aiden locked eyes. Finally, they'd discovered the link between Annabelle and Jackie—they weren't merely friends from the coffee shop who had bonded over a couple of lattes. They both worked for the same company that Adam was trying to hold to account in his article. Zoe wondered if there was any truth to what she'd dismissed as pure speculation.

"You and Jackie are from here, right? Pineview Falls,"

Aiden said. "Townies usually have families and friends. From her home, it didn't seem like she had many people in her life or even a boyfriend."

Amy blinked through her tears. "She... was very lonely. And we weren't nearly as close we should have been. She was kind of a mess." She couldn't keep the judgment out of her voice.

Zoe mulled over that information. Jackie was young and beautiful, having spent years walking the same streets and seeing the same faces and knowing the same corners of Pineview Falls. And yet she had managed to float through the dreadful town instead of putting down any meaningful roots. Did the dreariness of Pineview Falls get under her skin and cloud her mind? Did it dim her light and make her want to be alone?

"What mess?" Aiden asked.

"I feel bad..."

"You'll only be helping us," he explained gently. "The difference between you both is evident. I'm guessing you have seen the world, invested in your education. But Jackie wasn't interested in building anything, was she?"

Zoe resisted the urge to roll her eyes. Aiden was being Aiden—playing the vulnerable woman in front of him like a fiddle. He'd sniffed her superiority complex.

A flash of pride crossed Amy's face. "She was a hermit and obsessed with the fire. Her brother died in it." Her words chilled Zoe. All roads at Pineview Falls led to the fire. She imagined what the inside of Jackie's mind must look like. Every thought, every dream, every fantasy dictated by the tragedy she couldn't stop researching. "She was obsessed." She gave a small smile. "Who wouldn't be in this town? I kept telling her to do something with her life but the fire was a black hole she kept falling into."

"Do you know who MF is?" Zoe asked, remembering the calendar. "There was a date circled on a calendar at Jackie's house. September 5. It's MF's birthday. A boyfriend perhaps?"

"Oh, no, no. That's her brother. Michael. Michael Fink. What a shame for her mother. She lost one child to fire and the other child to madness."

* * *

Zoe didn't like the dark. Always slept with a night light. She imagined herself running around like a headless chicken, desperately trying to escape the total blackness. Outside, the wind snaked through the empty streets, rattling loose street signs and making the old lampposts flicker.

Sitting in the only Chinese restaurant in town, she rubbed the chopsticks between her palms, eagerly looking at the spread of cheap, greasy Chinese food, as she took her time deciding what to eat first. To her annoyance, Aiden neatly scooped a portion of each dish onto his plate. He tossed over a fortune cookie to her. She cracked it open—and imagined Rachel's hands instead of her own. It was their thing when they got Chinese food.

The answers you seek are not ahead but buried in you.

A thick stack of all research and case files into the Pineview Falls tragedy awaited her. It sucked out all the oxygen in the room. The tale of how six teenagers died together.

"Is that why this town feels like a cemetery?" Zoe wondered aloud. "Because of what happened all those years ago?"

"It's collective trauma response. Small towns are closed ecosystems, meaning everyone is either directly or indirectly connected to the victims. That grief doesn't dissipate. It lingers, passed down like folklore." He picked at his noodles, his eyes staring into empty space. "And then there is the displacement of time. These towns exist in a kind of psychological purgatory, where the past is more present than the future."

The wind whistled. Windows rattled. The velvety darkness outside folded and stirred. The town wasn't just scarred from the violent deaths; it was calcified. And even though Zoe had only been here four days, she could already feel herself becoming a part of the echo.

Her phone buzzed with a notification. She looked at it and a smile broke across her lips.

"What is it?" Aiden asked.

She laughed at the goofy picture. "My sister just sent me a picture of my nephew. Do you have any siblings?"

"Four."

She almost dropped her phone. "*What?* You have *four* siblings?"

He shrugged. "Why are you surprised?"

"I just assumed you grew up in a mental institution," she quipped. She caught him almost smile before his face became hard like granite. "Anyway, coming back to this, Jackie was obsessed with the fire. Do you think that has anything to do with our case?"

He narrowed his eyes at the files. "I want to say no. It's not surprising she was obsessed. She'd lived here all her life. I imagine a lot of people here are fascinated by it. But it will be useful to understand what happened."

Zoe licked her fingers clean, much to Aiden's horror, and divided the files between them. "Let's get cracking." She flipped through the pages, quickly absorbing the details. "Wow. So much here is handwritten. How many people do you think had carpal tunnel in the 1980s? November 1. Dispatch Center received a 911 call at 23:42 hours from an unidentified caller reporting 'bodies' at Fun House. Patrol units were dispatched at 23:44 hours. First officers on scene at 23:58 hours. EMS and fire personnel arrived at 00:07 hours. No survivors located."

"I got the medical examiner findings." Aiden read out from the file and his face fell. "Jesus. These kids range from the ages of fifteen to seventeen. They went through a ringer, Storm. Before the fire started, they were running around in total darkness, tripping over things and bumping around, trying to get out. They have physical injuries antemortem."

She cracked her knuckles, pushing aside the images trying to pop up in her mind. "It's hard to believe that *everything* went wrong in a haunted house. They have so many elements—fog machine, lighting rigs, automated circuits, mechanical props. How do all of them fail?"

"This was the 1990s. Safety wasn't a priority. And this Fun House was only three years old. More parts mean more failure points."

"I suppose." She scanned the notes and pictures. The skeletal remains of the haunted house structure, half-collapsed, with blackened wood and melted plastic. Props or animatronic figures fused into grotesque, half-melted shapes, their faces distorted. Floorboards with deep charring in streaks. She didn't dare to look at the pictures with bodies. Her blood curdled. "So this is what everyone in this town is obsessed with."

A deep frown marred Aiden's face as he focused on something, his eyes narrowing behind his thick glasses. "Do you see this?"

Zoe followed. There were faint impressions of something scribbled in the footnotes. "Someone partially erased their notes."

He picked up a pencil and began shading it, then he turned it over and read the words out loud. "Multiple ignition points. Charring underneath wooden floorboards. Downward fire pattern."

"They could have been just jotting down their thoughts before finalizing the report," she suggested but pulled out her phone and researched the observations. Surprise flickered on her face. "Interesting. These are indicators of arson."

His eyebrows shot up. "A deliberate act? Engineered to look like a malfunction."

"It's hard to say. Maybe they were just preliminary observations and whoever wrote this erased it, realizing their mistake." She glanced at the pictures again, trying to decipher if what was written was true. "We should try to verify this."

"There are a few people listed here as part of the expert panel. I'll get a handwriting analysis done to see whose writing this was."

She drummed her fingers on the table. "I can believe there were no witnesses and no one heard them, but what about the staff? There must have been at least one operator."

Aiden nodded, turned a page, and recoiled. "There was only one person on shift during this incident. David Harrington."

NINETEEN

"Jim, if you want to be a man in this town, you have to get used to violence. You have to know the smell and touch of blood." His father hugged his shoulders, pointing at the fallen deer on the ground. "Take the knife and make the first cut. Be a man."

The sound of a mediocre local band playing classic rock music drowned out his father's voice. Jim took another swig of his bitter beer. He didn't even like beer. He didn't like alcohol. It made his head swim and make the demons louder. But wasn't he supposed to like beer? Wasn't it manly to drink?

"Hey, Jim," the bartender said in his usual gruff voice. He gave him a nod. "How's it going?"

"Same old, same old."

"Going anywhere anytime soon?" He threw a rag over his shoulder and twisted open a bottle of rum.

Jim swallowed the bitter liquid, despising his weakness. "There's a gaming convention in Seattle in a couple weeks."

"Oh." He frowned. "I didn't know you were into video game designing now."

A hot flush crept up his face. He didn't correct him. He

didn't have a job. He wasn't into video game designing; he was into playing.

The bar wasn't exactly pumping on a weekday at this time. The few patrons were haggard, aging with vacant, dull eyes. Jim felt restlessness come over him. Is this what he'd become? He pulled out his phone to mindlessly scroll the Internet.

Somehow he ended up on LinkedIn, where all his buddies were announcing their new jobs and promotions. They all had fancy job titles and did important things. He was more qualified than most of them. And here he was rotting away in a bar, planning a video game excursion while his wife paid the bills.

His father must be turning in his grave.

"Isn't he the sheriff's husband?" he heard a man sitting a few seats away from him ask his friend. Jim stiffened.

"I think so," the friend replied. He cleared his throat and raised his voice. "Are you Sheriff Gray's husband?"

"Yep." He clenched his jaw.

"Did they find out who killed that woman?"

Jim's grip on the glass tightened. "I don't know. I stay away from all that."

He looked disappointed. "I know her husband. He's a mess. Single dad of two now."

"What a tragedy." The other man clicked his tongue. "The only big things that happen to this town. Did your wife tell you anything? She must be working late nights."

Jim had come across something in her files in the morning. He wasn't planning on it. He'd entered the kitchen and there it was.

Pineview Falls Big Fire. That's what was in her files.

"She's working hard," he said in a clipped tone.

They must have sensed his reluctance to elaborate and began chatting among themselves.

Why was Lisa looking into the fire of 1995? Why did everything revolve around one night in this town?

Jim finished the beer and slid a bill across the table. Curious eyes locked on to him—eyes that only saw him as the sheriff's husband, eyes that reminded him just how much he'd diminished.

His father was right. Even when Jim was just a boy, his father had picked up on something that haunted him.

"You don't have the stomach." He took the rifle from a sobbing Jim. *"Always a little boy, never the man. Nothing in your life will work until you learn how to go for the kill."*

* * *

"You're in a mood," Aiden commented dryly next to her as Zoe's foot almost got caught in gnarled roots jutting up like grasping fingers. She kicked the stones loose underfoot to keep her balance.

Zoe smirked. Watching Aiden navigate the ruthless terrain of Washington woods was entertaining enough for a moment. "Being in the field is different from sitting in a fancy office on a comfortable chair, isn't it?"

"Life is all about new experiences." His smile was tight as they weaved their way through the crowded trees. The drizzle wasn't heavy, but it came at them sideways, sharp and relentless, stinging her skin and blurring her vision whenever she lifted her head. "We should be close."

"This guy is a recluse."

The house was still out of sight. The path had narrowed, winding through dense woods, the branches overhead knitted too tightly together to let in much light. Everything felt damp: the air, the leaves, the ground beneath her boots.

She hated it. She cursed under her breath and pressed on, muscles aching from the climb, her breath visible in the chilled air.

"Are we looking at a revenge plot?" Zoe asked. "Someone

knew that David was on shift that night and maybe blames him? Now targeting his employees like Annabelle and Jackie?"

Aiden was unsure. "That's a roundabout way to hurt him."

"Well, they must be even more pissed at Dawn. David was still a teenager. The motive could be to destroy the Harrington legacy and name. Look at all the bad publicity they've been getting. That's got to have an effect on their stock price."

"Thank Adam Deader for that. The man is on a mission to ensure that everybody sees the names Annabelle and Jackie with Harrington Group in the same sentence."

The drizzle turned colder, harder, needle-like against her cheeks. "He could fit the profile," she said. "He's resourceful enough to pull this off. He's certainly creative enough to come up with the riddles for you."

"If you can't find a story to boost your career, then you can create one." Aiden remarked.

Then, finally, through a gap in the trees, the house came into view. It sat perched at the edge of the hill, dark and weathered against the slate-gray sky. Zoe could taste brine on her tongue. In the distance, she heard the waves crash against the rocky shore.

They knocked on the door and waited. It creaked open, revealing a muscled, weathered man in his sixties with gray at his temples and lines etched deep around his eyes.

Zoe showed her badge. "Ed Morgan?"

"Yes, yes." He wasn't surprised as he let them in. "What is it?"

She and Aiden looked at each other before stepping inside. The room was dusty and sparse, with an old television and some black-and-white photographs hanging on the walls. The only polished thing was a gramophone by the window.

Ed fell into a sunken armchair with torn upholstery. "Which case is this regarding?"

"You get a lot of consults?" Zoe guessed.

"Every now and then. No other reason for anyone to visit an old guy like me." His smile was tired.

"Yeah..." She cleared her throat. There was nothing old about Ed other than the wrinkles and gray in his hair. Under his clothes, he had bulging biceps and toned legs. Zoe wondered if he had a military background and then noticed some medals hanging on the wall.

"You were on the Pineview Falls incident case?" Aiden asked.

"Oh, yes." He made an *oof* sound. "That was a nasty one."

"You wrote some notes in the file that pointed at arson but then you erased them."

He nodded. "That was my assessment but my superior came to a different conclusion and told me to erase my notes."

"Was that an odd request?" Aiden asked.

"It certainly was. But you're young, you're new, you don't ask too many questions. You assume your boss knows best. A couple years later, I joined the army." He nodded toward an old picture of him with his buddies in uniform. "Didn't spend a lot of time thinking about it."

"Do you mind walking us through the pictures again?" Zoe handed him her phone. "We found deep charring in streaks across the floorboards. What does that tell you?"

He put on his glasses, which were taped together. "That's a pour pattern. You see how the burn marks are concentrated in elongated streaks rather than a single point? That suggests an accelerant was used. Fire doesn't naturally travel in lines like this. It spreads outward in a V pattern from a point of ignition. This? This is a liquid burn."

"So someone poured something?"

"Likely a fast-burning accelerant—gasoline, lighter fluid, something volatile. You can also tell because of the depth of the charring. A natural fire wouldn't eat through the wood that fast unless it was burning hotter than normal. I don't remember now." He frowned, his gaze looking out the window into the horizon. "I don't think any samples were ever collected to check what accelerant it was."

"You also mentioned finding ignition points in at least three separate locations," Zoe said.

He leaned back. "That's your biggest red flag right there. Accidental fires don't start in multiple places at once. Electrical faults? They have a single origin and spread outward. A system failure? It might trigger a fire in one area, but not simultaneously across different rooms."

"It was arson," Aiden whispered. "Do you still believe that?"

"Yes," he said stubbornly. "I don't know why I was told my conclusions were incorrect."

Zoe wouldn't be surprised if Dawn had buried the evidence by pulling in some favors. Anything to keep her son's name out of the scandal, even though her daughter had died in the fire. But if this was arson, then wouldn't Dawn want to know who'd killed her daughter?

"If I remember correctly, then the operations panel had also been tampered with." He skimmed through the pictures and zoomed in on one. "Here, you see that? That wire has been cut on purpose. It's too neat. It's why the fire suppression system didn't trigger and why the safety mechanisms failed."

"This was a thorough job," Aiden noted. "Someone knew exactly what they were doing."

Ed let out a low whistle. "Oh, yes. That was one of the bad cases. That's why they call it a massacre even though it's been officially deemed an accident."

"You never said anything? To anyone?" Zoe asked.

Ed shrugged. "Over the years, this thing has become almost mythic. I bet half the town already believes it was sabotage.

That half is called the conspiracy theorists. Setting up this whole thing would have taken some time too. I was surprised there were no witnesses."

The operations panel had been tampered with and David was the operator on shift. Was David responsible for the fire?

TWENTY

It was sitting in the lavish home of Dawn Harrington and eating a delicious muffin that Zoe realized how looming an absence could be. A picture of a teenage girl hung in the living room above the fireplace. And every expensive piece of furniture, handwoven rug, and crystal fixture was coated with a sense of incompleteness.

Aiden made a face. "David's sister was one of the victims."

"And David was the operator that night?" Something didn't sit well with Zoe. An uneasy feeling spread through her. She glanced at Lisa, sitting on the armchair, her knee bobbing incessantly. "You all right?"

Lisa pulled free of her racing thoughts. "Yeah... yeah... the warrant came through to seize Annabelle's computer at work."

"That's good news," Zoe said in a measured voice. "Isn't it?"

Lisa swallowed hard and nodded. She glanced at Aiden, who was watching a nervous Lisa bite her nails. Perhaps it was how rich the Harringtons were. A small town like Pineview Falls couldn't afford the wrath of a family that employed so many residents. Or perhaps Lisa was truly out of her depth. Zoe imagined what the sheriff's life was like—simple and predictable. A friend of the locals, she was more used to family feuds and rowdy men at the bar, not ruffling feathers of people who were way above her pay grade.

Dawn marched into the room, with David at her heels. "How can I help you? Lisa, what's going on?"

"Mrs. Harrington, we just have a few questions." Lisa got to her feet and sat down again after Dawn took a seat.

Dawn reminded Zoe of what Rachel would have been like had she not been killed. A sturdy woman in a flannel shirt and pants with a perpetual busy look on her face like she was juggling a gazillion things. Behind her David sank onto a barstool, his arms crossed.

"We want to talk about the fire." Zoe came straight to the point.

Silence. Dawn's face froze and so did the frenzy in her eyes. David threw his head back and closed his eyes, his shoulders visibly tensing. Zoe knew that she'd given voice to something that was *never* talked about in this house.

"What about it?" Dawn said, rather too quickly.

"David, you were the operator that night," Aiden said. "What happened?"

"We don't talk about that." David's voice was thick. "Tread carefully, detectives."

"It's important," Zoe insisted.

"Why?" His voice climbed an octave. "Don't you have bigger things on your plate like Annabelle and Jackie?" He stopped abruptly.

Zoe leaned forward, as she glanced at Lisa. "How do you know about Jackie? We never alerted the media."

"It was Adam," Dawn declared and poured herself a stiff drink. "He's been pathetically trying to link our company to the murder, so he wanted to get a quote from us."

"It seems that he's onto something. Jackie was working as a freelancer for you," Zoe said. "A video game tester."

Dawn stiffened before gulping down her drink. "I'm not privy to the identity of every employee, Agent Storm. Besides, it's only a coincidence. Adam wants more eyeballs on his articles, which is why he's using our status and company. This murder has nothing to do with us."

"David, what happened on the night of the fire?" Aiden repeated his question.

David avoided his eyes, his mouth a flat line. "Our family was destroyed that night. Do you really want to put to my mother through hell again by forcing me to rehash the events?"

"It's okay, David." Dawn squeezed his shoulder. "You'll find Pineview Falls to be an interesting study, Dr. Wesley. We never talk about the fire but it's always there, smoldering inside each of us. Even thirty years later."

David looked pleadingly at the faces waiting patiently for him to talk. His shoulders sagged as he gave up. "I was working there on the weekends to make extra cash. I was new to the job. I had a five-hour shift. All I had to do was push a few buttons and recite the same warnings to every new group of kids who got their rocks off by getting scared. Hayley showed up with a couple of her friends." His eyes glistened with tears. "She'd been to Fun House before but wanted to experience it again. I let them in, gave them the whole spiel, and then clicked those same buttons like I was on autopilot. After around ten minutes later, I got... distracted."

"Distracted?" Zoe raised an eyebrow.

He rubbed the back of his neck as a blush began creeping up. Next to him, Dawn's nostrils ballooned and she took another swig of her drink. "By a woman. I was nineteen and this beautiful older woman started chatting me up. I couldn't help myself. There was almost still an hour to go before the haunted house experience would be over. I checked that everything looked fine and thought just going across to get a hot chocolate wouldn't hurt anyone." He struggled to get the words out. "I got back thirty minutes later. I didn't realize how much time had gone by. That's when I knew something was wrong. For some reason none of the fire alarms had gone off. When I finally forced my way into the haunted house..." His voice trailed off. "It was all over. Fire everywhere. Everything was burning to the ground."

His words bled into a suffocating silence. Zoe desperately searched for something to latch on to, to avoid thinking about the grim picture David's words had painted. But it was impossible to avoid the haunting pain in Dawn's eyes. She stared past Zoe at the picture behind her.

"Why does it say that your shift ended before this incident and that the person on duty after you never showed up?" Zoe asked. "Nothing you've told us was in the case file."

Dawn took a shuddering breath, bracing herself. "Because I called in a favor to keep David out of it."

"Why?" Aiden was appalled.

"Because I wanted to avoid a lawsuit. There were five other kids who died in that fire. If their families found out that a Harrington was negligent, they would have jumped at the opportunity to milk whatever money they could out of us."

Zoe flinched at her ruthlessness. "You lost a daughter in that fire."

"And don't I know it with every breath I take." Her voice quaked. "You don't get to judge me. You don't know what it's like to live knowing your one child's carelessness took your other child's life." She glared at David, whose expression was blank and resigned. "Now, why you are here digging up old wounds is beyond me."

"We have two victims, and the only thing connecting them

is your company," Zoe said. "Jackie was obsessed with the fire. Did she ever try talking to you about it?"

"No." Dawn shook her head. "Lisa, are we done here now?"

"Yes." Lisa looked embarrassed. "I think we got everything we need."

The conversation was wrapping up. Dawn and David were about to leave the room when Zoe piped up. "We're getting Annabelle's laptop as we speak. If there's a time to come clean about anything, it's now."

The blood drained from David's face. He ran a hand down his face while Dawn stepped forward, tipping her chin up. "What I'm about to say doesn't leave this room. Is that clear?"

Zoe scoffed. Dawn reminded her of a strict high school principal who believed she had the authority to order everyone around. "Yes, ma'am. Anything you want."

Aiden elbowed her subtly, but Dawn didn't seem to have taken offense. "As you know, we are a data storage company but we have been reporting losses for the last consecutive four quarters. And then there was the SEC investigation of fraud that led nowhere. We've been branching out into gaming, working with small companies around the country and hiring developers. The idea was to innovate and diversify into what the market wants. So we developed something innovative to announce the new direction our company was taking. A video game."

"That's the top-secret project Annabelle was working on?" Aiden asked. "And that Jackie was a tester for?"

"Yes. The launch of the new game is critical. You don't understand but this could save our company." She took a shuddering breath. "We didn't want any of the details to get out because of how uniquely it was positioned. But ten days ago, an earlier prototype of the game was stolen."

"An internal investigation has started but we haven't got very far," David explained. "The prototype is *very* different from our final product. If it is leaked it will ruin our launch and impact the sales and perception around the game."

"So you're delaying the launch of your game?" Aiden guessed.

"Yes," Dawn said, her teeth clenched. "Whoever has stolen the prototype hasn't released anything about it, which means they're waiting for us to release the game so that they can undermine us."

David sighed. "Annabelle was spearheading the project. Her laptop contains all the details and specs that we are trying to protect. So please, whatever you do, do *not* let this information get out."

"All they care about is some video game, not one of their employees who was murdered!" Zoe huffed as the door shut behind them and they walked down the curling, cobbled driveway of the lavish home. It was an unusually sunny and warm day. When Aiden opened his mouth to reply, she raised a hand. "Yes, yes, I know how the world works."

Behind them, Lisa trailed in deafening silence. Zoe didn't fully understand Lisa—she had a quiet strength to her, always following up on tips and coordinating searches. She didn't speak much, but the deputies in the room would stand up straighter around her. That strength buckled when she was around the Harringtons. She transformed into someone inferior who didn't speak, not because she wasn't naturally assertive, but because she was afraid.

Aiden stopped in his tracks and a distracted Lisa almost slammed into him. "Sheriff, is there a conflict of interest we need to know about?"

Lisa bit her lower lip. "No. It's not like that."

"This is a high-stakes investigation. We potentially have a missing woman on our hands," Zoe said. "If the Harringtons are involved in any way, then we can't let them off the hook—"

"I know that!" Lisa snapped. "Look, they are the reason I got elected, okay? What you're seeing isn't subservience. It's gratitude. Besides, I don't have the luxury the two of you have. You will move on from this town and these people once this case is over. I'm stuck here. I can't afford to piss people off, *especially* people like the Harringtons."

"We just want to make sure that you'll be able to remain unbiased," Zoe said gently.

Lisa's eyes ping-ponged between them. She shook her head and sighed, pushing past them, muttering something inaudible under her breath.

Zoe watched her stocky frame head toward her jeep. "We weren't being unreasonable, were we?"

"No, we just found one person who isn't charmed by you," Aiden teased.

"Are you saying I've charmed you?" she blurted out without thinking and then bit her tongue. Was she flirting? She could retract and deflect but she waited. She actually wanted to know his answer.

Aiden adjusted his glasses and smiled. A brief pause. "Yes."

She rolled her eyes and took out her sunglasses despite her heart doing a little skip. "Wish I could say the same. Anyway, what do you think?"

"The only connection is the Harringtons and the video game that was supposed to launch," he said thoughtfully as he leaned against the car door. "We should get a list of everyone that was involved in the project."

"That shouldn't be too hard now that we have Annabelle's laptop. Do you think the fire is just a red herring?" Zoe said. "There was no hint that Annabelle was interested in it. Maybe it was just Jackie."

Aiden stroked his jaw and stared at his feet. "I can imagine every other person we find in this town will at the very least be fascinated by the incident, if not somehow related to it. This could all just come down to whatever's going on with Harrington Group. Like you said, someone who stole the earlier prototype. Maybe Annabelle found out who it was."

A thought occurred to Zoe. "Dawn is very concerned about competition. What if that's what this is? Some corporate spy? Only a competitor would benefit from this theft."

"Who enjoyed killing a little too much." Aiden completed her train of thought.

Zoe's mind raced with question after question. She didn't want to admit it out loud but the biggest question still remained —what was *her* connection to all this? She imagined a dark, shadowy figure always following her around, blinking in and out of existence. Her phone chirped with a notification.

"It's an email from the crime lab." Zoe opened it. "They were comparing the DNA from the lock of hair in the mail to Jackie since it didn't match Annabelle." Blankness spread through her synapses. "It doesn't match Jackie either."

"*What?*" Aiden closed the distance between them, looking at her phone over her shoulder.

"Enough nuclear DNA was preserved to determine it is male DNA. It wasn't a match but there was an overlap."

"They are related."

Zoe skimmed the long report. "Around fifty percent match..." She scrolled down to the summary. "Mitochondrial DNA was identical, which means—"

"Siblings."

"There's more." She waded through the tide of information. "They did keratin degradation analysis and amino acid racemization testing to get a rough timeline of decomposition. It's around thirty years old."

"That old?" Aiden sounded skeptical. "Wouldn't it have degraded? The hair you got looked fresh enough."

"Hair is one of the most durable tissues. Far more so than skin and other organs. It's possible for it to be just fine if the body was embalmed or placed in a sealed coffin." Something clicked inside Zoe. "The fire was thirty years ago."

The revelation simmered between them.

She spoke through the knot in her stomach. "Jackie's brother, Michael Fink, died in the fire. The killer sent me his hair. But why? And how did he have access to his hair?"

TWENTY-ONE

The first time Zoe had stepped foot in a cemetery was when Rachel was buried.

She still remembered that day. The pain had been so monumental and consuming that she had almost fainted. She'd had no appetite for days. But she couldn't marinate in that grief for long.

Mist was trapped on top of the thick trees. Their branches so crooked and lush with leaves that the mist simply hung there, blocking the sunlight and cooling the ground.

Zoe buttoned up her leather jacket, a chilly breeze slapping her face as she trudged, avoiding the patches of puddle from the rain earlier. The headstones appeared, like white dots popping out of a brown ground. Most of them were worn and leaning with time. Weathered and chipped. Others were sharp and shiny.

"There it is!" Aiden pointed to a faded headstone, tucked away in a corner under a wild weeping willow, its branches sweeping the ground.

The inscription on the headstone read:

IN LOVING MEMORY OF MICHAEL FINK 1980–1995. BRIEFLY
HERE, ETERNALLY LOVED.

A thick silence crystallized between them; their eyes fixed on the words. Zoe's heart squeezed. A single crow called out in the distance, the sound cutting through the hush like a broken bell.

"How did Lisa know where he was buried?" Zoe asked Aiden.

"The entire town knows where the kids from that fire are buried. She told me how in the first few years strangers would leave flowers…" His voice trailed off at the barren headstone. "I guess no one cares anymore."

Zoe studied his angular face, pinched in tension. She was used to Aiden behaving like a chess player—always strategizing and carefully plotting his words with a glimmer of something raw here and there. But right now, he was almost shaking, his foot incessantly tapping, his hands fidgeting in the pockets.

Was it being in a cemetery or the grave of a child?

"The soil doesn't look disturbed," she noted, analyzing the ground, which looked even. "Unless someone is really good at this. It's the only cemetery in town. Would the killer risk doing something like this? Break open a coffin, cut a lock of hair, and bury the body again? It seems very convoluted,"

He frowned. "Well, he's sending you riddles and hunting down women." He looked around, his eye catching a middle-aged man hunched a few feet away between two headstones with a damp cloth and shears, wiping away moss.

"Excuse me," Aiden said. "You work here?"

The man straightened slowly, squinting. "Every day."

"We're with the FBI." Zoe flashed her badge, clipped to the waistband of her jeans. "Do you know if anyone's visited the grave plot belonging to Michael Fink?"

His mouth pressed in a hard line. "Yeah. One woman used to. Came regular, flowers every time. Talked to her once. Said she was his sister."

Jackie. She and Aiden exchanged a look.

Aiden narrowed his eyes. "No one else?"

"No. Just her." A pause. "Haven't seen her in a couple weeks, though."

Zoe glanced at the headstone behind him, its edges slick with dew. "And no one has tampered with the grave?"

He raised his eyebrows, alarmed. "Of course, not! I've been coming here twice a day for the last ten years. Rain or shine. Nothing's been touched."

"And have you ever seen anyone acting suspiciously?" Aiden prodded. "Lurking around too often or anything odd?"

He shook his head. "It's a safe place for the dead. Now, if you'll excuse me." He pointed a finger at the sky, which was churning with clouds. With that he walked away, heading toward a shed.

"Well, no one has dug up a grave." Zoe sighed. "Then how the hell did the killer get his hands on the hair? Did he know Michael from before?"

"Or he got it right after Michael died," Aiden suggested. "Like someone who worked on the case and had access to the body."

Just as the caretaker had warned, the sky cracked open with a low rumble, and thunder rolled in behind a sudden, sharp gust of wind.

Zoe ducked beneath the sweeping branches of the weeping willow as the rain came down in sheets. Aiden followed her. The long, slender but soaked branches formed a curtain that swayed and shimmered with the wind. Raindrops pattered on the canopy—a muffled drumming noise.

"I don't like rain," she complained, even though they were well hidden in the cocoon, where only a few drops hit them.

"I've noticed," he said wryly. "I like storms."

So did her mother.

"I don't like morose things, Aiden." She didn't know why she said it and she didn't know where she was going with it. "I don't like feeling sad."

"No one likes feeling sad, Zoe." He called her Zoe. It oddly felt even more intimate than the fact that their shoulders were brushing against each other. "But why do you run away from it so compulsively?"

She didn't really run away from it. There was a place where she indulged all the pain she had felt, a place where she could be free. "Ever heard of 'fake it till you make it'?" She tried cracking a joke.

He threw his head back and laughed, the corners of his eyes crinkling. "That's one way to look at it."

It was a pleasant sound to the ears. "You should laugh more. It sounds better than you psychoanalyzing me."

He scoffed, looking down at her. Suddenly, she almost felt shy about the height difference. "Should we just hang out here until the rain stops?" He shifted uncomfortably.

"I guess." She took a deep whiff, the scent of wet earth and bark hitting her nose. Maybe rain wasn't entirely bad. After a few minutes, the noise inside her muted, swallowed by the hum of the rain. She was acutely aware of Aiden's gaze on her. But she was pretending not to notice.

Why was he staring? And why was she letting him?

When she turned to look at him, he tore his gaze away and frowned, catching himself. "We should go. Just brave the rain."

"Are you okay?" she asked. He looked pale and itchy. "Do you not like cemeteries?"

The lingering tenderness on his face evaporated, as did the moment. An aloof and hard expression captured his face. "It's nothing. Let's head out."

Zoe watched in disbelief as he ducked out from the canopy

and into the rain. Irritation fluttered through her. How hypocritical of him trying to find out everything about her but clamming up when it came to himself. Once again, Aiden had reminded her never to let her guard down.

Once again, she regretted liking him a little.

TWENTY-TWO

"Adam, you've made some bold claims in your latest article, suggesting that Harrington Group isn't just linked to the murder of one of their own, but that there's—what was it—'a deeper rot beneath the surface'? Let's start with that."

Adam was suited up in the studio. Giddiness oozed out of him at the attention he was getting. "Look, I don't just throw things out for clicks, Julia. I follow the facts. And the facts? They don't look good for the Harringtons."

"All right. What facts?" Julia raised an eyebrow.

"You've got an employee who is high-level security clearance working on AI infrastructure and is found murdered and buried in the woods."

"That's circumstantial at best. Where's the link to Harrington Group?"

"The link, Julia, is in the timing. Harrington Group was about to make a big announcement and then boom. They backtracked. The woman—Annabelle Stevens was an internal asset —was sitting on something. A project, a concern, something she wasn't supposed to talk about. And what happens? She winds up dead. And what does Harrington Group do? They button up. No comment, no transparency, just... silence."

"Or they're following legal protocol and respecting an active police investigation?" she challenged.

"Come on. You've been in this business long enough to know better. The minute her death hit the news, they started scrubbing connections, sealing files, locking doors. My source told me that they were reluctant to hand over Annabelle's laptop to the authorities. Why is that? What are they hiding?"

Julia gave it some thought. "You're making a very serious allegation with no direct evidence. This is all speculation."

"I've got sources, and I've got a trail." A dramatic pause. "Annabelle Stevens isn't the only victim."

Julia leaned forward. "What are you saying?"

His cheeks lifted in a clandestine smile. "My sources have told me that a woman called Jackie Fink has also gone missing. She was hired by Harrington Group to do some freelance work. Now, tell me, Julia, does it still feel like mere speculation to you? What you call speculation, I call pattern."

"Are you saying we have a missing woman?" Julia was alarmed.

"Yes. And trust me, it all comes down to Harrington Group."

* * *

Zoe turned off the television and groaned. "It's out now. Jackie Fink's disappearance."

Aiden was perched on a desk, his nose buried in paperwork. "Why didn't we make this public sooner?"

"Because there is no evidence of her being taken." She picked up an apple she had swiped from the break room and tossed it between her hands as she paced the office. "And she's an adult. Protocol doesn't dictate publicizing every disappearance. Now watch the staff here get busy with tips."

Their workroom was cozy with brown walls and lime-green carpet. The rain drummed against the roof in steady, uneven rhythms, a soft patter turning into a muffled roar. Every so often, the wind sent sheets of rain slapping against the siding, a hollow, rattling sound that made the walls feel even thinner than they were.

For a moment, she felt comfortable. But then as she looked out the window through the rivulets into the blurry, gray scene, a shape took form. The shape of a man. She stumbled back and the shape dissolved.

"What is it?"

She was about to confide in him about her fear, about how she wasn't entirely surprised that someone was keeping track of her, but there was a knock at the door.

Their heads turned to find Trevor with a stroller and holding Kevin's hand.

"Mr. Stevens," Aiden exclaimed. "What are you doing here?"

Trevor looked like hell—his hair unruly and shirt covered with milk stains. But it was Kevin's blank stare and hollow eyes that made Zoe's heart stop. A little boy afraid of how the world would treat him without his biggest shield to protect him. Was that the look she had when her mother died?

"I'm here to report a break-in," Trevor said bluntly.

"A break-in?" Zoe's eyes widened. "What happened? Sit down."

Trevor collapsed onto a chair with Kevin. The baby in the stroller stirred and Aiden began rocking the stroller back and forth. Zoe's heart did a little flip before she chided herself. She didn't even like Aiden, did she?

"I... I haven't been sleeping well in our bedroom, so I sleep in Kevin's room," Trevor admitted bashfully. "I have nightmares. This morning I went into the main bedroom to get some clothes and noticed that a lamp was on the floor and some of the drawers on the nightstand were open. I thought it was odd but then I went into the closet and I swear it looked different." His red, tired eyes searched theirs. "I don't know how to explain it… but I think someone was there."

"Could it have been the kids?" Zoe looked at Kevin, who was staring out the window and rubbing his eyes.

"I asked him. He doesn't lie. He has no reason to." Trevor ruffled Kevin's hair.

"Do you have a cleaner or a babysitter—?" Aiden began to ask but Trevor shook his head vehemently.

"I was in that room yesterday morning and the lamp was standing and all the drawers were closed."

"Someone snuck in the night," Zoe whispered. "Was there anything missing?"

"Nothing valuable. But I didn't really keep track of things around the house. Annabelle was much better at that." He dragged his hands down his face. "Why would anyone do this? What are they looking for?"

Zoe's eyes kept drifting to Kevin. "Trevor, why don't we get your official statement? Lisa's right outside. I'll keep an eye on the kids."

"Thanks." Trevor exited the room, followed by Aiden.

When Zoe was alone with Kevin, she leveled with him. He looked like he had tears pressing into the inside of his eyes, his nostrils flaring. "Kevin, I'm so sorry for what happened." He didn't reply. "I lost my mother too when I was fourteen years old."

Finally, he looked at her. He probably didn't even know how to communicate how he was feeling, how to express it. Boys, especially, were rarely taught how to.

"Did you see anyone in the house? Can you think of anyone

who would break in?" she asked. Kids were intuitive. He shook his head. "Everyone liked your mom, huh?"

He looked over his shoulder at his father. A moment of hesitation. "My dad and her were fighting a lot."

"Do you know why? You heard something?"

"Just a lot of shouting."

Zoe made a mental note of it. But every couple fought. She watched Trevor give his statement, haggard and unshaven. His whole life had been turned upside down. "Okay, I'll look into it. Is there anything else I can do for you?"

"Find who killed my mother."

TWENTY-THREE

Hours flew by as Zoe combed through Annabelle's phone records and emails. There was a renewed energy at the station—the kind that Pineview Falls wasn't used to, not because nothing bad happened here but because people had grown complacent. Now, with one murder and two disappearances, everything had changed.

"The hunting darts were laced with adrenaline," she said, reading out the latest report sent by the coroner.

Aiden threw his head back and squirted in eye drops. "Adrenaline? That's interesting."

Zoe shuddered at the thought. "She must have been subjected to extreme stress. She was already abducted and was likely chased through the woods."

"It also accelerated the process leading to a heart attack. The hunting ground will be remote, wooded, deliberately chosen, and offers both symbolic and practical value. It grants the killer dominion over the setting and reinforces the predator-prey dynamic."

She chewed on the tip of her pen. "Do you think Kevin was onto something? Trevor and Annabelle had been fighting."

"Highly unlikely. But the break-in is interesting."

"Ethan is there with CSU to see if there are any prints to lift. I don't understand why anyone would break in. Are they looking for something?"

When Aiden became distracted by something else on his laptop, Zoe returned to dissecting Annabelle's life. She had made several calls to Jackie in the last few days of her life. But no other number stood out. According to Aiden, the women knew the killer. It was the only plausible way for both of them to be abducted by him. Perhaps, Jackie's phone records would reveal someone. But they would take some time to obtain.

"I might have found something from your old case files," Aiden said suddenly. Zoe was so engrossed in the victims that she hadn't spent much time thinking about her own connection to the case. "Do you remember Darren Galanis?"

Zoe shrugged. "Not really. Who's he?"

"A year ago, you worked on a homicide during your stint at Lakemore. A stay-at-home mom was killed by the man she was having an affair with. Ring a bell?"

She blinked. "Oh yeah. I was on like ten homicides in six months. That place is crawling with criminals."

"He was the perpetrator's roommate..."

Flashes of a short man of medium build, with a missing tooth, zapped through her mind. "I think so... he always wore Hawaiian shirts, I think. Didn't leave an impression though."

"Not to you but his statement didn't sit right with me. Too structured, too rehearsed. Gave unnecessary details, kept his narrative fluid so nothing ever caught him out. Classic counter-measure. His priors include breaking and entering and work-place harassment, altercation with ex—"

"So what?" She pressed her fingers against her temples, the information dump making her dizzy. "What does that have to do with me?"

Aiden hesitated, as if carefully choosing his next words. "I pulled his movement patterns. Traffic cam hits, ALPR logs, and cell tower pings. That's the part I was confirming. I don't know if it's a coincidence but he's been orbiting you. Left Lakemore and moved to Seattle when you did, was in Harborwood when you were, and now he's in Pineview Falls."

Zoe's tongue felt heavy. Was this man stalking her? She already suspected someone was watching her. How else would Viktor Axenov know where to show up and to take the deposit box key from her? Or could this be related to why *she* had been sent the lock of hair and letter?

"I have to talk to Simon," she exclaimed without thinking. "He said he'd look into the letter."

Aiden's jaw clenched but he didn't say anything. Fat drops of rain began cascading outside, making the asphalt slick and shiny. She winced, rotating her shoulder, still stiff from her beat-down. It was a miracle she had won the fight. She must have completely surrendered to her rage to win a fight so brutally.

"You're still hurting," Aiden said blankly.

"And you won't let it go," she hissed.

They stared at each other, neither of them backing down, until Zoe tore her gaze away, suddenly in a foul mood. She couldn't let Aiden wear her down. She had a recurring night-mare that she was back in his office for a session, except this time Aiden was holding sharp knives. And he intended to use them to cut into her brain and feed his academic curiosity.

But could Darren be following her? From Lakemore to Harborwood to Pineview Falls? Aiden suspected he could be involved in the murders, but Zoe wondered about his connec-tion to Viktor.

Viper.

The name echoed in Zoe's ears, drifted around in her brain aimlessly, looking for some logic or context to latch on to.

Zoe didn't say anything. He wouldn't understand. She

cleared her throat. "So, the fire was indeed a massacre. It was arson."

He flattened his mouth in disapproval. "This level of arson takes preparation. This wasn't a crime of passion. It was premeditated."

"Why would anyone want to kill six teenagers?" she said. "And they didn't even entirely know each other."

"Unless we are missing something? Teenagers can be nasty. Maybe they bullied someone and this was payback?"

"They weren't the same age, Aiden. The youngest was fourteen. Unlikely they engaged in some coordinated activity that led to this."

He brooded for a while. "Unless... there was only one target." A eureka moment. "That's the only thing that makes sense."

"What do you mean?"

"There's no reason to kill six kids—especially when they didn't really know each other. Then there's the fact that they made it look like an accidental fire and circuits shorting leading to everything going haywire. Maybe there was only one target and the fire was to make it look like an accident?"

Dread filled Zoe's senses. "Why would anyone want to kill a kid?"

"I have no idea," he whispered.

A knock on the door and Lisa poked her head in. "Good time?"

"Yeah, of course. Where are we on Annabelle's laptop?" Zoe said.

Lisa set the laptop on the desk. "They definitely deleted a lot of data and files before we got our hands on it. Our IT department is very basic. Could you guys retrieve everything that was wiped off?"

"For sure," Zoe said. "Did you find anything useful?"

Lisa beamed and turned the screen in their direction. "She was in this chatroom talking to someone."

Zoe and Aiden leaned forward to read the screen.

AnnPlays: So? You finally tried it?

Specter: Yeah. Spent a couple hours in. Looks basic on the surface, but it pulls you in.

AnnPlays: Right? It's not even complex, just… *real*. Like your brain stops questioning it after a while.

Specter: That's what got me. After a bit, I forgot I was wearing a headset.

AnnPlays: I felt the same. Lost all track of time. The world design is unreal.

Specter: Everything feels… too real. Like it's waiting for you to mess up.

AnnPlays: It's just good VR. I'm glad you liked it.

Specter: Maybe. Or maybe it's more than that.

AnnPlays: What are you talking about?

Specter: What if it doesn't stop when you log out?

AnnPlays: Okay, weird take.

Specter: Just saying. Some things in there feel like they're watching you.

AnnPlays: That's not funny.

Specter: I'm not joking.

AnnPlays: I'm done with this convo.

Specter: No, you're not.

"Who is this Specter?" Zoe asked.

"I don't know. It kind of works like Reddit. It's a username and there's no way to track unless we get a court order…"

Zoe hung her head low. "Yeah. That will be fun. Was this their only interaction?"

"No. I think they chatted two more times. It's all archived though. I can pull it out. This could be something, right? This creep that she was talking to online?" she asked desperately, like she was clutching at straws.

"It's hard to say," Aiden said softly. "Online spaces operate within a psychological boundary. An artificial detachment from reality that allows people to express darker impulses without consequence. For most individuals, that boundary remains intact. They compartmentalize. They understand the distinction between online persona and offline consequence."

"Right." Lisa let out a frustrated breath. "So this Specter might just be some harmless freak."

Zoe nodded, but Aiden's words loitered in her head about how online space provided hard boundaries for dark impulses. A sharp discomfort tugged at her chest, questioning how strong *her* boundaries were to keep her dark impulses from hurting someone.

TWENTY-FOUR

Zoe incessantly clicked the end of a pen, her mind racking through Annabelle's autopsy reports. There had to be something here. Some pattern or some clue concealed beneath the brutality of her torture and her death. But her brain was too frazzled and worked up.

She needed peace. She needed to feel rooted. She needed to fix *something*.

She wandered down to the break room to find something to snack on. The sky outside was bleeding black. She had been at it for over three hours and hadn't realized where the time had gone. Opening the fridge, she took out a loaf of bread and decided to make a peanut butter sandwich when someone caught her eye.

A man walked into the substation in a black leather jacket, his hair shaved close to the scalp. His mouth moved as he chewed gum. No hesitation, no uncertainty. Just an easy, measured pace, boots tapping against the tile, hands slipping into his jacket pockets like this was nothing more than a mild inconvenience.

Like a shark smelling blood, Zoe knew he was trouble. She closed the fridge and waited.

His eyes zeroed in on one of the deputies—Ethan. He didn't even shake off the rain as he stopped in front of a deputy's desk. "You need to stop wasting my time."

Ethan's eyes flicked around, his jaw tightening. "We have to follow proce—"

"Bullshit," he spat. "This is the third time CPS has given me a clean chit. If this doesn't stop, then I'm suing you for harassment. You hear me?" His jaw moved, his eyes rude and harsh. He glanced around, undeterred by the men and women in uniform surrounding him. Ethan's face reddened but he didn't say anything as the man turned and dragged his feet back out. He stopped when he saw Zoe watching him.

"You like what you see, sweetheart?"

Zoe's nose scrunched in disgust, which amused him as he left the station. She went to Ethan who was still fuming at his desk. "Who was that?"

"No one." He shrugged.

She offered him a sandwich. "You look hungry."

He hesitated and then took it. "Thanks, I guess."

She smiled on the inside. Food always did the trick. She leaned casually at his desk like they were friends. "So he looked like an ass."

"Yeah." He sighed. "He's been on our radar for some time now."

"I heard him mention CPS."

"He's got two boys. Seven and nine years old. The bruises aren't the kind to raise huge flags. No hard proof. Just a string of concerned neighbors, hushed whispers from teachers. The kids aren't talking—maybe too afraid, maybe too well-trained."

"Any chance they are just rumors? A shitty father doesn't always equate to an abusive one."

"I agree but there is no smoke without fire. These kids get injured way too often. He always explains it as football injury. And he's known to have a temper at work. I've been here long enough to know when something's wrong." Ethan flipped a file close. "But no evidence. No charges. Nothing to hold him on." He got up and walked away, leaving Zoe to ponder.

Her instincts were wired. She opened the file and absorbed the man's name and address. A smile curled up her lips. She'd found an avenue to expel the rotten feeling that was growing inside her. She went back to her office, already formulating a plan. She knew his address now—she'd just have to corner him at night with no witnesses around.

No. No. No.

She zapped out of her thoughts. There had to be another way. She didn't believe in vigilante justice or being defined by her rage. There was one person who deserved her wrath—the Viper.

Once she'd exterminated the Viper, she'd redeem herself.

"Z. Z!" A familiar voice echoed in the distance like someone was trying to wake her up.

"Simon?" she said, bleary-eyed. "What are you doing here? This late?"

He closed the distance between them in long strides, his trench coat dripping with water, his hooked nose tinged red from the chilly night. "The FBI received another letter." He pulled out an evidence bag from his pocket. "From the killer."

A sharp static force gripped her as she read the words.

Ticktock goes the clock,

Jackie won't hear it anymore.

No way forward, no way back,

She's left behind, behind the door.

Last step taken, last stage set,

No reset, no second bet.

Final round, final scene,

Find her where the game turns clean.

TWENTY-FIVE

Knock.

Knock.

Knock.

Zoe's eyes refocused. Her lungs burned like twin hives of fire. She realized she wasn't breathing. Simon's hand clasped around her arm and she drew a breath and then another, until her muscles began to relax.

A click and the door swung open. Aiden appeared in the doorway, shirtless and without his thick glasses.

"Doesn't he own a shirt?" Simon mumbled under his breath.

"What's going on?" Aiden squinted, sleep clouding his dark eyes.

"We got another letter from the killer. It's about Jackie." Zoe spoke through the unease tingling in her bones.

"Shit." Aiden let them inside his motel room. "When did you get it?"

"A few hours ago. It wasn't addressed to Zoe. It was sent to the Seattle office," Simon replied.

That was odd. But her thoughts were too faint. Idly, she

inspected Aiden's room and the immaculateness of it. While Zoe hadn't bothered to unpack her suitcase, Aiden had his shirts ironed and hanging in neat rows. He pulled on a hoodie, while Simon lingered at the doorway.

"What do you think?" Zoe handed Aiden the evidence bag with the letter in it.

He read the letter. "It's different from the last one. Much less poetic and flowery. More direct. Short sentences. I don't see any hints like with the previous one. Maybe it's more concealed. I'll need more time." He stifled a yawn and then looked at Simon. "Why did you come all the way here?"

Simon suddenly appeared awkward. "I-I had to be in the area for work anyway. Thought I'd hand this over personally."

"I'm sure you did." Aiden bristled slightly. It didn't take a profiler with a doctorate to know that Simon was lying. But Zoe didn't care, not at this moment, not at this ungodly hour in a town held hostage by the six young people who died almost thirty years ago.

"It says final and last. Final round. Last step," she recited quietly. "Is Jackie the last victim?"

"That's what it looks like," he agreed. "And if we are going by what happened with Annabelle, Jackie might be dead already."

* * *

Lisa couldn't sleep. There was a slimy feeling under her collarbone. She gave up on counting sheep and climbed out of bed, fastening a robe around herself. Next to her, the bed was empty. It was one in the morning. Where was Jim?

And where was Jackie?

She slid out of the room and heard the faint sound of gunfire. She tiptoed to the guestroom and found the door slightly ajar. A soft, blue glow emanated from inside. Jim was playing a video game, his face enthralled and his thumbs moving with dexterity.

A sharp focus that he lacked in every other sphere of his life.

She ground her teeth and marched away, deciding to do some chores instead to distract herself. Her phone rang.

It was Ethan.

"Why are you up so late?" she asked as she began rifling through the laundry hamper.

"I just can't sleep with everything going on..." he said. "How's it going on your end?"

"Fine." She felt stupid. Always cleaning up after Jim. He stayed home all day. Couldn't he do the laundry? "You got anything?"

"Remember the break-in at Annabelle Stevens's house?"

"Yeah..."

"CSU picked up DNA on the window that didn't match Annabelle or Trevor. We'll run it through CODIS to see if there's a match."

Lisa's brain fired in all directions. "Why would anyone break into Annabelle's house? Some crazy person following this story?"

"Or the killer trying to get rid of evidence."

Lisa considered it when her hand felt something soft in the hamper. She yanked it out without thinking and froze. A scarf. It was red with a blue border. And it definitely wasn't hers.

Ethan was still babbling on the phone, but it slipped from Lisa's grip. She sank to her knees, her hands shaking and her breath tearing in her chest. It was right in front of her—the evidence. The signs were always there—his disinterest in her fertility treatments, him spending most of his time in front of a screen, always getting himself checked out.

He was having an affair.

* * *

Only one bar in Pineview Falls was open at two in the morning. It was one of the town's three bars, where nothing ever changed but nothing ever went unnoticed either.

Zoe was plopped on a barstool and stuffing fries into her mouth. Her stomach was queasy and the latest riddle had sent both hot and cold sensations through her body. She glanced at the handful of patrons hunched over their drinks, their eyes fixed on the game playing from a half-buzzing TV mounted in the corner. It was the highlights of high school football. Lakemore's Sharks playing against the Ravens.

"I never got the appeal of sports." Simon slid next to her and ordered a whiskey. "It's too brutal."

"There's darts over there. More to your speed," she said dryly, pointing at the dartboard hanging on the far wall.

He suppressed a smile. "I think sometimes you forget I'm your boss."

"I think sometimes *you* forget that," she said, instantly regretting it.

Silence descended over them—the air thick with the cloying scent of old wood, spilled beer, and a faint trace of cigarette smoke that clung to the walls. The jukebox hummed low in the background, playing some old country song that no one seemed to be enjoying but no one bothered to change.

When Zoe couldn't take it anymore, she asked, "Why are you here, Simon? And don't give me your bullshit that you had work in the area this late."

"I didn't know where to go." He drank his whiskey. "Nancy wants to talk."

"That's good, right? She wants to get back together with you?" It wasn't long ago when Nancy had accused Zoe of meddling in her marriage, but her only crime was being in the orbit of a man who still harbored feelings for her.

He took another swig and winced at the bitter taste. "It's complicated. I love Nancy. I really do, Z. She's really amazing but..." He paused and bit his lip. "How do you force yourself to fall in love with someone?"

"You didn't think of that when you married her? Seriously?"

"No." He traced the rim of the glass with his ring finger. He still wore the wedding band. "I didn't need to. I was *there*. Now I'm not. It's like something wore off."

"It could just be the seven-year itch. I don't know why you've come to me."

His eyes searched hers pleading, desperate. "Do you think we made a mistake breaking up all those years ago?"

Zoe's throat went dry. She blinked, trying to pluck words from the air. Memories of them together burst behind her eyes. "It fizzled out."

"But we were happy. It's more than what most people get."

"You like the *idea* of us, Simon. Your marriage with Nancy is growing stale and you are glorifying us."

"Spending all that time with Wesley is making you a shrink too, huh?" He didn't bother trying to hide his distaste.

"If you don't like Aiden, why do you put him on cases?"

His smirk didn't reach his eyes as he rubbed his chin. "I like the guy. He had it rough when his wife died. He used to smile a lot more back then."

Zoe's chest tightened. "He's a widower?"

"He didn't tell you? Sorry. I figured he had, with all the time you spend together."

She didn't know what to think. She thought his emotional map was clean while she had drawn hers with smoke, blood, and tears. "He didn't. I guess we don't get that personal."

"I have to say that's a relief," he confessed, his eyes boring into hers. She noticed the whiskey in the glass was almost gone. "I was a little jealous."

"Simon—"

"I'm separated, Z. Have been for months now." There was a beat of silence. Zoe felt the air between them turn electric. When was the last time Zoe felt wanted? She was happy, bobbing through life like a buoy. But there was a glaring hole in her otherwise full life. At the end of the day, she came home to an empty house, drank that glass of wine alone, and slept in an empty bed.

So when Simon closed the distance between them and pulled her into a kiss, she didn't resist.

His hands came around her waist. Warmth expanded in her belly. She cupped his face, seeking comfort in the familiarity. When so much in her life and about her past was an unknown, there was nothing to do but cling to what she knew. It felt good —the delicious weight of him pressing into her and the scent of whiskey assaulting her nose. He was filling up her senses, making it easy to forget about everything else.

She ran her hands down his muscular arms, brushing over his hands. Then, she felt it. His wedding band. She tensed. She pulled back and swallowed a hot rush of tears. What the hell did she just do? Did she even like him?

"We can't do this," she whispered.

"Z, I'm not with Nancy."

"You're still married."

His arms around her went slack and he held his head low. She stomped out of the bar.

TWENTY-SIX

Fun House loomed ahead. Its silhouette jagged against the dimming sky.

Zoe stood in front of it, feeling like the only person in this world.

Peeling paint curled at the edges like dead skin, wooden beams bowed inward as if the whole structure were exhaling a slow, rattling breath. The wind blew softly as if it were assessing her, gauging her response, trying to understand her. The shadows on the uneven ground were long, shivering, but here—right in front of the house—there was only stillness.

The wind stirred. The old porch groaned like it was shifting in its sleep. Loose shutters clapped softly against the warped frame. Zoe stood motionless, her gaze tracing the details—the skeletal remains of a house, the windows gaping and black, like sockets where eyes used to be.

The air around it was infested with the tragedy. Six teenagers died inside while the carnival outside raged on. Why would the killer send her the hair of one of the victims? She swallowed, her pulse drumming in her ears. It was just an old house. A carnival attraction. A collection of wood and dust and neglect. But it was hiding more than the lives it had stolen. Was it hiding injustice? A secret that was threatening to spill out?

So why did it feel like it was waiting for her? She exhaled slowly, trying to shake the feeling that the house was... watching her. But then her antenna started blaring. It wasn't the house that was watching her. It was something else.

From the corner of her eye, she spotted a black sedan with tinted windows a block away from where she stood. It was just the two of them on the stretch of the road. The window was slightly rolled down. It was too far for her to determine who it was. But something was visible.

A bright Hawaiian shirt. There was only one person who dressed like that in Zoe's memory. Someone who Aiden said might have followed her to Pineview Falls. Darren Galanis.

Zoe took off like a bullet leaving the barrel, her legs sprinting with speed and intention toward the car. A moment later, the car kickstarted its engine and swerved dramatically, its tires hissing on the asphalt, spraying dirt on either side. It began gliding away from Zoe but she didn't slow down. She pushed herself harder as the car gained speed.

"Hey! Wait!" she yelled but the car zipped away.

She came to halt, panting, and pressed her hands into her knees. Her lungs burned, drawing shallow breaths. Frustration clawed at her. She was *so* close. But she had memorized the license plate.

She called the local police dispatch. "I need you to run a plate." She recited the number and waited.

Darren Galanis.

* * *

The next morning, everyone was out searching for Jackie Fink. The substation was crowded, stretched thin, everything happening at once. Fax machines beeped, printers rattled, and chairs scraped against the tiles. The walls were lined with cluttered bulletin boards, a mix of wanted posters, departmental notices, and half-torn flyers for upcoming events no one had time for.

Zoe threaded her way through the buzzing place, searching for Aiden. Lisa was on the phone, getting K9 units to comb through the woods where Annabelle's body was found. She spotted him in the break room, thumbing his phone.

"Hey."

"Simon went back?" he asked.

"Yep." She flushed. "Did you get anything from the letter?"

"Not yet. Why wasn't it sent to you like the first one?" He frowned. "And why was it sent to the Seattle office? The killer must be watching you and know that you're in Pineview Falls. He could have just addressed it to this station."

"Good questions." She walked past him and poured herself a coffee with three cubes of sugar. "I'm more worried about Jackie being found dead. Annabelle was killed within twenty-four hours of being taken."

He drummed his fingers on the counter. "We don't know what the abduction site was either."

Zoe's phone beeped. "It's the crime lab. They analyzed the first letter with the poem sent to me."

"I thought there was no DNA or prints."

"There isn't. But they found pollen. It's called *Viola glabella*." She read from her phone. "Shaded forest floors in the Pacific Northwest, common in Washington's old-growth forests and stream banks. It doesn't disperse easily via air, meaning direct contact is required for transfer."

Aiden set his coffee down and straightened up. "Jackie had a bouquet of flowers at her place. Stream violets, remember?"

"I think so." She quickly checked her phone. "That's where the pollen's from. So the killer has been in Jackie's house."

The wheels in his mind spun. "I have to go."

"Where?"

"Jackie's place. I'll take Lisa." He was almost frantic, like his thoughts were racing and he was struggling to catch up. He began backing away.

"What are you looking for?"

"She was obsessed with the fire – rather the massacre. More so than the regular folk in this town. I'll be back. Following a hunch."

"Okay." Zoe headed back to the office and locked the door behind her, shutting out the humming at the substation. The events from last night still clung to her skin like grime. Shame stirred inside her. She wanted to crawl under a rock and die. What was Simon thinking chasing her like that?

She pulled out her phone and shot a message to Benny.

Z: Book me in ASAP, please.

She didn't wait for a reply. He always took his sweet time. Instead, she decided to go through Annabelle's autopsy reports again. There had to be something she was missing. She began reading through the notes and reports again, absorbing everything piece by piece. She didn't know how much time had passed.

Multiple contusions and abrasions across the anterior torso, bilateral upper arms, and thighs, indicative of repetitive blunt force impact.

Linear impact marks across the lateral ribs (T5–T9 bilaterally), consistent with compression injuries caused by sustained external force. The absence of fractures suggests sublethal force applied over time rather than a single crushing event.

And then something caught her eye.

Distinct heat demarcation lines present, inconsistent with exposure to an open flame. The pattern suggests radiant heat exposure at close proximity rather than direct flame contact.

There was fire damage but not from the actual flame. It was stimulated heat exposure. She flipped through the report again.

No soot in nares, trachea, or esophagus, ruling out inhalation of combustion byproducts.

She sat back in her chair, her mind reeling. Annabelle was put through extreme stress and torture. Stimulated heat. Blunt force trauma. Hunting darts. It was elaborate and specific and psychopathic. She scanned the autopsy reports of the teenagers from the Pineview Falls Massacre, her eyes flicking between the forensic details. Bruising patterns. Thermal injuries. Signs of prolonged psychological distress. Each detail echoed back, a perfect match to Annabelle.

Same impact zones. Same heat exposure. Same biochemical markers of extreme fear before death.

Her stomach twisted. This wasn't just similar; it was identical.

Annabelle and the victims of the big fire were tortured and killed the exact same way.

TWENTY-SEVEN

PAST

The music made the air vibrate. Zoe felt the rhythm reverberate from the ground up to her legs, soaking into her bones. The strobe lights pulsed, slicing through the darkness in jagged bursts, revealing the dingy nightclub in disjointed glimpses.

Shadowy figures dancing. Sticky floor. Dark corners. Leather booths.

It was a messy club—not the kind for a nice night out, but the kind where people danced as if their lives depended on it, with sweat dripping down their backs and mascara running down their cheeks. Zoe was feeling messy too as she moved and danced, chasing some kind of resolution she knew deep down she would never find here. A nameless guy had his arms wrapped around her waist and was kissing her neck. She allowed herself a moment of fancy.

She was supposed to be celebrating. She had gotten into Quantico. But the pleasure in the pit of her stomach felt hollow. Her eyes scanned the dimly lit club. For a second, she saw Rachel. Then another burst of light and she saw Rachel again. Every glimpse of her was the same—she stood motionless, unblinking, her skin almost slimy like her flesh was hanging off her bones.

Zoe clenched her teeth and her nostrils ballooned. Rachel was dead. Rather than her absence, it was her secrets that loomed over Zoe's life. Her blood ran hot and heavy in her veins. This is what her mother had left her with—lack of closure and guilt. She had no right to convince a little Zoe to not go looking if anything happened to her and to do everything in her power to cover it up. Silly little Zoe had fallen for it and tampered with her mother's crime scene.

How dare Rachel now haunt her?

Zoe couldn't breathe. She dragged the man she was making out with outside the club. A blast of cold air hit her face and a chill skipped up her sides. She almost tripped over a crack in the pavement as she pulled him into a dark alley. They were kissing again. She didn't even know his name. She was young and stupid. And she deserved to be, after her mother made sure to rob her innocence, because she loved her secrets more than she'd loved her daughter.

But even this distraction failed to silence the chaos building inside her.

"This isn't working for me." She pushed him away and decided to go back in, when he grabbed her by the elbow.

"Come on. Don't be a tease."

"Sorry. But I'm not interested anymore. Find someone who is." She took one step away when he grabbed and twisted her arm, slamming her against the brick wall.

"You little slut," he sneered, his grip tightening on her arm. "Who do you think you are rejecting me like that, huh? I'll do whatever the hell I want to do." He pressed his lips onto hers, shoving his tongue down her throat.

She slammed her hands against his chest, trying to push him away but he was strong. She struggled against him for a minute and then something snapped inside her. Her teeth bit his tongue.

He yelped, staggering back and peeling away from her. Instead of running away, she struck him across the jaw with her elbow. He tripped and landed on the ground. She could have walked away then. Instead, she swung her leg into his chest over and over again. He curled into a ball to absorb the blows, moaning in pain. And she got high on it.

This feeling was intoxicating. This is what she was seeking at clubs, in alcohol, with strangers. Whatever this liberating feeling was. When someone came around the corner, she broke out of her daze. Her attacker was whimpering, still on the ground. But he deserved it. It felt good to fix something, to dispense a little justice. She wiped her mouth with the sleeve of her top and walked away. Her legs were still shaking.

What had she done? Why did it feel so good? And why did she know she would do this again?

Rachel's ghost appeared. Zoe walked past it, not even sparing her a look. But this time she heard Rachel's voice carry in the wind.

"Don't become this, Emily."

* * *

Mothers.

The bond between a mother and a child is disturbing. Calling it pure is an insulting simplification. It's a quiet, consuming need that blurs the lines between love and possession. It isn't just maternal devotion. It's ownership, dependency, something far heavier than affection. A bond forged from the undeniable—one life carved from another, flesh stretched, insides rearranged to make room, to grow, until the split is inevitable. Separation isn't just an event; it's a brutal tearing, a before-and -after written into the body itself.

How do you come back from that? How can you exist as separate entities?

Zoe stared at the picture of Dawn's daughter. The girl who died at Fun House after someone sabotaged the ride's mechanics.

"What do you want now?" Dawn came into the room clad in a robe, looking frail.

"We need to talk." Zoe sat across from her and locked her fingers tight. "Is the prototype a simulation of the big fire?"

She didn't need to wait for Dawn's reply. Her face gave it away. Surprise mingling with shame. "How do you know that?"

"Because someone used the prototype... on Annabelle." She didn't know how else to frame it. "How does it work?"

She drew a deep breath. "It's a VR headset with a device that when put on simulates mild sensations like heat. Highly sophisticated, offering a full immersive experience. As if you were in the haunted house that night."

"It's total sensory immersion? It inflicts real-world trauma through controlled stress."

Suddenly, Dawn turned a sickly pale as she began rubbing her chest with her palm. "I still remember when it was presented to me. It was too much. Some people on the board were all for it. It was bold, it would get everyone talking. That's what our company needed to stand out in a crowded market. Build something rooted in a real incident. But there weren't enough votes. Most of them feared it was tasteless."

"If anyone found out about the prototype, your company would have gotten bad publicity," Zoe said. "Why didn't you just destroy it?"

"Because it was remarkable and involved the hard work of a lot of talented people. We kept it, thinking one day in the future we could salvage something from it or maybe consider releasing it after more time had passed."

"How could you?"

Dawn's mind was adrift. She lifted her eyes to her daughter's picture. A churn of emotions brewed in her tired eyes. "Around three years ago, our company needed a big pivot. Something to drag it out of the financial mess it was in. This isn't about AI or VR or whatever new tech is on the rise. The reason is always psychological. People want to *feel*. People today are disconnected. Lost in their screens, numbed by routine, afraid of real emotion. So they chase intensity—horror, violence, chaos, all kinds of taboo behavior—anything that makes them feel something, even for just a moment. That's where immersion comes in. And now we have the technology to make that possible. For people to feel completely at one with something, to totally forget who they are and live an intense experience."

"I meant how could you, given your daughter died in the fire?"

"It wasn't my idea, Agent Storm. It was David's." She struggled to maintain her composure. "I wanted to create a game and he came up with linking it to the massacre. It was unique, it would put Pineview Falls on the map, it would benefit this wretched town. A homegrown product based on a homebound tragedy. It was a marketable idea."

"You are making money off of her death."

"You perceive it as me making money. I view it as all my hard work and this family's legacy being saved. My daughter's death isn't about increasing my yearly bonus, Agent Storm. I don't give a rat's ass about any of that." She was furious now. "I have more than enough money to walk away from all of this and live out the rest of my years in luxury while making sure that David can afford to buy another property in Aspen. Her death is saving our family, our purpose. That's way more important than us sitting around moping about how she was killed. This way she gets to do something for us from beyond the grave."

The words felt flimsy to Zoe. "How do you relive that violence?"

A bitter laugh. "When I discovered what had happened that night, I spent months thinking and researching what she must have gone through. I learned how the biochemical mechanisms of the body respond to fire, the injuries from falling, the effect on the heart from the stress. I had gone positively mad." She poured herself a stiff drink, blinking rapidly. "But the more I read about it, the better I felt. I don't know why. It was almost therapeutic. And when I tried the prototype, when I played the game, I finally came close to being with my daughter in her last moments. I felt I was there. With her." She took a huge gulp without hesitation. "And now once again some asshole is ruining my daughter's legacy."

Everyone in Pineview Falls was invested in the massacre. But how many of them knew of Zoe to send her *Michael's* hair? She needed Aiden—to her surprise—but he was at Jackie's with Lisa, following up on a hunch. "Why would Annabelle steal this prototype? Was she being poached by your competitors?"

"I don't know. Maybe she stole it for ethical reasons." She rolled her eyes.

"She wouldn't be entirely wrong. Other parents lost their kids in that accident too. How do you think they would feel about you making a video game out of it?"

She smiled sadly. "Absolutely gutted. But those who spend their lives worrying about not offending others never make it big. And morality is not the warmest blanket on cold, winter nights."

She opened her mouth to say something but noticed Dawn's trembling hand around the sculpted glass and her teary eyes still locked on her daughter's picture. She could see Dawn was torn, but she couldn't comprehend the path Dawn had taken. Perhaps, she operated in a different world. Maybe after losing the most important thing, nothing else mattered. An idea came to her. "I'm not into video games but I believe there are levels?"

"Yes." She frowned at the line of questioning. "Based on difficulty."

"And these levels take place in different locations in the game?"

"Yes. The game is based on the massacre but we had to make the game more interesting and dynamic. Keeping one location throughout would not be enjoyable; it traps the player and diminishes their reward for reaching the next level."

Zoe already knew the answer to her next question. "Where is the final level in the game set?"

"Fun House. The grand finale."

She shot up from her seat and dialed Lisa's number. When she saw Dawn watching her, she moved away, out of earshot. Lisa answered the phone in two rings.

"Lisa? I think I know where Jackie is."

TWENTY-EIGHT

Thirty years later, the tragedy still clung to the walls of Fun House. It swelled with the events. If Zoe turned over a fallen prop, a trapped scream would escape. If she pushed into the walls, blood would spill from the cracks. If she sucked in a deep breath, she would smell something charred. Which is why when she entered the house, she held her breath.

Her flashlight beam cut through the darkness, sweeping over the hollow-eyed mannequins left behind from the carnival days. Their plastic faces stared blankly, cracked with age, their faded costumes stiff with dust. The boards beneath each step groaned, the sound swallowed by the emptiness.

"Everything is so old," Zoe commented.

"They never switched out the props," Lisa said. "They upgraded the safety protocols."

Zoe shifted uneasily. "Have you been here? For the haunted house?"

"Just once," she confessed, sweeping her flashlight in arcs, searching for a clue. "I was eighteen and even then I felt horrible."

"Why?"

"I think it's despicable making a franchise out of this."

Zoe headed to the stairs when it hit her. A smell. It was strong, sickly sweet, and metallic. She glanced around and the light passed over a shadow slumped against the far wall. At first she thought it was just another forgotten prop—until the light shone on pale skin, not plastic.

A woman.

Zoe's skin prickled. Goosebumps dotted her arms. Slowly, she approached her, irrationally afraid that she would come back to life.

Jackie sat against the rotting wallpaper, her head tilted at an unnatural angle, her body stiff with the first stages of rigor. Her clothes were damp with sweat and something darker—a patchy spread of blood seeping into the warped wooden floor.

Her arms were lined with the purple bruises, just like Annabelle's. Thermal injuries on her neck. Wounds on her face and feet. No scratches, no defensive wounds.

"No sign of a struggle or heat marks this time." Zoe's voice came out hoarse. She crouched on the floor next to her, using a handkerchief to plug her nose. Behind her, Lisa was already on the radio calling for backup.

She had been placed carefully. Legs stretched out, arms carefully arranged, head tilted just enough to look like she were staring at something across the room.

"Clothes torn in places but mostly intact," she noted. "She's covered in injuries from the darts. He hunted her down too."

* * *

Another knock on the door—this time it was Ethan. "Pulling an all-nighter, are we?"

His smile was watery, his eyes frantic. "You have to see this."

Minutes later, Zoe, Aiden, and Lisa were huddled around

Ethan's ancient computer. The grainy image on the screen kept flickering.

"They still make these computers?" Zoe asked.

"We don't have the budget the FBI does," Ethan retorted grumpily. "Lisa told me to get CCTV footage from Annabelle's place of work."

"The Harringtons turned over their security tapes?" Aiden cocked an eyebrow. "The court order only covered the victim's laptop."

"I didn't need access to their cameras. A museum across the street voluntarily gave us access to their tapes." Ethan's finger hovered over a button. "Nothing on the day Annabelle disappeared. But this was two days before the disappearance."

The images on the screen started moving again—albeit jerkily. Zoe had to squint to decipher faces. The camera faced the side of a street with people walking back and forth. The time-stamp read 6 p.m. Annabelle appeared, stepping out of the building. She paced up and down, checking her phone.

"She's waiting for someone," Lisa said.

Two minutes later, a man approached her, his back to the camera. She turned around and they began chatting, animatedly. After a minute, Annabelle ushered him into a corner, disappearing from the view. The man followed, his side profile captured on camera.

If it weren't for the thick glasses and the fact that his face was plastered all over the local news, Zoe wouldn't have recognized him.

"Did he tell you that he met Annabelle two days before she went missing?" Zoe asked Lisa.

Lisa was taken aback. "He didn't even tell me that he knew her."

"Bring Adam in."

TWENTY-NINE

Adam Deader had no qualms about being dragged to the substation. He was positively delighted as he was escorted into the room, looking around and soaking up every ounce of the experience. He reminded Zoe of her nephew's first time at Disneyland.

"Why is he so giddy about being called in?" Zoe stifled a yawn, wincing at Adam's megawatt smile.

"He's delusional narcissist bordering." Aiden cracked his neck. "How deep that delusion runs, I don't know yet."

Her nerves jangled at Adam's glee but she managed to form a polite smile. "Thank you for coming in this late, Adam."

"Of course." He gave her an impish smile, like they shared a secret. "I'm hoping you have come to your senses and require my expertise to solve this case?"

"Maybe." She placed a printed copy of his meeting with Annabelle captured on camera. "Why don't you start with this?"

Adam's smile faltered. "Where did you get this?"

"An advanced piece of technology called CCTV," Zoe quipped. When Adam didn't reply, she continued, "For someone who has a lot to say on the evening news these days, you've gone awfully quiet."

Aiden's eyes shifted as if he were doing a mental calculation. "There is no point in denying it."

"Is that it?" Zoe sat back and leaned back in her chair, enjoying dismantling some of his arrogance. "You wanted to help us solve the case and didn't care to mention something this important?"

He pressed his lips in a thin line. "I didn't realize it would be important. I didn't know her that well. This was the first time I was meeting her. Before that, we only talked on the phone a couple times."

"Why?" she asked.

"She reached out to me." His chest puffed as he regarded them. "It was about a week before her murder. She had some information she wanted to share."

"Am I supposed to do a drumroll?" Zoe asked flatly.

"She stole a product from Harrington Group," he declared.

Zoe's chest deflated. Her grumpy, sleep-deprived mood melted away and her curiosity piqued. She looked at Aiden who narrowed his eyes in suspicion.

"What product?" Aiden challenged.

"It was a video game. She stole the code and the prototype."

Adam was telling the truth. Dawn was keeping the theft under wraps—specifically, it hadn't been made public that the product was a video game. "And she told *you* about it? Why?"

"Because she wanted to sell a story, obviously. That's why we are all here, aren't we?" His titillating eyes landed on Zoe. "This whole notion you have about dispensing justice and doing the right thing, it's all fiction. It's a man-made construct. And while you are living your fiction, I am merely recording it."

"Morality is fiction?" Aiden countered. "It's interesting you say that considering you're a suspect in a murder."

His face fell. "I'm a suspect?" And then excitement unfurled on his face. "What a most thrilling development."

"Okay, cut the crap. Why didn't you tell us that you knew Annabelle and met her days before?" Zoe said, exasperated.

"Because I didn't have any information related to her demise. She didn't tell me she was being threatened. She simply wanted me to write an exposé on the Harringtons."

"What exposé?" Getting information out of him was like untangling a knot one thread at a time.

"There was something about this prototype of the video game that was controversial and disturbing. That's why she stole it. She thought it was unethical of the company to develop this in the first place. She never told me exactly what was so troubling about it. I even asked to see the game but she refused. She didn't trust me entirely, I suppose. It's why I met her that day. I was trying to convince her that I can't write anything if she doesn't give me more."

Zoe sieved through his words. "I'm still not convinced about why you didn't come forward. And then you went ahead and told everyone that Jackie is missing. You've been gaining a lot of visibility and traction since this case started. How many clicks are your blogs getting?"

"Enough for *The Seattle Times* to offer me a job." He smiled shamelessly. "As much as I'm relishing finally becoming a big fish in a small pond, I have nothing to do with this. I'm merely recording what is going on and adding a slight twist to it. Though, me becoming a suspect was something I didn't see coming. Writing myself into a story. Now that's a challenge."

She stared at him dumbfounded but Aiden was enthralled. Adam wasn't just thirsty for gossip, weaving stories to keep himself entertained; there was a component of something twisted in him. The glaring lack of empathy. Like he viewed the rest of the world as characters in a story.

"If you don't mind, I think I have more writing to do." He

stood up and buttoned his coat. His twinkling gaze lingered on Zoe. "Something tells me you will be an intriguing character in this story, Agent Storm."

A blazing, hot energy jolted up her spine as Adam walked away. "If he were innocent, he'd be defensive, uncomfortable. Instead, he's reveling in it," she said to Aiden.

"That's the first problem. He's reducing people—real, living people—to characters in his personal story arc. That level of depersonalization? It's dangerous. It means he doesn't see them as people. He sees archetypes, players, set pieces."

She shuddered at Adam's reveries. "Aiden, what was that?"

"That, Storm, is our top suspect." He began gathering his things. "I'd check his alibi. Are you not going back to the motel?"

"No." She stifled a yawn.

"It's one in the morning."

"I... can't," she admitted. She didn't feel well. A fury was gathering pace inside her. Her mind felt as though it were trapped in a box with the sides closing in on her. She needed answers in order to escape but the questions kept piling up. "Do you think Jackie was also involved in the theft of the prototype?"

"Possibly. It also means the Harringtons have another motive to want the women dead." He stopped by the door. "You sure you're staying longer?"

She nodded. He lingered, waiting for her to change her mind or confide in him. She felt his looming presence suffocating. When he finally left, she exhaled and dove back into work.

Zoe spotted Lisa also toiling at her desk. "Want some?" she said, offering her Sour Patch Kids.

Lisa looked up, tired and fighting tears. "No, thank you."

"Is everything okay?"

Lisa opened her mouth but didn't say anything. Didn't she have a husband? But now that Zoe thought about it, lately Lisa had been avoiding going home, working long hours, and often staring at her phone with a haunted look. Her home life must be in turmoil, but Zoe didn't feel close enough to her to comfort her. "How long have you known Adam for?"

"A couple years. I'm surprised he hid this information from us. Thought he would have loved to be involved from the beginning."

"Perhaps he planned it this way." She chewed on a piece of candy, savoring the taste exploding in her mouth. "He's been attacking Harrington Group. Maybe he's been doing more than just reporting the story. He's creating it too."

"I found something," Lisa said abruptly. "Remember we talked about any competitors of Harrington Group? Anyone who would benefit from this?"

"Yeah..."

"I was just looking at other gaming companies in the state, digging through announcements and calling in a few favors. Look at one of the websites."

Zoe took the phone. It was a page showing the team behind a midsize company out of Seattle with offices in Port Angeles and Tacoma. The director of R&D was a familiar face. Pudgy face, doe-like eyes, and golden curls.

Jackie's half-sister—Amy Andrews.

THIRTY

Because the future of gaming isn't a boys' club.

Built by Women. Played by Everyone.

She who codes—conquers.

Zoe read the words written in giant block font on a white marble wall. The office was like a beehive of activity. Women in power suits and steely demeanors strutting around and working behind large monitors. The walls plastered with empowering quotes and news articles. It was all very efficient and orderly. The only welcoming feature were the plants on the windowsills.

"This looks interesting." Zoe felt like an outsider in her shabby jeans and Gina's old leather jacket she'd snagged last Christmas.

Aiden looked bored. "Identity management."

"What is that?"

"Women often develop a culture of overperformance to disprove stereotypes like they're too emotional or soft. The internal pressure to perform often leads to hyper self-monitoring."

She cocked an eyebrow. "Do you get bored often?"

"What do you mean?"

She hitched a shoulder. "Being a know-it-all must get boring."

He stared at her blankly. "And carrying that chip on your shoulder must be exhausting."

"Chip on my shoulder?" Her eyebrows shot up as she stepped closer. "It's called being normal. You wouldn't understand."

His smile was sarcastic. "It was my job to evaluate you, Storm. And normal is the last word I'd use to describe you."

"I knew that's why you volunteered to be on this case," she said, losing control of the situation. "You see me as a patient to prod and poke and lock up in whatever dungeon you came from."

"I volunteered to *help* you. If you really were this happy, cheerful person you pretend to be, you wouldn't be so cynical whenever you saw a friendly face."

She opened her mouth to retort but was distracted by a sweet scent of gummy bears laced with an airy ocean breeze. Was it coming from him? And then she looked at her reflection in his glasses. Why was she blushing? And why was she standing so close to him?

"Darren Galanis is in town," she blurted out when she didn't mean to, suddenly changing the subject.

Aiden's hard face faltered. "You saw him?"

Zoe nodded. Why was she telling him anything? "I swung by Fun House one morning. He was in his car watching me. I chased him on foot but he got away. I have a stalker."

Aiden ran a hand through his hair. "He's dangerous, Storm. As it turns out, I don't think he has anything to do with this case. I highly doubt he dug around Michael's hair."

A lump hardened in Zoe's throat. She couldn't confide in Aiden. No matter how much he sniffed around, she needed him to mind his own business. But she wasn't brave enough to hide her fear completely. Uneasiness unfurled in her belly. She knew she was being followed, being watched, but now she had a name and face.

And she fully intended to hunt him down and beat the truth out of him if she had to.

"Don't, Storm," Aiden said suddenly, as if he'd read her mind. "Don't go at it alone."

"Can I help you?" A woman appeared, hiding her smile as she glanced at them.

Zoe jerked away, hating that he was unaffected by their proximity. "FBI. We need to speak with Amy Andrews."

"Sure." The woman's eyes lingered on Aiden a moment longer before she escorted them to one of the rooms with bleached white walls that hurt Zoe's eyes.

Amy was busy typing away at a computer, her eyes fixated on the screen. "We're not just making games here; we're fixing the industry." She was wearing a headset. "Harrington Group is ancient. They have no skin in the game. Trust me—" She stopped when she noticed Zoe and Aiden standing at the door. "I'll call you later." She removed the headset, a confident smile planted on her face. "How can I help you?" She stood up and then her face fell. "Did you find Jackie?"

"Not yet," Zoe said. "I didn't know you were such a big shot."

"I'm sure you have a work persona as well, Agent Storm. You're also in a male-dominated industry. Please take a seat." Amy gestured them to the little sitting area.

The office was covered with Amy's accomplishments. Framed university degrees, certifications, awards, and pictures taken at glamorous events. Zoe couldn't imagine working in a room with her face everywhere.

"Do you know who killed Jackie?" Amy asked solemnly.

"We're doing our best. We wanted to talk to you about Harrington Group," Zoe said.

Amy pursed her lips, her gaze bouncing between them. "What about them?"

"You're one of their key competitors," Aiden stated. "Did Jackie know that when she began freelancing for them?"

Amy threw her head back and laughed. "I never talked shop with Jackie. She wasn't interested in the business side of things."

"But given that she was testing video games for your competition, do you not see the conflict here?" Zoe said.

"Harrington Group isn't competition. They think they are. It's just that old hag's desperate attempt to reinvent herself. I couldn't care less about what they're doing." She blinked rapidly and clenched her fists in her lap. Zoe noted Aiden watching her carefully. "What does this have to do with Jackie?"

"We're just trying to get a clearer picture around the events," Zoe said. "Are you sure Jackie never mentioned an Annabelle Stevens? She worked for Harrington Group."

Amy shrugged. "Like I said, my step-sister and I didn't discuss every aspect of our lives. While she was stuck on the big fire, marinating in the trauma it caused our family, I only care about the future."

"Where were you the evening of November 2?" Zoe asked.

Amy stared at them blankly. "Are you serious? You think I have something to do with this?"

"We have to cover all the bases."

She scowled and flared her nostrils. "I was working. Here. In my office."

"Can anyone vouch for that?" Aiden asked.

"No. I work overtime many days." There was a knock on the

door and the same woman poked her head in. "Amy, they need you."

"Yes." She stood up and smoothed out her pantsuit. "Agent Storm, Dr. Wesley, please keep me in the loop about Jackie. And don't worry about what's going on with our company and Harrington Group. It's just business."

As she gestured to lead them out, Zoe felt a tickle of frustration. She exchanged a look with Aiden. They couldn't divulge the prototype theft to Amy and sabotage Harrington Group. Especially not when they only had a theory.

On their way out, Zoe paused, her eyes locking on something. A rifle. It was mounted on a wall in a glass display. "What's that?"

"Oh. That's a Winchester Model 94." Amy beamed. "It belonged to my grandmother. We used to go hunting together. She was my biggest inspiration. I learned to be unapologetic about my ambition. She taught me women shouldn't just be represented, they should dominate. Now, if you'll excuse me."

They were about to head back, disappointed and frustrated, when Zoe's phone beeped with a message from Lisa.

"What is it?" Aiden asked.

Zoe's eyes thinned and her mind sharpened. "Remember Jackie's neighbors reported a red Prius outside her place and some shouting?"

"Yeah..."

"Guess who owns a red Prius. Amy."

The car glided through the empty, monotonous streets of Pineview Falls. Zoe didn't know if it was an adjustment period going from a city girl to living in a dead town, or if there was something truly sinister or dull about such places that sucked the joy out of everything.

She brought the car to a sudden stop at the red light.

"Sorry," she said to Aiden.

"Don't worry about it." He had been engrossed in his phone since she'd picked him up from the station.

"Did you find anything at Jackie's?" she asked.

"Not yet." He scowled, putting his phone away. "But I've asked Ethan to bring in her trash. I'll sift through it."

"You really think there's something in her apartment?"

"Since the killings are related to the big fire, I'm certain she must know something. Is that why she was chosen? There are a lot of people working on the project. There has to be a reason why Annabelle and Jackie were the victims." He scratched his head, thinking out loud.

Zoe held back a smile. Aiden was always measured and deliberate around her. Every word that came out of his mouth, every movement he made, came off as rehearsed and planned. Unlike her, who talked and acted out of impulse. It felt good to know that Aiden could also think out loud and didn't always speak with certainty.

"Amy has another link to both," Zoe pointed out. "She wasn't super close with Jackie. Jackie was working for her competitor. Do you think Amy fits the profile?"

"Originally I had us looking at a male offender, probably between twenty-five and forty years old. He's methodical, structured. This level of planning doesn't come from someone impulsive or reckless. He's intelligent, definitely above average. Socially detached. Not a recluse, but distant. Financially stable. Likely not close with family, not estranged, but emotionally distant. Few or shallow relationships. He can interact socially but prefers online engagement. An architect who wants to shape the experience and wants full control. But two people potentially fit that profile if we disregard sex."

"Amy and Adam," she said. "The killer hunted Annabelle down after shooting her with darts dripping with adrenaline, leading to a heart attack. I'm assuming the same thing happened with Jackie."

"The killer is fixated on the original incident, not just as a tragedy, but as an event that is significant to them personally. Maybe they believe the event was incomplete, flawed, or not executed properly... maybe they wanted to be the one to execute it properly this time."

"Is that why the killer sent me Michael's hair?" She swallowed hard. "He was hinting at being unhappy with the past?"

"You know who could potentially have access to Michael's hair? Jackie's step-sister Amy."

The car hummed under her as she breezed through the freeway. The evening sky unfolded in layers—burnt orange to deep indigo. The last glimmers of sunlight pooled into the horizon and stars began winking into existence.

And then a flash in the mirror.

A car. Didn't she see the same car three turns ago? Maybe she wouldn't have thought twice if it had passed her once, maybe even twice. But every time she switched lanes, it did too. Every time she slowed, it kept its distance—close enough to shadow, far enough to not raise alarm. But she wasn't a casual spectator, was she? A bad feeling took hold of her.

She slowed down suddenly so that the car could get close enough for her to read the license plate. It was the same one from the other day. The one registered to Darren Galanis.

Her pulse spiked.

"What is it, Storm?" Aiden asked. "Why are you driving erratically?"

"We're being tailed."

"*What?*" He looked over his shoulder. He said something but she didn't hear. She was laser-focused. This was her chance. She took the next exit and as expected the car was right behind. Her heart jackhammered.

She flicked her blinker right. A test move. Nothing ahead,

just an empty side street. The tailing car hesitated, then mirrored her turn. Without warning, she jerked her wheel to the left, hard, cutting across two lanes. The tires shrieked against the pavement as she veered into an empty parking lot.

He had followed her.

"Jesus Christ, Storm. We should call for backup!"

Zoe ignored him. Instead of taking the exit, she cut the wheel again, using the curve of the lot to swing around in a wide, brutal circle. Darren had already committed to following her original trajectory—it was too late to correct.

By the time he realized what she'd done, she was already behind him.

A cold, electric rush snapped through her nerves. She slammed her foot on the gas.

The car surged forward, the gap between them vanishing in an instant. A crunching, gut-punch sound of metal on metal split the air as her bumper connected with his rear. The car in front lurched forward and skidded sideways, crashing into a fence.

Zoe didn't bother to kill the engine as she jumped out of the car. Her hand hovered over the Glock in her waistband as she marched toward the stalled car. She threw open the door and grabbed the man inside by his collar, dragging him out.

"Hey!" he growled as Zoe dropped him on the ground and pointed a gun at him.

Darren—a face she had forgotten, wearing his typical Hawaiian shirt.

"Why are you following me?" she hissed at him.

He got up, unsteady on his feet. He was mildly disoriented from the crash, but uninjured. He grabbed his head and swayed. "I will sue you!"

She smiled sweetly and then rammed her leg into his shin. He let out a shriek and doubled over, clutching his leg. "Speak up or I'll put a bullet through your empty head."

"Storm, what the hell are you doing?" Aiden whispered frantically in her ear but she paid no attention.

Darren looked up at them, frowning and panting. "I have rights, you know." She sighed impatiently and clicked off the safety of her gun. Darren panicked and raised his hands in the air. "All right, all right. He paid me money to watch you."

"Who?"

"Viktor."

Her heart leaped in her throat but her face remained expressionless. Moments ticked by and the sky grew darker and larger. She lowered her gun and leaned into his ear. "Tell Viktor Axenov to come find me or the next time I see you following me, I'll mail him pieces of you. Got it?"

THIRTY-ONE

Zoe could breathe fire. She didn't fear anything anymore. Not about threatening Darren, not about being watched by Viktor, and not by Aiden sniffing around.

She didn't even fear the twisted person responsible for torturing and killing women in Pineview Falls.

"When will Rodney be done with Jackie's autopsy?" She asked Lisa, who was huddled in front of a computer with Ethan.

"He should have preliminary reports for us by later tonight. We just got through Jackie's cell phone records."

"Good, good." She shifted on her heels and bit her nails. Adrenaline pumped through her like little electric blades plucking her ribs and humming through her veins. Her muscles were coiled tight—ready to be snapped into action. She realized her unusual demeanor was drawing attention. The typical Zoe with a skip in her step and smile on her face was unraveling.

She had messaged Benny again. He finally replied.

B: You never ask for fights this quickly.

Irritation danced on her skin. Why did he care? She

messaged him to mind his own business and find something for her. She dreaded what she'd do if he didn't. Because whatever was building inside her had to come out. Aiden walked into the room, holding a garbage bag. He dumped it on the table, his features drawn tight.

"This is from Jackie's place?" she asked.

He nodded curtly and put on gloves before delving into the bag. The ride back had been fraught with tension. Aiden had tried to prod further but Zoe had clammed up. He already knew too much. Zoe sat across from him and began pulling out contents from the trash.

"What are we looking for?" she asked with a bounce in her voice.

"Anything related to the massacre." He didn't look at her. To her bewilderment, she realized that she really wished he had.

She sifted through receipts, used napkins, lipstick-stained coffee mugs, broken rubber bands, and crushed medicine bags. Aiden had some pieces of paper laid out in front of him—torn and stained. He was deep in thought as he tried to arrange the papers. crumpled paper scraps, torn edges, and half-shredded words spread out in front of them.

He worked methodically, sorting through the discarded pieces, smoothing them out, aligning jagged edges like a puzzle. Every now and then, he'd pause, turning a fragment sideways, testing its fit against another. Ink bled at the seams where words reassembled themselves and incomplete sentences began to take shape.

She exhaled, arms crossed, resisting the urge to drum her fingers on the table.

"Almost there," he murmured, not looking up. A strip of paper slid into place. A sentence emerged. "Shit."

"What?"

Aiden froze. "It was Jackie."

"What do you mean?"

He showed her the pieces. Words stuck out—ticktock, rock, marrow, blackens... words from the first poem that had been sent to Zoe. Words scribbled in Jackie's handwriting as if she were trying to come up with a riddle and jotting down words and rhymes.

Zoe stared at Aiden in shocked silence. Her brain tried to restart. "Jackie sent that letter? Did she kill Annabelle?"

"Then who killed Jackie?"

THIRTY-TWO

"Jackie killed Annabelle?" Lisa wasn't convinced, her eyes darting between Zoe and Aiden. She looked down at the pieces of paper that Aiden had carefully assembled. "This is from her garbage? Are we sure someone else didn't write this? Perhaps the person who had access to her home."

Images came to Zoe's mind unbidden—a frenzied Jackie scrawling words, her heart pounding, her eyes coated with a violent glint—an obsession that had quickly spiraled into a delusion and needed to be acted upon.

"The handwriting is an obvious match," Aiden said. "Though, of course, when evidence is handed over to the DA it will be verified by an expert."

"Could someone have coerced her to write this?" Lisa asked.

"If she were coerced, she wouldn't have been the one coming up with the riddle, testing out different words and rhymes," Zoe pointed out. "This riddle was her brainchild. The pollen came from the flowers in her apartment. The two victims knew each other."

"But why?"

"Obsession isn't static. It escalates. It feeds on itself. The more you indulge in a thought, the more it demands. What starts as fascination becomes fixation. Fixation becomes immersion," Aiden explained. "A moment like that—a tragedy, an act of chaos—becomes an itch, a loop that won't stop playing until they step into it themselves. Until they become a part of it. Especially in this case, Jackie, who was related to one of the original victims, Michael. This wasn't just an intellectual interest in the fire. She was connected to it. One of the victims was her family, her blood. This is what we call identity fusion. When someone can't separate their identity from the trauma they're fixated on."

Lisa removed her sheriff's hat and held her head in her hands. "Annabelle was *hunted* too with those darts. That wasn't part of this real-life video game."

"Fantasy can become more real than reality itself and the boundaries start to disappear. And once those boundaries are gone? The only way to make the fantasy real... is to turn it into action. Which is what happened here."

"But who killed Jackie?" Zoe asked. "Someone else who has a personal connection to the tragedy?"

"Most likely." Aiden removed his glasses and cleaned them with his tie. "Though in this town, even someone with no direct link could feel they are connected and develop an obsession."

"But we are looking for someone Jackie would know," Lisa surmised. "How else would the killer have known that Jackie sent a riddle to the FBI?"

"It also explains why there were differences between the notes," Zoe said as the realization dawned on her. "The second riddle was stylistically very different from the first one. Because they were written by different people."

"So we are thinking Jackie had an accomplice," Lisa said. "But then they turned on her."

Aiden nodded. "This person knew Jackie had sent a riddle,

which is why they did the same thing, and they used the game on Jackie."

"What's the point of sending us these riddles? Pure psychopathy?" Lisa asked.

He shrugged. "He's playing. He needs someone to play against. That's us."

A cold nub settled in the pit of Zoe's stomach. Outside the wind lashed against the windows, rattling them against the hinges. The trees swung and writhed; resisting being uprooted. She swallowed hard. "Now that Jackie is dead, are they going to take someone else to torture and kill?"

Zoe didn't head back to her motel. She should have, but a lot was playing on her mind. Two women were dead—an innocent victim and her killer. Whoever killed Jackie had to be in her orbit. Her hands fidgeted at the leather wheel. Annabelle stole the game—but what if Jackie had encouraged her?

Zoe pictured how it could have played out. Annabelle and Jackie becoming friends, Annabelle confiding in Jackie about an immersive game related to the fire, and Jackie, with ulterior motives, convincing her to steal it. But there was a third person involved. Someone else who shared Jackie's obsession and was still playing the game.

She chewed on a sucker and glanced at the rearview mirror and side mirror every few seconds. Her mind drifted to Darren Galanis. At least Darren wasn't following her anymore. She wondered if he'd given Viktor her message and if Viktor was going to retaliate. She hoped he would. This time she would be prepared—this time all that poison and rage that lived inside her would be vented on someone who deserved it.

But for now this man was going to do. The man who had walked into the sheriff's station like he owned the place. The man everyone believed to be abusing his kids. He wouldn't be missed. He didn't deserve to be missed.

A fading voice inside her told her to stop. Her mind was being pulled in all directions. She really needed to stop doing this. The world wasn't hers alone to fix. And this wasn't the way to do it. But what if it was? What if she could save those children this way?

A messaged popped up on her phone. It was from Simon.

S: I'm sorry for making you uncomfortable, Z. I was in a bad place. Talk soon.

She sighed. That was the last thing she wanted to do. It didn't help that Simon wasn't someone she could avoid forever —but nor did she want to. He was one of the rare few people in her life who wasn't in transit.

The wind howled through the railyard, whipping between the freight cars, rattling loose metal, sending dust and grit skidding across the gravel. She parked her car just outside the reach of the floodlights and rolled down the window. The cold air snaked through the seams of her jacket, nipping against her skin.

He was right there. Hard hat tilted back, sleeves pushed up, standing like he had nothing to fear. He was ugly—the way he talked and moved was crass and jarring. Like he thought he was better than everyone else. Like he was doing them a favor by being there.

Zoe clenched her jaw, flexed her fingers against the cold. She could go to him. Right now. Let him feel powerless. Let him feel the pain he inflicted. Let him feel that agonizing helplessness of injustice.

Don't do it.

She climbed out of the car. The wind pulled at her, pushing her forward, dragging at her like it was urging her on. She took a step. Just one. The itch was too strong; her insides were coated with it. This was a line she'd never crossed. But maybe now was the time. Who was she going to find who was worse than someone abusing their own children?

She took another step and a gust slammed into the freight cars, making them groan against the rails. The floodlights flickered, and in that brief second of darkness, his shadow stretched long across the ground, swallowed by the night.

She could do it, right? It wasn't the worst thing. Happy, sweet Zoe could do something wrong. She was someone who apologized to fire hydrants and streetlamps if she walked into them. Surely, she could do something bad for once.

And then her phone rang. A sharp, trilling sound pierced through the dark. Luckily, she was far away enough that no one had noticed her. It was Aiden. What the hell did he want now?

"What?" she snapped.

"Hello to you too," he said, instantly making her frown. Since when did a stoic Aiden develop a personality? "What are you doing?"

"I..." She blushed like she was a child caught stealing candy. "Running an errand. Why?"

"I just came back to the station because I left my wallet here and I ran into Ethan, who was working late going over Jackie's cell phone records and looking very distressed."

"What did he find?" Her heart rose in her throat.

"He ran one of the numbers on her call list in the weeks leading up to Annabelle going missing. It belongs to Jim."

"Who's that?"

"Jim Gray. Lisa's husband."

THIRTY-THREE

"I want to live your life!" Gina whistled on the phone. "Look at you, Zoe. Making out with a married man."

"Shut up, G! He's separated. And I gave in only for a second after *he* initiated it." Zoe groaned. She had done a good job of burying that memory somewhere deep inside her. "Please tell me I wasn't a total asshole."

"You weren't a total asshole."

She pinched the bridge of her nose, an ache pulsing in her stomach. "His wife would hate me. And rightfully, so."

"She would but she did walk out on him. It's not cheating. Meanwhile the most exciting thing to happen to me is that I learned from a teacher that your favorite nephew has expanded his vocabulary by learning the word 'dick.' Yes, Zoe. Dick. I can feel Mom judging me."

"She'd be proud of you," Zoe said. It wasn't often they spoke of Rachel. Zoe always thought it was too painful for Gina, who didn't have that many memories of her. Though Zoe had promised Rachel to forget about her and move on, it was Gina who had kept that promise. Gina with her husband and her children and her house in the suburbs. Gina with her summer evenings spent drinking lemonade on the porch. Gina with her Sunday mornings busy trying to shepherd the kids for morning hockey practice.

Meanwhile Zoe had autopsy pictures of Jackie laid out in front of her.

"Well, you're overthinking this." Gina's voice disrupted her train of thought. "We're all allowed to be messy sometimes, sis."

"I guess you're right." She bit her lip. But Zoe didn't like being messy. She was unfiltered but she wasn't a trainwreck. She made good decisions.

"I have a question for you…"

"What's that?"

"If Simon and his wife get a divorce, would you date him again?"

The thought hadn't crossed her mind. She hadn't even considered the possibility. Now she toyed with it. She imagined a world where she was with Simon and didn't care about what happened to Rachel. The lightness with which she would float about her day was tempting. But was Simon just a remnant from her past offering her a false chance at freedom?

"I don't know. I mean… we did share something special but it was so long ago, Gina. I haven't thought about him that way in years."

"Is there anyone you think of?" she teased. "Not that I'm someone to put pressure on anyone to have kids, but I'd like my boys to have cousins! My husband is an only child, remember?"

Zoe caught a glimpse of Aiden outside, heading toward her. The image of him shirtless when he opened the door flashed through her mind. She blinked it away. What was that about?

"I have to go, Gina. I'll talk to you later." Her voice came out shrill and she hung up.

"Who was that?" Aiden gripped the edges of the doorway.

"My sister." She cleared her throat and willed herself not to blush.

"Jim Gray is here."

"Oh." She stood up. "Does Lisa know?"

He faltered. "Nope."

"You didn't tell her. Why?"

He shrugged. "I want to see her reaction."

Zoe didn't fully understand the way Aiden worked. And she was rudely reminded that this was who he was—methodical and shrewd. He was always testing people like he was prodding and disassembling a toy to decipher how it functioned.

Stepping outside, she saw a tall, heavy man with unkempt dark blonde hair, wearing a hoodie, being brought in by Ethan. His eyes were round and puzzled. Lisa was coming out of the break room and frowned.

"Jim? What are you doing here?"

Ethan leaned to whisper something in Lisa's ears. Her mouth dropped open and her eyebrows pulled together. Her eyes flew to Jim, who shrugged helplessly. Voices overlapped, chairs scraped against the floor, and the steady hum of conversation filled every inch of space.

"I would say she's genuinely surprised," Zoe murmured.

"I agree."

"We'll take this one," she said, raising her voice. The laughter in the room stopped, the chatter thinned out. Everyone was acutely aware of the silence as Zoe headed to one of the rooms in the back to interview Jim.

"What do we know about him?" she whispered to Aiden.

"Software engineer. Unemployed for the last seven months after getting laid off. That's all Ethan told me. And no priors."

"In here, Mr. Gray." Zoe ushered him into a room.

A simple metal table, scuffed at the edges, and three chairs sat in the middle of the room. The walls were a dull, muted brown. A single fluorescent light buzzed overhead, casting a cold, flat glow.

There was no window, no clock. Nothing to give a sense of time passing. Just four walls and stale air.

Jim sat down gingerly, across from Zoe and Aiden. His face was crumpled and teeming with worry. "Please, can I talk to Lisa first?"

"I'm afraid this is more important," Zoe said. "How did you know Jackie Fink?"

His mouth flattened. "Shit. I mean, it was..." He sat back, his hands stuffed inside the pockets of his hoodie, and looked at the closed door. "It was a mistake, okay? It meant nothing. It was barely anything."

Zoe and Aiden exchanged a look. "So you were having an affair with her?"

"No!" He was appalled. "It was just three dates, okay? It was so stupid." He hung his head low and pinched the bridge of his nose. "What the hell do you think I've done?"

"Walk us through this, Jim," Zoe instructed. "Jackie Fink was found murdered. You're the sheriff's husband. This doesn't look good for you."

"I know! I know! Look, Lisa and I are going through a rough patch. She has it in her head that a baby will fix everything but I'm not even working right now. And her fertility treatments have been so..." He caught himself and clasped his hand into a fist. "Just please let me talk to her first."

"I'm just going to wait until you accept that you're talking to us first," Zoe said.

His shoulders sagged in defeat and he wiped his nose. "We met at the café where she worked. I used to get an Americano almost every afternoon and we got talking."

"What did you talk about?" Aiden asked.

"I don't know. Regular stuff."

"And you said you went on three dates?" Zoe asked.

"Yeah, it lasted only two weeks. I realized what an asshole I was being. And she was kind of weird."

"How?" Aiden narrowed his eyes.

"All she ever talked about was the fire." He grimaced. "Don't get me wrong. We all talk about it. When I was a kid, we played Survivor. We would role-play being the victims and added a twist that one of us was the killer." A wan smile crossed his lips. "Well, it was stupid and we all grew up. I have other things I wanted to talk about but she was only interested in one topic. I sent her flowers and ended things with her over the phone like a gentleman."

Zoe struggled to hold back a burst of laughter at him referring to himself as a gentleman after cheating on his wife. "Did she mention any other person in her life? Friends or family?"

"Not really. I don't think she had a life. Everything was about the fire. I think someone in her family was a victim, which started this obsession. Though... I think she mentioned someone else." He closed his eyes. "I'm trying to remember. She was doing some freelance work and said someone was pushing her to do something she wasn't comfortable with. I thought it was sexual favors or something but she said it wasn't that but it was illegal."

Zoe threw a discreet glance at Aiden. Her mind raced. It didn't make sense. Why would Annabelle come up with the idea to steal the product? Was she truly that disturbed by the ethics of it? She didn't need to steal it to leak the story to Adam. Jackie, on the other hand, had a reason to want to take it. She intended to use it to escalate her obsession.

"David!" he said suddenly. "She said some guy called David was pressuring her. She didn't say about what."

Zoe went blank as his words slowly permeated her brain and traveled through the cells, forming into a realization that Aiden seemed to have reached already.

"David Harrington."

THIRTY-FOUR

David sat with his hands clasped, jaw set, his tie just a little too tight. Across from him, Dawn leaned back in her seat, tapping a pen lightly against the arm of her chair. Measured, calm, controlled.

This was who she was. She wasn't any different at work. She wasn't a mother at home and chairwoman of the board at work. She was always the chairwoman. Her warmth and affection calcified by tragedy. His nervousness pitched higher. It wasn't the board members with stiff faces that made him uncomfortable. It was his mother. He was once again trying to prove himself. It was all he'd ever done.

"This isn't personal, David."

It was the first lie and first slap to his face.

Across the table, a man—gray-haired, three decades too comfortable in his position—cleared his throat. "We've reviewed the candidates thoroughly. The board has made its decision."

David's fingers flexed slightly against the table. "The board," he repeated, eyes moving across the room. Half of them wouldn't meet his gaze. The other half wore the faint, unreadable expressions of corporate survivors—people who knew when to stay silent, when to stay clear of the blast zone.

Dawn's lips curled slightly, not quite a smile. "It's not about your qualifications or your commitment to the company. You are valued."

Another lie.

He sat back, exhaling slowly through his nose. "Then what is it about, Dawn?"

A silence stretched, just long enough to make it clear she wasn't going to answer. She didn't have to.

Instead, it was Landers, one of the younger board members, who finally spoke. "It's about stability." He shifted uncomfortably. "Things have been in flux with the product launch indefinitely delayed, our company reporting losses this past quarter *again*, and the stock price down nineteen percent this week alone. We can't be seen to be making too many changes."

There it was. An excuse disguised as corporate diplomacy.

He gave a slow nod, jaw tightening. "Right. Because when something isn't working then a change in strategy is the last thing to try?"

Markson sighed like he wanted to get out of here before the valet shift changed. "This is final, David. We're sorry."

David turned his gaze back to Dawn. She was watching him the way a surgeon watches a patient before the first incision. And then there was the glint of *I told you so*. She loved inflicting pain on him, putting him in his place.

"You should be grateful, really," she said smoothly. "This is me protecting you."

He let out a short, humorless laugh. "You always were generous."

The irony of Dawn protecting him when really it was the other way around. He could let it slip that the product launch had been canceled not because it had failed quality assurance but because it had been stolen. He could reveal how Dawn had lied to the board previously. But the words remained stuck inside his mouth. It was the power his mother held over him—and she knew it.

The meeting ended without ceremony. And just like that, his candidacy—his shot at real power—was gone.

By the time he reached his office, David was fuming.

He pulled at his tie, undoing the knot in one sharp motion. The office lights were dim, the city skyline stretching beyond the floor-to-ceiling windows. His reflection stared back at him. All he saw was a man who had spent his entire life being wronged.

His phone buzzed.

He let it ring once while trying to still the gibbering of his mind. Saliva thickened in his throat. This was the last thing he needed today.

"I'm doing everything I can," David said, answering the phone.

The voice on the other end was curt, impatient. "How much more time do you need, Mr. Harrington? Because we're running out of patience."

"I know," he muttered. "Just... one more week. One more week and everything will be in place."

A pause. Then, without another word, the line disconnected.

Sweat beaded David's hairline. He opened his laptop. A few keystrokes. A confirmation screen. His finger hovered over the button. It was a huge amount. Then, with a final press of a button, the wire transfer was sent. He typed a message.

I've sent more. You need to step up.

Across the office, beyond the glass walls, Dawn's office was visible. She marched back inside, her posture stiff and proud.

He watched as she reached into her purse, pulled out a small vial, and dry-swallowed two pills.

David was puzzled. But then a smile curled up his lips.

* * *

Lisa didn't know who her husband was. She didn't even know who she was. Her life suddenly seemed completely foreign to her. Her memories felt fabricated. Was anything real? She sat in her living room, surrounded by the furniture she'd handpicked, in a house that she'd chosen as a newlywed many years ago. Now everything felt infected and impersonal. She resisted the urge to dig her nails into the walls and tear down this false life she'd naively constructed with Jim.

Her heartbeat was erratic, and chaotic thoughts swarmed her mind like a flock of birds. She caught her reflection in the mirror. Her face was bloated—a side effect from the treatments she was subjecting her body to.

The glass hit the wall before she even realized she'd thrown it. It exploded into a thousand jagged pieces, scattering across the hardwood floor. Rage, hot and consuming, climbed up her throat.

Her hand found the nearest object, a framed photo on the console table. The frame hit the ground face down, the glass fracturing beneath it. She stared at it for a moment, at the memory now shattered. She spun round, yanking the lamp from the side table and hurling it to the ground. The bulb burst in a violent pop, plunging the corner of the room into shadow.

It wasn't enough. Nothing was ever going to be enough.

Her fingers fisted her hair and pulled at it. She sucked in a shaking breath and backed up against the wall. Her knees buckled, and she slid down the wall, her breaths coming too fast, too ragged.

"Lisa? Lisa!" Jim's voice rang in her ears. She looked up and his worried face hovered over hers. "I'm so sorry."

"Shut up!" she screamed. He froze. She was a rabid animal. "How could you? How could you?" She stood up and shoved him backward.

"Let's calm down and talk about this rationally," he said, backing off with his hands raised.

"You're telling me to calm down?" Everything inside her burned. "You're a piece of shit, Jim. And you know what, I'm glad that I didn't get pregnant because I don't want any part of you."

Anguish was written all over his face. He dropped his hands to his side limply. "Nothing even happened between me and her. We didn't sleep together. It was only—"

"Don't!" She whirled back round, unable to face him. Her breathing still uneven. She tried taking long swallows to calm herself. "Don't downplay what you did. I was trying so hard, working long hours—"

"Maybe that's the problem," he snapped. "I'm sick of you trying so hard and constantly rubbing it in my face, Lisa. These past months, every moment with you, I've felt *less*." His voice climbed and quailed. "You've made me feel like a sloth, like a chump. So yeah, I slipped for a moment because it felt good to get away from the constant stress of being around you!"

She stared at him wide-eyed. "Are you seriously blaming me for being too supportive? You were the one who rejected plenty of opportunities because you thought you were too good for them."

He dug the heels of his palms into his eyes and shook his head. "I'm sorry, Lisa. I didn't mean to hurt you."

"Nothing matters. You don't matter to me," she whispered, numbness silencing her churning thoughts.

He staggered back from her words like he'd been hit. With a curt nod and tight jaw, he stormed out of the house, slamming the door shut behind him. She didn't care where he went, she didn't care if he came back or not. Sobs raked her body as tears streamed down her cheeks.

The warning signs had been right in front of her. He'd been too disengaged. But she'd ignored all the signs and let them slowly carve into her like a blunt knife.

THIRTY-FIVE

"Fight! Fight! Fight! Fight!"

The faces were delirious. Their eyes hungry for violence. Zoe could feel the primitiveness pulse through this basement that lay beneath a shuttered warehouse. She smelled the sweat, blood, and the sharp sting of cheap liquor. The only light came from flickering overhead bulbs, casting long, jerking shadows against the stained concrete walls.

Through the cacophony of voices, only one sound stood out: that of bone meeting flesh.

In the corner, a man wiped his nose with the back of his hand, blood smeared across his knuckles. He smirked, wild and reckless, teeth slick with red. Cigarette smoke curled in the stale air, distorting his smile. He liked the challenge.

Zoe's body was wired and drenched in sweat, her muscles throbbing and drawn tight under the sickly yellow light. The ring was marked by flimsy ropes atop a bare slice of concrete at a slight elevation. Outside the ring bodies pressed tight, shouting, jeering, fists raised in anticipation.

She was winning this round. She'd fought stronger men

before. But she needed this. She didn't come here to seek a challenge; she came to quell the guilt.

Promise me you won't look into it if anything happens to me. Promise me.

A dull thud echoed as a punch landed solid across her face, the wet sound of spit and blood hitting the floor. Her head felt like it was going to explode. She stumbled back, almost losing her balance. Shockwaves rocked her skull, leaving her vision blurred. She clenched her hands into fists, twisting her arm, ready to deliver an uppercut.

But she stopped. She gave him a window to hit her again. And he did. A brutal kick to the stomach and she was on the floor, curled into a ball, white-hot agony ripping through her body.

Another kick to the side of her face, and her teeth rattled from the impact.

A punch to her ribs, and her world tilted.

She could have fought back; she had the strength. But she didn't even try. The sharp pain searing through her body in dizzying waves was almost addictive. She deserved this pain. She deserved it because she'd let Rachel's killer walk free, because she had been lying to Gina for years that Rachel killed herself, because she was sick of seeing too many wrongs.

Benny jumped in and declared her opponent the winner. Money exchanged hands in the crowd. But she didn't care. As her eyes swept over her surroundings, something—or someone—caught her eye.

Aiden.

He stood in a corner, his arms crossed and his eyes unreadable behind thick glasses.

Panic roared hot in her blood. He *knew*. She closed her eyes and let the darkness swallow her whole.

. . .

A few hours later, Zoe was staring at her bruised reflection.

Damn it. How was she going to explain any of this at work?

After being woken up by Benny and convincing him she didn't have a concussion, she had searched the crowd for Aiden. But he was nowhere to be seen. For a moment, she wondered if she'd imagined it. But she hadn't. She knew it in her bones.

The rain battered the motel window, unrelenting. There was a low roll of thunder, and the thin walls shook. The dim glow of the bedside lamp stretched long shadows across the room, flickering every time lightning split the sky outside.

A knock.

She sighed, knowing exactly who it was, and opened the door.

"We need to talk," Aiden said.

Moments later, they were sitting on the floor, their backs against the side of the bed, inches apart.

"You should see the other guy," Zoe said out of nowhere, trying to lighten the mood.

"What?" He stared at her, confused.

"It's like in the movies. I always wanted to say that line," she admitted, staring ahead.

"You hear that?" he murmured, tilting his head toward the window.

"The storm?" she asked, her voice low. "We're talking about the weather now? Just do it, Aiden. Say what you want to say."

"What were you doing in that place, Storm?"

"Why were you following me?" she volleyed back.

He exhaled slowly. "I have been worried about you and you refuse to tell me what's going on with you. So yeah, I followed you."

Zoe shivered at their proximity. Close enough to feel the heat radiating between them, but not close enough to touch. "I go to this underground fight club to blow off steam. It isn't that deep."

"Then why did you lose on purpose today?" he asked. The silence between them stretched and Zoe's heart sank.

She wasn't ready for this conversation. But tonight, she was too tired and defeated to fight it. "Because I'm angry, Aiden." Her eyes turned glassy. "This whole happy-go-lucky thing I have going on isn't a façade. I swear it isn't. I'm genuinely happy but... this darkness exists inside me and I don't know how to get rid of it."

"It looked like you were punishing yourself there, Storm."

"I guess I was." Her knee brushed his. Not by accident. "What do I do then? I really am a happy person. But that's not enough. How do you actually move on?"

"Move on from what? You have to give me something."

She gave him a look. "Why don't you give me something for a change?"

He flinched and adjusted his glasses—an unconscious habit, Zoe realized. "I'm the shrink here."

"I thought we were becoming friends."

His jaw clenched. He turned his head, looking at her now, really looking. The space between them became as thin as a breath. "I'm a widower. That's what you wanted to hear, right? Now who is Viktor Axenov?"

"The man who beat me up in Harborwood," she confessed too readily. She turned to see his surprised face.

"And why did he do that?"

"Because I think he killed my mother."

Lightning flashed, and for an instant, she saw the way his lashes flickered and saw him notice how her lips parted just slightly.

"And now he's after you?" His voice sliced the thickening air.

"Kind of. I was looking into my mother's life. She had so many secrets. I discovered something in Harborwood. An old acquaintance who gave me a key to a safety deposit box in

Chicago. My mother kept something in there. But somehow Viktor found out, beat me up, and took that key."

"And now he is in possession of whatever object your mother was concealing?"

"I don't think so." Her gaze lifted to his, steady, unreadable. "He doesn't know which safety deposit box it is. But he does have leverage. He's been keeping an eye on me in case I start digging around her death again."

"Darren Galanis. He paid someone to follow you and report back." He connected the dots. "You're the one with a badge and a gun, Storm. Why haven't you gone after him?"

Her fingers curled slightly, resting on the floor beside his. One inch closer, and she'd touch him. "He belongs to a shadow criminal organization. Even the FBI barely has any information on it."

"What is it called?"

"Red Trigger."

He froze. The air between them went from electric to cold. Zoe hadn't realized how close they had been sitting, how intimate it had felt. But now a bucket of ice-cold water had been thrown on the moment. "Zoe, I—"

Zoe's phone rang, puncturing the heavy silence. It was Lisa. She answered.

"Hey."

"Agent Storm, we have a problem. Amy Andrews..."

"Yeah, did you check her alibi?"

"She's missing."

THIRTY-SIX

It was that in-between hour when the night had mostly bled away, but the sun hadn't fully risen, just a faint, cold light creeping over the horizon. The streetlamps, still on, flickered weakly against the encroaching daylight. Heavy morning dampness clung to Zoe's skin. A light mist drifted over the lot, curling in the distance where the trees stood in eerie silhouettes.

Amy Andrews's Prius was parked at the edge of the lot at a rest stop, the driver's side open a crack. Not wide, just enough to feel wrong. The windows were fogged at the edges, dew clinging to the windshield, untouched. Like it had been sitting there for hours. Waiting.

But she was gone.

"What do we know?" Zoe asked.

"The manager at 7-Eleven started his early morning shift thirty minutes ago and noticed this abandoned car. Dispatch ran the plate. It's registered to Amy. Ethan made some calls and learned that Amy never arrived at work and no one can seem to reach her." Lisa's voice was clear but her eyes were swollen. Zoe resisted the urge to give her a hug. Finding out in such a public way that your husband had cheated on you was a punch to the gut. Zoe thought about her kiss with Simon and felt like throwing up.

"There are signs of a struggle here." Zoe pointed at a set of scuffed footprints, sharp against the damp ground, like someone had dug their heels in, then a drag mark leading toward the edge of the pavement. The gravel was disturbed, scattered.

"The CSU is on the way. Her phone's under here!" Ethan was crouched on the ground. He shoved a gloved hand under the car and retrieved an iPhone with a blue case. The screen was fractured like cracked ice, the battery flickering at two percent.

"Any cameras around here?" Aiden looked around, the wind tousling his hair.

"There's one but it doesn't work. The other one is inside but there's no view of this spot," Lisa said gruffly. "I've alerted the Washington State Patrol. Do you think this is related to our current case or something else altogether?"

"We should knock on doors just in case but what are the chances?" Aiden said. "Amy was Jackie's only family and hence related to one of the original victims."

"Did the FBI get a riddle?" Lisa asked. When Zoe shook her head, she sighed in relief. "Well, that's good, then. The last two riddles have directed us to bodies. No riddle means she might still be alive."

"And getting tortured as we speak." Zoe's scalp prickled at her own words. "We need to talk to David."

"David's going to lawyer up," Lisa said. "And he wouldn't get his own hands dirty. He's got money. He'd hire someone."

"It will be a bitch to get his financials and go through them. Wealthy people like him are experts at hiding money." She bit her lip. "There has to be another way to dig up the dirt on him..." She paused when she spotted something in the distance. On the other side of the road was a red Toyota parked with the window rolled down. "Who's that?"

Lisa turned around and sighed, shaking her head. "It's Adam. Following us around everywhere to be the first one to break the story."

Zoe's heart constricted in her chest. This town had found a new tragedy to obsess over.

"I found this a few feet away." A deputy came running over. "You gotta see this. It must have been blown away by the wind."

Zoe's breath caught in her chest as she read the words.

Ticktock goes the clock,

She's out there past the cedar rock.

Ticktock, fading fast—

Something laughs where the branches snap,

And blood runs cold in the hunter's trap.

Find her soon, or she breathes her last.

THIRTY-SEVEN

Zoe dumped the entire jar of maple syrup over her waffles. Saliva pooled in her mouth and pangs of hunger rocked her stomach. She didn't stop until the waffle was soaked and soggy.

"Looks healthy," Aiden said dryly as he dug into his quinoa salad, which made Zoe suppress a gag.

"At least I feel good," she muttered. Her eyes darted to the impenetrable, green wall of trees surrounding the diner. Somewhere Amy was getting tortured and if Zoe didn't find her soon, she would receive another tingling riddle.

Lisa was out with the entire force, covering more ground in the area around where Amy was abducted and coordinating with the other counties.

"I told Ethan to get Amy's phone records and canvass the area," Zoe said. "Adam was watching."

"I saw that."

"Why did the killer take Amy?"

"Annabelle and Jackie stole the prototype. Jackie's decision to kill Annabelle wasn't driven solely by greed or betrayal, it was psychologically rooted. The triggering event appears to be the death of her brother in the fire, which acted as a trauma activator for underlying psychopathic tendencies." He drummed his fingers on the table. "They were partners, so Jackie must have easily lured Annabelle and pulled one on her. But then someone killed Jackie the exact same way."

"Why Amy? Because she's Jackie's sister?"

He stroked his jaw. "Amy is a high-status woman—confident, educated, and successful. Perhaps the killer's sense of identity is so fragile, female agency becomes a threat to his core self."

"Someone must have known what Jackie did to Annabelle, which is why he hunted Jackie in a similar way."

"Someone like Adam who knew Annabelle," Aiden suggested.

"Or David Harrington. Maybe he planted the idea of the prototype theft. There are rumors about familial conflict."

"But we can't touch David Harrington without further proof. He's already lawyered up."

"Do you think he'll stop?"

"Who?"

She made an obvious face. "The killer."

"Oh." He thought about it. "I'm surprised actually. His last riddle about where Jackie's body was rang with finality. *Last step taken, last stage set. No reset, no second bet. Final round, final scene.* He literally said in the riddle to find her *where the game turns clean.* Where it all began. He wasn't subtle that Jackie was the end."

"But then what changed his mind?"

"The thrill of the hunt."

Her stomach turned to ice. "He's hooked?"

He nodded. "Unless there is a specific reason to take Amy— a personal vendetta or Amy somehow discovered his identity. He took her because torturing and killing Jackie was too much fun. Either way, we might have a longer window to find her."

"Why do you think that?" She idly glanced at a group of

teenagers as they sat huddled in a booth behind Aiden and took their phones out and ordered fries for the table.

"Because he's going to have to think twice about where to leave the body. Fun House was the final destination. A full-circle moment. He'll likely hunt for a place that has some significance."

Zoe opened her mouth when one of the teenager's voices cut through her train of thought.

"No, listen, I'm telling you. This is just like what happened in 1995," a girl said, leaning forward, eyes wide.

Across from her, a girl in an oversized hoodie rolled her eyes, sipping her milkshake. "Dude, you weren't even alive in 1995. It was a fire in the haunted house. Not random women going missing."

Zoe and Aiden locked eyes. She strained her ears to listen to the conversation.

"I know, but I've been listening to that podcast—*Buried Hollow*. They're covering this and said that the second woman was found in Fun House, and her uncle, Michael, was a victim of the original fire."

The third teen, scrolling through his phone, nudged his screen toward them. "Tell me this isn't creepy. Someone on Reddit has a thread tracking down all the family members of the fire victims."

The girl took the phone and huffed. "Why do they even care so much?" She tossed the phone back. "It was an accident decades ago. This town needs a hobby."

"What if someone's coming after the descendants?" The first boy's voice dropped to a whisper. "Or—" He grinned. "Do you think I can predict the next victim?"

"You've been watching too many Netflix documentaries," the girl muttered, pushing her fries toward him.

The boy grinned but didn't argue.

"Everyone's an armchair sleuth now," Zoe tsked. Her

phone vibrated. "Just got back the particulate evidence from Jackie's clothes." Her eyes scanned the report. She wasn't expecting much—Jackie's autopsy report was standard. But then her eyes caught something unusual buried in the trace evidence section. "They found a canine hair sample on her jeans. Silver-gray, approximately two centimeters. A borzoi breed."

His eyebrows furrowed. "A borzoi? That's not a breed you see every day. Expensive. Rare. Selective owners."

A thought itched in the back of her mind. "Jackie doesn't own a dog. It must have come from the killer, then?"

"You know who could afford a dog like that? David Harrington." A slow smirk curled at the corner of his mouth.

"We didn't see any dogs at his place."

"Did you see how big their property was? Can we look at the city's pet ownership registry?"

"We'd need a subpoena. No time for that." Her thoughts were tumbling ahead. "I have an idea." She did a quick search for pet groomers in the area. There was only one. "If this guy owns an expensive dog like a borzoi, he's definitely taking him to a groomer." The phone rang thrice before an elderly lady answered.

"Madeleine's Canine Boutique. How can I help you?" She sounded like someone who wore cashmere cardigans and pearl necklaces.

"Hi there!" Zoe said cheerfully. "I was thinking of getting a borzoi and wanted to know if you guys work with that breed. I'd like to, you know, make sure I find the right groomer before I commit."

"Yes, we groom borzois, but we're appointment-only. And they're not a breed you just... pick up on a whim."

"Oh, I know. I've done my research," she said smoothly. "I actually ran into someone in town with a stunning borzoi. Not sure of his name, but the dog had this incredible silver-gray coat.

Thought I'd call around and see where he might take it for grooming."

The silence dragged for more than a second. "A man, huh? Well, there's only one borzoi in Pineview Falls. Beautiful animal. His owner is one of our regulars, very particular about how he likes it done."

"Do you mind giving me his name?" she asked innocently. "I've had bad experiences with groomers in the past and would love to just chat with him about his experience. I hope you understand."

"Of course, of course! We understand the importance of references... ah, here's his name." Zoe didn't know what to expect but then the lady said the name.

"Adam Deader."

THIRTY-EIGHT

The air smelled of stale coffee at the overworked station. Zoe was convinced that the substation had been barely active before she'd arrived armed with a riddle that led her to the first murder victim of Pineview Falls in many years. The doors creaked, the windows jammed, and the refrigerator in the break room constantly hummed. The substation was brimming with activity. Deputies from the neighboring towns had pitched in to find Amy Andrews.

Her picture was pinned to the bulletin board. Zoe stared at her unremarkable face. The printer under the board spat out missing person posters. She picked one up and frowned at the fading ink and poor paper quality under her fingertips. It would wash out in the rain, which was a frequent occurrence. Outside sheets of rain pounded against the pavement. Water cascaded from awnings, dripped from the edges of street signs, and splattered onto windshields of cars in the parking lot. The town was painted in smears of gray.

"He's waiting for us." Aiden appeared.

Zoe gathered the printout and tucked it under her arm.

Upon entering the makeshift interrogation room, she was immediately put off by Adam.

He sat with easy elegance, legs crossed, fingers tapping against the arm of his chair as though he were waiting for a drink at a jazz lounge instead of a police interview.

She dropped the folder on the table in front of them and perched on the chair across from him.

"Ah, the infamous folder drop," he said, flashing a lazily amused smile. "A detective classic. Next, you're going to dramatically flip it open, lean forward, and say something ominous. Something like"—he deepened his voice mockingly—"we both know why you're here, Adam."

Zoe's jaw ticked. "That's not what I was going to say."

He arched an eyebrow. "Oh? Do surprise me, then."

She leaned in slightly, his voice quiet but sharp. "Tell me about your dog."

Adam's eyes jumped between Zoe and Aiden, like he was trying to decipher some hidden code. "My dog? Aesop?" He placed a hand over his chest, as if deeply offended. "You dragged me all the way down here to discuss—what? Canine nutrition? Breed temperament? I assure you, Agent Storm, Aesop is the perfect gentleman. Is the FBI really *that* clueless about the murders?"

Zoe flipped open the folder. Inside was a forensic report, a few photographs clipped to the top. One showed Jackie's body, another the silver-gray borzoi hair found on her clothing. She tapped the photo with one finger.

"This hair," Aiden said, his tone almost conversational, "is from a borzoi. Not a very common breed, is it?"

Adam exhaled dramatically, leaning back in his chair. "Tragic," he mused. "And here I was, thinking we were talking about my dog, not forensic hair samples. You must forgive me—I do have a flair for the romantic, but this feels a little too... forensic noir for my taste."

She stared at him. "The hair matches your dog, Adam. It was found on Jackie's body."

Adam tilted his head, his expression curious rather than worried. "Are you implying," he said slowly, "that my beloved pet has become some kind of murder suspect? That he's leading a secret life—roaming the streets at night, luring unsuspecting women into alleys? I must say, that would make for an excellent short story."

Zoe's patience thinned. "How did your dog's hair end up on a dead woman?" she asked flatly.

Adam hummed thoughtfully, tapping his fingers against the table. "What if I told you I met her a few days before she went missing?"

He was testing her reaction. "I would say that's bullshit because this hair wouldn't have stayed stuck on her jeans for several days. I think she touched your dog shortly before she went missing and was killed."

Suddenly, he dropped his fake charm act rubbed his temple. "I didn't do anything. I swear. I'm just a storyteller."

"And this way you get to be in the story you created. Every writer's dream," Aiden said.

"I... I was there." His lips quivered and he leaned forward.

"Where?" Zoe asked. "I don't have a lot of time, so hurry up."

His chin trembled. "I was at Fun House before you showed up with the sheriff. But I swear I didn't kill her." He raised his hands.

Zoe masked her surprise and kept her face rigid. "Convenient you were at Fun House."

"I was there for my story! I was walking Aesop and thought I'd get some inspiration too. I'm working on a podcast, if you must know. A real-time account of my journey during this string of murders. Even though Fun House is closed for the season, I have been going there from time to time. But you can't just write about a place like Fun House from memory, Agent Storm. You have to breathe it in."

"Why Fun House?" Zoe challenged.

"Well, obviously because it all comes down to it," he scoffed. "The game that's torturing and killing the women is based on the massacre and Jackie was related to a victim. I was at Fun House so that I can soak it in and capture its true essence." Horror crossed his eyes. "I was walking through the hallways when I saw her. Jackie. At first I thought it was some fallen prop but when I got closer, I saw her skin and all that fresh blood." A violent shudder rolled through him. "It was barbaric."

"How do we know that you didn't move the body there yourself?" Zoe asked.

"I didn't!" His eyes blazed. "Check my whereabouts. I was at an interview with News 9 before that. The day before I was at work all day. You can confirm my alibi. I didn't do this."

"Don't worry, we will." She smiled sweetly. "Why didn't you call the police when you discovered the body?"

He avoided their scrutinizing gaze. "I... I wanted to be the one to break the story. But I was so disgusted and shocked by what I saw. And then I got scared, thinking what if the killer was still around? My dog was with me, barking crazily. I ran out of there and was figuring out how to use this for my podcast when I saw the sheriff's car approaching from the end of the street. Next thing I knew, the scene was swarming with cops. I don't know how you guys got there first."

Zoe didn't like Adam—disingenuity poured out of him. Here was a man with a distorted vision of the world, where the only thing that mattered was a story for people to lap up. And then there was his penchant for wordplay—a quality he shared with the killer, who had left riddles.

"Did your dog touch the body?" Aiden asked.

"Yes. Obviously. It's a dog. It smelled something and went

sniffing around." A moment of hesitation, his smugness withering. "He might have swallowed something he found."

Zoe rolled her eyes. "Jesus Christ. The crime scene was tampered with. Do you realize how serious this offense is, Adam?"

"I'm sorry! I told you I was in shock and I struggled to control Aesop before I finally dragged him out of there! But I think he was sniffing around the pockets of her jeans quite a bit." He pulled out his phone and after a couple swipes, showed them an image. "This came out in his excretion this morning. I didn't recognize it but I think Jackie had it on her."

Zoe and Aiden stared at the photo of a keychain, a piece of paper inserted into it with *INV-W7-D4-1553* written on it.

"Is that a fob or what?" Aiden wondered out loud.

He shrugged. "No idea. It's not mine. It must be Jackie's. I don't know what it means. I was hoping to find out for myself—that's why I kept it."

Zoe stared at Adam. His colorful flamboyance that once eclipsed the station had gone, replaced with desperation.

"Agent Storm, Dr. Wesley," he said. "I wouldn't *kill* anyone for a story. For starters, I'm only good with words and reading people." His eyes zeroed in on Zoe. "Like I can look at you and know that you carry shame that you hide behind your infectious, dimpled smile." Zoe flushed red. Adam looked at Aiden. "And I can sense that you know deep loss and struggle to be understood. But I'm not smart enough to get away with murder. And the worst nightmare for any writer is never being able to write again."

Zoe held the evidence in the palm of her hand. INV-W7-D4-1553. What did it mean?

THIRTY-NINE

Adam's words clung to Zoe like an itchy blanket.

Shame.

The shame of being stupid enough to listen to Rachel, clean up her crime scene, and then lie to Gina festered inside her like something rotten her body was constantly trying to expel. But it couldn't. No matter how happy and content she was, the shame was a permanent resident, slowly swelling and expanding until there was only one thing left to do. She cracked her knuckles and rolled her shoulders. Her body was still sore from the beating she'd deliberately taken.

"What are you thinking?" Aiden offered her coffee. She took it and didn't answer. "Storm... what we talked about—"

"Don't." She looked at him. He stood innocently, the sleeves of his shirt rolled up, one hand in his pocket, thick glasses resting on an aristocratic nose. It bothered her how polished he was. "I just want to focus on the case, if that's okay."

He nodded after what seemed like forever. "I have to head out. I'm due in court in a couple hours."

"Oh?"

"Another case I was on. Have to testify." He picked up his coat. "I'll see you later?"

She nodded, returning to her pile of folders. She felt his gaze linger on her before he finally walked away. She released a sigh of relief that loosened some of her knots.

The station was quiet, but not in a peaceful way. A silence built from exhaustion, the type that made everyone double-check everything, waiting for the moment something would crack open.

She sat at her desk, rolling her pen between her fingers, her eyes locked on to the forensic report.

Both Annabelle and Jackie had been targeted with hunting darts. The darts were the only element that was introduced by the killer—by Jackie and then adopted by the person who used it on Jackie. According to Aiden, the darts were meant to make them feel like they were part of the game, like an active player.

She studied Jackie's picture. What pushed her to torture and murder a friend? She had no priors, no history of any known mental illnesses, but that didn't mean there wasn't a darkness growing inside her slowly. She was isolated from her family, didn't have any close friends, no boyfriend or girlfriend. All that time she spent deeply marinating in the massacre with nothing to lift her out of her spiraling thoughts.

Zoe dropped the picture and shot a message to Gina.

Z: I will come see you after this case wraps up.

Gina's reply was instant.

G: YESSS.

A smile tugged on her lips and she returned to the notes. Based on the dimensions of the bruise, the forensic team had identified a potential candidate that was a perfect match. A slim metal shaft that looked light but weighted. Balanced. Built for precision. The barbed tip gleamed, sharp enough to bite into flesh.

A voice broke through her thoughts. "You're staring at that report like it's about to confess."

"Lisa..." Zoe hesitated. "We haven't had a chance to talk and I know we don't really know each other, but I'm really sorry."

She snorted without humor and crossed her arms. "I knew."

"About Jackie?"

"No..." She licked her lips. "About Jim having an affair. I found a woman's scarf at home. Red with blue border. It's imprinted in my brain."

"You didn't confront him?"

She lolled her head. "I think I was trying to pretend it wasn't happening for as long as I could. But anyway, I'd like to focus on work."

"Of course."

Lisa slid a piece of paper in front of her. "Just got back Adam's financials. We had probable cause since his dog's hair was found at a crime scene. Look at that." She tapped her finger on the highlighted deposits into Adam's account for the last two weeks. "Since the first disappearance, someone's been wiring him money. And it's not his employer."

"Can you contact the bank for more information on the sender?"

"Already did." She hooked her thumbs into the buckles of her belt. "They're looking into it."

Lisa's face had grown gaunt. Her complexion pale. There was always a strain on her face, like she was constantly fighting tears. Zoe racked her brain for words of comfort when Lisa cleared her throat. "What's that?"

"The hunting dart that was used on the victims. I just

searched it online but I can't find anything quite like it. It has this pattern on the tip that is unique."

Lisa looked closer. "It might be local."

"Is there a place in town?"

"Yeah, Hollow Point Outfitters. They sell a lot of outdoor and gaming gear. If it's not a major retailer, then I can't think of anything else." Zoe was already grabbing her coat. "Agent Storm! The owner doesn't like people. Especially cops."

Zoe beamed. "Good thing I'm such a charmer."

The bell above the door jingled as Zoe stepped inside, shaking the rain from her coat. The shop smelled like leather, gun oil, and sawdust. A hunter's paradise, stocked with weapons, camouflage, and everything needed to kill something big.

Rows of rifles, crossbows, and hunting knives lined the walls. Mounted deer heads stared blankly from above, their glass eyes frozen in permanent shock. A deep horror seized Zoe. She understood the thrill of the hunt but couldn't fathom staring at a dead creature hanging on a wall.

At the counter, a woman in her mid-forties, auburn hair tied back, was counting inventory when she saw Zoe. Her expression shifted immediately. Mild irritation curdled into distrust.

"Unless you're here to buy something," she said, not looking up again, "we're closed."

"How do you get customers with that attitude?" She couldn't help herself. When the woman sneered, ready to retort, Zoe dropped her badge on the counter between them.

"We're licensed." The woman's voice was sharp.

"I didn't doubt that." She showed her a picture of the dart. "You sell these?"

Her eyes flicked to it. A half-second hesitation. "Yeah," she admitted. "Not to just anyone, though. That's restricted stock."

"So you'll know who has bought these?"

Her shoulders tensed. "Let me check." She pulled out a register and flipped through the pages. "In the last six months, just one. Jackie Fink. She paid in cash." Her startled eyes looked up. "Isn't that the woman in the news? The dead one?"

"Was she alone?" Zoe said, ignoring the question.

The woman hesitated. "Yeah. But she took a call while I was ringing it up. Seemed agitated."

Zoe's pulse kicked up a notch. "Did you hear a name? What were they talking about?"

The woman's face scrunched as she tried to recall. "It was a man, for sure. But I was busy with some other customer too, so I didn't pay attention to what they were arguing about." Then she snapped her fingers. "Spector!"

Zoe's breath hitched. "Spector?"

"Yeah." She nodded. "Repeated the name a few times. Like she was confirming details."

A cold weight settled in her gut. The name rang a bell. It was the username from the chatroom that Annabelle communicated with. Jackie knew Spector too. But who was he?

FORTY

Dawn stood barefoot on cool tile in the washroom, wearing a robe, a towel wrapped loosely around her damp hair. It was a muted morning with soft amber light leaking through linen curtains. The faucet was dripping again. Another thing she needed to fix.

There were many things that needed fixing. Her company was sinking. And her body was betraying her. It wasn't until the diagnosis that Dawn understood the distinction between her body and mind. All her life, she had prided herself on her efficiency and performance. Sharp as a tick. Her entire being working in coordination.

Ever since she'd found out just how sick she was, she had grown detached from her body. But what about her mind? Where would she go after she died?

She moved slowly, methodically, brushing moisturizer across her cheek with one hand, the other reaching up into the mirrored cabinet above the sink.

The pill bottle was where it always is. Tucked behind a half-empty bottle of mouthwash and a travel-size sunscreen she rarely used, living in a town under a constant cover of clouds.

She pulled out the bottle and twisted the cap open, shaking out two small pills into the palm of her hand.

The routine was built into her. She froze.

The pills were the same color. The same shape. But there was a slight chip on the edge of one of them—a little crescent bite that wasn't there yesterday. And the other? The coating looked dull... Maybe it was the light.

Dawn tilted her hand. The pills rolled slightly on her palm. She set them down on the counter.

Doubt brewed inside her mind, curling in the corner of her thoughts and shaking her confidence. Something felt wrong.

She reached for the bottle again and peered inside.

Maybe she was just being paranoid after all the stress at work. She was seeing the worst in everything. But still she decided to count them.

Sixteen.

She did the math in her head. She should have seventeen. Or was it fifteen? She hesitated, her fingers tightening around the bottle. A week ago, she'd skipped a dose. She was working late, had a headache, and fell asleep early. Or was that two weeks ago?

"Damn it," she muttered, frustrated. She didn't like uncertainty.

She picked up the chipped pill again and turned it over. It could've broken in the bottle. That happened. Except the cut was too clean. It wasn't jagged like she'd expected it to be. She held it to her nose and took a whiff. It smelled less metallic than the other ones.

She put it back down and her heart picked up rhythm. Frantically, she checked her cabinet again and the label. Name, dosage, instructions. Everything looked fine. And she didn't have any other pills. But this pill was different. She was sure of it. But where did it come from?

And what if she'd consumed the wrong one before?

The staff would have no reason to do this—would they? Dawn was a powerful woman with enemies. But how many enemies had access to her washroom?

Her eyes flicked to the mirror again. And she glanced out the half-open window beside the sink.

David was in the backyard, trimming the rosemary bush near the fence. A random hobby he had picked up in recent years. He wore a linen shirt with the sleeves rolled up, his fingers deftly plucking dead leaves. A watering can sat nearby. He hummed softly to himself. Something tuneless, low.

Dawn watched him for a long while. Could it be possible?

She felt guilty for even thinking it. David was her son. As much as he resented her for their differences, he wouldn't stoop this low. Except he could have. She knew how she'd punished David every single day since his negligence that night of the fire. Much more recently, she had blocked his attempt to get on the board, even though he'd had some support.

She turned away from the window.

The pills were still on the counter. Her mind jumped back to two weeks ago. The night she woke up in a fog. Her mouth dry, heart thudding in her chest. She'd chalked it up to one of the symptoms, even though it was relatively a new symptom and not something she had expected. But her medication was strong and everyone responded differently.

But then last week, David had offered to refill her prescription for her.

The memory settled in her stomach like a stone.

* * *

The truth was that Lisa was out of her depth. She had never dreamed big or complicated. She had been raised by a teacher and a storeowner, graduated with average grades, and enrolled into the academy. It was supposed to be a simple, uneventful life in this simple and uneventful Washington county.

Nothing bad happened here. A couple of overdoses and a hiking accident here and there. But now Lisa was dealing with a missing woman who was very likely being tortured. She went over everything she was supposed to do—conduct search parties, recruit volunteers, follow up on tips from the hotline that had been set up.

Her phone buzzed against the kitchen counter. She glanced over from where she was rinsing a glass in the sink. The caller ID read: *Dr. Khalid—OB/GYN*. A moment of hesitation. She hadn't thought about this at all for a while. It felt like a lifetime ago.

"Hello."

"Hi, Lisa. It's Dr. Khalid. I just wanted to follow up with you after your last check-in."

Lisa's stomach tightened. She knew what was coming before the words landed. "I'm really sorry, but your HCG levels came back negative. The embryo didn't implant this cycle."

A pause. Did she even care anymore? Jim never did. And she had been too blinded by the idea of a baby to see that her husband had been flirting with women online.

"I see," she said softly. Her head was already hurting.

"I know how hard you've worked for this," the doctor continued gently. "I want to reassure you that it doesn't mean we're out of options. It's just one outcome, and it's more common than most people realize."

Lisa leaned against the counter, rubbing her temple. "What... what happens next?"

"Well," Dr. Khalid replied, her tone shifting. "We have a few directions we can go in. If you want to try another round, we could adjust the hormone protocol slightly. Sometimes a different stimulation can improve egg quality or increase retrieval numbers. That's an option. We could also talk about doing a freeze-all cycle. Retrieve and freeze the embryos, then transfer to a separate, more controlled cycle. Or even preimplantation genetic testing if you're open to it—just to give us more information on embryo quality."

"Right," Lisa murmured, though the words barely made it through the fog forming in her mind. It was all so dizzying.

"There's also the option to pause. Let your body reset. Take a cycle off. Emotionally and physically, that can be important too. You could try naturally for a while again to give yourself a break."

Dr. Khalid paused, her voice softening. "But this is your timeline, Lisa. We'll go at your pace. I'm here whenever you're ready to talk more."

"Thanks," she whispered. "I'll... think about it."

"Of course. Take care of yourself."

The call ended with a soft beep. Lisa stood motionless in the kitchen, staring at the darkened screen, the doctor's words still floating in her mind like faint echoes. She didn't realize her hand was trembling until she set the phone down and saw it shaking.

Suddenly, her life didn't seem like hers anymore. Everything was drastically different from two weeks ago. She wandered to the bedroom in a daze. The air felt thick and soupy. Her bones grew heavy as she plopped on the bed and slid under the duvet. But her eyes stayed open as she stared into the darkness.

She didn't know how much time had passed when the door creaked open. It must be Jim. The fabric rustled as he undressed. The bed shifted as he lay down beside her. He reached out, his hand just grazing behind her back for a second too long. Then he withdrew it.

Lisa forced her breathing to be slow and rhythmic. Pretending to be asleep was easier than trying to deal with him. It was their new routine that they had fallen into. He would try to talk to her and she would pretend to be asleep. It was easier than looking at his face.

But not tonight.

Something came over her. A fire. A need to assert. She rolled over to him.

"Lisa, I—" She swallowed his words with a furious kiss. He protested, mumbling something against her mouth but she didn't stop. She kept the pressure and slid her hand down. He wrapped his hand around her wrist and forcefully pushed her away. "What are you doing?"

In the dark, she could barely make out the silhouette of his face. Instead she kissed him again, this time more aggressively, letting him know what she wanted. Finally, with a groan he gave in and responded, molding his body into hers. Her skin burned not with passion but with the memories of his betrayal.

She didn't want to talk to him. She didn't care to. She didn't care about anything anymore.

FORTY-ONE

PAST

The elevator doors slid open with a hushed chime. The woman stepped out onto the top floor of one of the tallest buildings in Seattle. The dim glow of recessed lighting cast an amber tint over the plush carpeting. She inhaled deeply, smelling the familiar polished mahogany, aged whiskey, and expensive cologne. The hallway stretched long and silent before her. Most of the offices had already gone dark for the night, their glass walls reflecting the city skyline beyond.

She could still remember the first time she'd arrived at this building. She was just a child, holding a big hand she'd once trusted. It didn't take long for her to smell the secrets this building drew its power from. It didn't take long for her to become one of its secrets too.

A storm brewed outside, flickering threads of lightning illuminating the high-rise buildings like silent explosions.

Her heels sank into the carpet as she made her way to an office. Not hers, she didn't work here. There it was at the end of the hall, behind a set of double doors carved from dark wood and brass. The nameplate gleamed under the dim light. She came to a halt, her heart rattling. In the pregnant silence, her erratic breathing was loud in her ears.

Her resolve hardened. She had no choice.

She glanced over her shoulder—nobody there. The security guard wouldn't do his next round for another fifteen minutes. Slipping a gloved hand into her coat pocket, she pulled out the duplicate key she had swiped weeks ago. The lock clicked too loudly, making her hesitate. She glanced up and down the hallway. Still no sign of anyone. She had disabled the security cameras to play on a loop.

The inside of the office was lush, oozing power—from sweeping views of the city and first-edition books to an expensive scotch decanter. She could feel his eyes on her even though she was alone. That was the chokehold he had on her. That's why she had to leave.

She moved quickly.

The safe was behind the bookcase. She knew because she had watched him enter the combination once before. He had spun the dial with a practiced ease, making no effort to hide it from her. His tendrils were embedded so deeply in her that even she believed she would never betray him.

She crouched down, pushing aside the row of leather-bound volumes to reveal the sleek steel door behind them. The lock gleamed under the glow of the desk lamp.

Her breath slowed. With every click, the knot in her chest tightened. Guilt washed over her. What was she doing? Betraying the hand that had fed her and raised her.

No. It was time to the cut the cord. If not for her then for Emily. Because Emily deserved better.

The dial turned smoothly beneath her fingers. One wrong move and the alarm would trip. She swallowed hard and then the final click. The safe door swung open.

Inside were stacks of crisp bills, an envelope filled with passports, and a single leather-bound diary.

There was only one thing she cared about and she now held it in her hands. Grazing its soft and worn-out cover with her fingertips, a thrilling sensation jolted her nerves. She tucked it away in her coat and closed the safe.

At full speed, she sprinted out of the office and down the hallway. She turned a corner to head to the elevator and bumped into someone.

She gasped, her heart lurching violently. "Oh, it's you!"

Tall, polished, his suit still crisp despite the late hour, he held a folder under his arm, his dark, beady eyes narrowing slightly as he looked down at her. "What are you doing here this late?"

His voice was smooth and buttery but she knew it wasn't genuine. She'd once watched him beat someone to death. She forced a quick smile, adjusting her coat to keep the diary pressed against her chest. "I thought I left my wallet somewhere here when I was in for a meeting. But it's not there."

He arched an eyebrow. "I see." He glanced at the office door behind her.

She let out a small, forced laugh. "I have to go. I have a birthday party to chaperone tomorrow. See you later?"

He studied her for a second too long. The air between them thickened, charged with something unreadable. "You're a very dedicated mother," he said finally, his lips curving into something that wasn't quite a smile. "Well," he continued, glancing down at his watch, "I won't keep you."

She exhaled a little too sharply. "Yeah, I should go." She stepped past him, willing herself not to rush. Then, his hand wrapped around her arm. Her spine snapped straight.

"Did you get information on the next target?"

She didn't look at him. "Yes."

"I know you got a little... involved with your previous target," he hissed softly, like a serpent, sniffing its prey. "Being a mother has made you soft."

She forced another smile but this one was hard. "It hasn't made me soft. It's done the opposite. I'm willing to do *anything* for her. A feeling you wouldn't understand."

His lips and nostrils twitched, like he was holding back a jab. Their relationship had always been tense. They were opposite sides of the same coin.

She turned again, her steps even and measured. The diary burned against her ribs. With her heart in her throat, she walked away from Viktor Axenov.

FORTY-TWO

The music thumped, glasses clinked, and bursts of laughter cut through the crowded bar.

Zoe nursed her drink in a corner, shrouded in darkness. She had driven to a bar just outside of Pineview Falls, where she hoped she wouldn't recognize anyone, and vice versa.

A soft amber glow spilled from the vintage lights lining the walls, illuminating carefree faces.

Faces that laughed and joked and teased and engaged. Faces that lived in the moment. That was how Zoe lived her life. She was chirpy and bubbly. One of her instructors at Quantico had described her as "a meadow on the first day of spring"—full of sheer optimism.

But inside she wasn't rooted in that feeling. She didn't lie to herself. For someone who had lived almost a decade in witness protection during her formative years, she knew exactly who she was. But then why wasn't she filled with joy and peace? She was only ever partially immersed in it.

There was only one emotion that penetrated her entire being and tethered every strand of her. A thread of darkness that sutured her together. A need for violence, a need for blood, a need for *pain*.

She took out her phone and scrolled to find Aiden's phone number. Her thumb hovered over it. Confusion flared inside her. Was she actually thinking about calling him? For what? Business or personal advice? It was awkward enough that he'd caught her at the club and in a moment of weakness, she'd let her guard down. The very man who had tried to surgically extract information out of her during her psych evaluation.

She smacked her lips and put her phone away. There was a reason she'd come to this place. It was the perfect bar to find a douchebag. Someone who could use a lesson. Someone who deserved a dose of pain like she did.

"We now turn to the developing story of the string of murders at Pineview Falls, which now includes a missing thirty-three-year-old Amy Andrews," a woman with a blonde bob announced from the flat-screen TV mounted on the wall. Luckily, Zoe had been sitting close enough to hear. A few other patrons turned their attention to the screen. "She was abducted from a gas station..." The screen flashed to the parking lot but there was a group of teens dancing and posing in the dark. The anchor's voice floated over the disturbing scene. "Videos posted to TikTok show teenagers gathering at the location, using the scene as a backdrop for viral content..."

A group of teens performed a choreographed dance. One girl threw a peace sign and shouted to the camera, "Okay, so this is where that girl disappeared, like right here, and it's sooo creepy but also iconic."

Another boy turned to the camera. "We're calling it GhostTok now. Come and get haunted at Pineview Falls!"

Zoe's blood felt thicker, sludging through her veins. She couldn't bear it anymore. What was the world coming to? She took a sip of her beer when she overheard two men ahead of her at the bar, watching the news and chatting. Pints in their hands and lazy grins on their wrinkled faces.

"You see that one? The blonde in the crop top?" he said, referring to one of the dancing TikTok girls. "Jesus. At a crime scene, no less. Bet that girl's got OnlyFans at fifteen!"

His friend guffawed. "Time to get on that then. Look at her shake her ass. Practically begging for it."

"Hey, I'm not complaining." He grinned and they clinked their glasses.

Bile rose in Zoe's throat as she watched them—two grown men easily in their fifties, sexualizing teenagers and laughing about it. Would she break their fingers one by one or would it feel better to repeatedly bash their heads against the bar? One required patience, a slow trickle of that anger, the second was diving in headfirst, pure liberation. She chewed on the idea as they paid the bill and grabbed their coats.

Her nerves twisted under her skin, a visceral sensation blooming inside her. This would solve it. She was going to go after them. She was going to beat them up, unleash the wrath on those who deserved it, and undo some of her bad karma on this planet. She slid a twenty-dollar bill on the table and hopped off the chair to follow them outside.

Stepping out, the cold air had sharp teeth, biting into her skin. Her breath fogged and the soft wind snaked its way down the collar of her jacket. She was orchestrating when to attack them, her body wired with energy, when her phone trilled.

"Damn it," she muttered, sighing in exasperation. It was Simon.

S: *Lab finished inspecting every inch of the letter sent to you. You might want to take a look.*

All thoughts of starting a fight evaporated and she marched

in the opposite direction from her almost victims, toward her own car, climbing inside. She opened and assessed the attachment.

Microscopic inspection of the envelope flap revealed non-uniform adhesive patterns. The inner glue layer was cracked and absorbed, which was typical of an envelope that had been opened once. The outer glue was viscous. This implied that the envelope was manually resealed after someone had tampered with it.

She frowned. Why would Jackie open the envelope again before mailing it to her?

The report said that the letter and envelope were mismatched. One was a standard white office stock while the other a premium brand. But that could easily be explained—maybe she just used whatever was lying around.

And then came the kicker. Adhesive label analysis under UV light revealed Zoe's FBI address appeared slightly misaligned and showed raised corners, indicating it had been applied after the envelope was sealed. Under UV fluorescence, traces of the original ink from the previous label were partially visible beneath the current one.

Recovered fragments included:

Name: "J. GOL—"

Address Number: "28—9"

ZIP Prefix: "94—04"

Zoe got to work. Frantically, she combed through the public database and cross-searched the address until she came across a match.

Her pulse quickened and her thoughts scrambled. Jeff

Gold. The name didn't ring any bells. A quick search told her it was a prosecutor.

So Jackie never sent Zoe the letter. She'd sent it to Jeff Gold. How did they know each other?

And more importantly, why did Jeff Gold forward the letter to Zoe?

FORTY-THREE

PAST

"Thank you for seeing me again, Mr. Gold." The woman's voice was so small. Blood pounded in her ears. Her clammy hands rested on her lap and she wondered if she was wearing enough perfume to conceal the smell of sweat pooling in her cleavage.

Since when did she become this meek?

"Nice to see you again. You know you can call me Jeff, right?" His smile was warm as he took a seat across from her and put on his glasses. He was older than her by at least ten years and large enough to engulf her frame.

Behind his desk, the windows stretched high, revealing only the reflection of the room against the blackened cityscape. Rain streaked the glass, blurring the outside world. His office was cozy—a room she imagined finding in the pages of a book. Floor-to-ceiling bookshelves lined the walls, stuffed with leather-bound books competing for space. A heavy mahogany desk sat in the center of the room, its surface pristine except for a few neatly stacked papers and a single half-drunk glass of amber liquid.

"How's your kid? Emily, right?" he asked.

"Good. She's doing well. Thank you."

He picked up a pen and twirled it between his fingers. "We've had many conversations where you've pled your case. We've decided to grant you full immunity pending your testimony in court, of course. Have you given it some thought?"

A shudder raked through her. "I don't really have a choice, do I?"

"I know you're concerned about your kid. But the day you decided to work for him, you put yourself and your future in serious danger." Jeff didn't sound judgmental despite his words.Her hand tightened around the strap of her tote bag that she refused to put down. Suddenly, it weighed a hundred pounds. She couldn't imagine parting from it. It was going to stay glued to her side for the rest of her life—it was her only guarantee, her leverage.

"Now, let's talk about witness protection. It's a fresh start for you and your daughter," he explained. "The name I've chosen for you is generic so that you'll be hard to find. You are going to be Rachel Sullivan. Do you like the name?"

She sounded the name. *Rachel.* A common name she'd once used before with a man she'd loved—but not enough. But it felt different on her tongue this time. She had never realized how intimate a name was. That fierce sense of belonging, that link to expectations, history, family, and culture. In stories, names held magic. In this life, her name had become a vulnerability.

"Can I ask you something?" Jeff hesitated. "What made you decide to leave that life?"

"It's not the first time I've been faced with this decision. Over the years, I've had moments where I wanted to leave. I came very close once, but before I could make the jump, I got pregnant." A man's face flashed in her mind—his dark skin, deep eyes, and strong arms. Promises were made; dreams were imagined. "But there was a job a few months ago."

"What was it?"

She looked down at her hands. The words felt heavy in her

mouth. "I was supposed to plant myself in the target's life and make sure he was at a specific place at a particular time."

"That's unusual. I thought you didn't interact with the targets. You were only dispatched to… remove them from the equation."

She didn't deserve his politeness. He could have easily judged her. "He was only fifteen years old."

"Oh." He winced, reeling back in his chair. "What was his name?"

"Michael. His father was a developer who refused to sell a pretty big lot even though we landlocked him. He was adamant. No one ever expected me to go after children, and we never did up until now. I was told this was a kidnapping and that because the boy was an extreme introvert, I needed to lead him to a haunted house, where my colleague would abduct him. A haunted house in a local fair, where it would be dark and loud. Once we got what we wanted from his family, we'd return him home. I was instructed to distract the operator on shift so that the abduction could take place. Instead, my colleague sabotaged the haunted house and started a fire that killed Michael and five other teenagers." A look of horror crossed Jeff's face. Shame ripped through her. "I swear I didn't know they were going to do this. They didn't tell me because they knew I wouldn't have agreed to the job had I known. Apparently, kidnapping the boy wasn't enough; killing him was the message they wanted to send." The truth spilled out of her in desperate sobs. "My daughter isn't safe. Nobody is. And I hate myself that it took me inflicting this much damage to find the courage to leave."

"You were very young when you entered his orbit." His lips thinned. "You were brainwashed. The important thing is that you have agreed to testify. Now, what's your favorite type of weather?" he asked out of nowhere.

"Why do you ask?" She arched an eyebrow.

"You'll see. Just humor me."

She gestured at the window behind him. "That kind." Her voice was swallowed by thunder rolling in deep, bone-rattling waves. A fork of lightning illuminated the room.

He laughed. "That fits just perfectly with your current name—Celina Storm."

FORTY-FOUR

The drive to Jeff Gold's house felt like slipping off the edge of the world.

Zoe gripped the steering wheel, her eyes flicking between the winding dirt road and the thinning signal bars on her phone. The deeper she went into the backwoods, the quieter everything became. No streetlights, no passing cars, just the occasional scatter of wildlife disappearing into the brush.

She had racked her brain for any connection to the retired federal prosecutor. But she came up with zilch. Why had he decided to send Jackie's riddle addressed to him her way? Why had Jackie sent this to him in the first place?

Questions rattled around in her head. She hadn't seen a house for miles.

And then, there it was.

A weathered old cabin, half-swallowed by the surrounding trees, its wooden exterior scarred. The front porch sagged slightly, and the single yellow porch light flickered dimly, like it was struggling to survive.

She killed the engine and stepped out. The scent of pine and wet earth surrounded her.

Her boots crunched against the damp leaves. A flutter rose in her chest. Without thinking, she knocked at the front door.

A long pause.

The sound of locks shifting, bolts sliding open. The door cracked just enough for her to see him.

Jeff Gold.

His face was lined. His hair was silver-streaked, unevenly trimmed, as if he hadn't cared enough to do it properly. There was stubble on his jaw, deep shadows under his eyes. He smelled like old books and whiskey, and he gripped a half-full glass in his hand.

Despite the wear and tear, his eyes were wide and alert. And they stared at her like he'd seen a ghost.

"Hello." Zoe's voice was hoarse. "I'm—"

"Emily."

She suddenly realized why the name had sounded so familiar. The floodgates in her mind opened. Memories of her mother yelling at her, *Emily! Finish your banana!*; a teacher at school, *Well done, Emily*; the kids at school playing with her, *Want to play hide and seek, Emily?* A cacophony of voices hurtling around her head at full speed and making her ears bleed.

She closed her eyes, trying to suppress the long-buried memories. A different name, a different person. The truth was right in front of her, hidden by layers of the years that had gone by. Why didn't she remember? How could she have forgotten?

Her dreams hadn't forgotten.

"How do you know?"

"You look exactly like your mother." His voice was rough. His eyes glanced behind her in paranoia. "Come inside."

The cabin was dark, save for the weak light filtering through the window. The fireplace was cold, the air inside tinged with stale whiskey and old paper. Books were everywhere. Not neatly arranged—piles stacked on the floor, crammed onto shelves, scattered across the table. Some with faded covers, others with handwritten notes stuffed between pages.

She ran her fingers over one, brushing off a thin layer of dust. This was a man who had buried himself alive in books and whiskey, cut off from everything that had once tethered him to the world.

Jeff went through the elaborate process of locking the door. His robe swished behind him as he crossed the room to the window, peered outside, and drew the curtains shut. "Does anyone know you're here?"

"No." She frowned. "How did you know my mother?"

He set down his glass and rubbed his lips, deep in thought. "I was a federal prosecutor. Your mother and you went into witness protection. Connect the dots."

"Who did my mother testify against?" she asked. The answer was in this room. The name of the man who killed Rachel. "What's his name?"

WITSEC was a notoriously secretive program. Even as an FBI agent, Zoe had no access to court records. Since Rachel's death was "natural," her records were permanently sealed.

"You want to get straight to the point," he said dryly. "How did you find me?"

"I asked you first."

"It's my house. My rules." His face hardened. "How did you find me?"

Her heart thudded. "You sent me a riddle that was addressed to you. Even though you tried to hide your involvement."

"Ah, I see. You're sharper than I thought. Did you solve the case?"

"That's not why I'm here." She paused. "We're working on it. Why did you send it to me?"

He sank into the armchair and raked his eyes over her. "You might not like what you find out, child."

"It's always better to know."

Silence stretched between them, thin and taut. Zoe curled her hands into fists in her pockets. Bolts of energy climbed up her legs. But she willed herself to be patient.

"Have you heard of a shadow criminal organization called Red Trigger?"

"Yes. But I don't know much about it."

He nodded. "Your mother worked for them. She was a contract killer."

Hollowness grew behind Zoe's navel and crept its way into the rest of her body. All air left her lungs as she exhaled. "No."

"I know it's difficult for you to hear, considering the honorable path you've taken in your life." He picked up his glass again and turned it in his hand. "Your mother was very young, just a teenager, when she was sold to Red Trigger by a trafficker who had abducted her. She was groomed from a young age to kill. It was all she knew. It wasn't her fault." Dazed, Zoe let his words wash over her like water. "Whenever the organization needed to assassinate someone, they sent your mother. Over the years, she experienced a crisis of conscience many times. But it was the only life she knew, so she was never able to walk away. Even after having you. It wasn't until she indirectly caused the death of a teenage boy at Pineview Falls that she finally had the courage."

"Michael," Zoe whispered.

"Yes. Her task was to lead the boy to a haunted house and then distract the operator. What she thought would be an abduction turned into a massacre. That's when she approached me."

Zoe recalled David mentioning a pretty woman had begun talking to him and he'd stepped away from his station. The whole time it was her mother who had been at the center of the massacre at Pineview Falls.

"We worked together for several months. I even met you

twice but you were too young to remember." A smile formed on his lips. "I heard Rachel committed suicide. After that I kept tabs on you and your sister." He hesitated. "How is she?"

"Who?"

"Gina."

The way he said her name. It carried so much love. Zoe stared at him blankly and then she saw it—a slightly upturned nose and almond-shaped eyes that were too familiar. Her nerves sizzled. "Oh my God... you're her father."

Jeff whipped his head to look the other way. "I had a wife and kids, Emily. I couldn't... well, you understand."

Zoe didn't understand anything. "So you know who I am. Jackie, Michael's sister, sent that riddle to you. Do you remember?"

"Oh, yes." He blinked, frowning. "It was so long ago but... I remember there was a little girl with the family. It must have been her. I had visited the family on multiple occasions, trying to gather more information on Michael and why he had been targeted."

"She must have remembered you. That's why she sent it to you. The only person she knew who had worked on the original case."

"And I forwarded it to you. I'm an old man and Pineview Falls stirred up memories of your mother. I know how great you are at what you do. She would have been proud of you. You have her killer instincts."

Rachel a *killer*? Zoe still couldn't get her head around it no matter how long she held that thought. It percolated inside her like a foreign body. A thought her brain kept rejecting like a failed transplant.

"Who did she testify against?" she asked.

Jeff opened his mouth. "He's—"

The front window shattered, the sharp whine of a bullet slicing through glass before burying itself into the far wall.

Jeff barely had time to move before another shot rang out, this one slamming into the wooden bookshelf behind him, sending a shower of splinters raining down.

Zoe reacted on instinct. Her crowded mind emptied and she became a machine.

She reached for her gun, flipping the small table in front of her as makeshift cover. Jeff cursed, ducking behind the armchair.

A voice, sharp and laced with amusement, drifted in from outside.

"All you had to do was stop asking questions, Agent Storm."

Zoe knew that voice. Viktor Axenov. Rage seared her skin, turning her blood hot. She tightened her grip on the gun.

She peered through the shattered window, her heart pounding.

Viktor stood just beyond the porch, his silhouette sharp against the flashing lightning behind him. He had a pistol in one hand, a smirk on his face, and was absolutely calm.

"Viktor," she called out. "I should've known you were too much of a cockroach to stay buried. I see Darren sent you my message."

Viktor laughed, tilting his head slightly. "He did. I thought I should oblige and pay you a personal visit. Clearly, you didn't get my message in Harborwood." He took a step forward, tapping the barrel of his gun against his thigh. "Now, be a good girl and step outside. I only want to talk."

Zoe shifted slightly, silently signaling to Jeff to stay put. Her heart raced as she quickly tried to figure out how to get to safety. She pulled up her phone and dialed 911, but before she could tap the call button, there was an ear-splitting sound and the front door blasted open.

"Ah!" Jeff shouted.

Zoe fired a bullet but Viktor ducked, laughing, dodging her

shot by inches as he disappeared behind a tree just beyond the porch.

"You aren't as good a shot as your mother!" Viktor called out.

Zoe's pulse was a roaring drumbeat in her ears. He knew her. Of course he did. She wasn't surprised. She moved fast, cutting toward the side of the cabin, her gun steady. She caught sight of Jeff moving behind the kitchen counter, trying to get to his phone.

Zoe's phone was lying a few feet away from her after falling out of her grip. She contemplated reaching for it when another shot blasted through the air.

This time there was another sound that followed. A squelching, sickening, wet sound. Zoe lifted her eyes to Jeff standing in front of the window. Blood poured from a hole in his chest, trickling down his white robe and turning it red.

"No!" she screamed.

Jeff staggered against the counter, eyes wide, his breath coming in short, shallow gasps. He slipped down the wall, landing on the floor with a thud.

Viktor stepped into the house. "Tsk, tsk," he mused. "Are you going to put up a fight, Emily?" Zoe was still crouched behind an armchair, her heart thundering. "Your mother certainly did before I killed her."

Zoe didn't stop to think.

She fired three times. Fast, sharp, her aim clean.

Viktor barely had time to react before one of the bullets slammed into his shoulder, another grazing his ribs. The last one lodged in his stomach. His laugh twisted into a grunt of pain, and he stumbled back.

Zoe didn't hesitate. Her instincts took over. She advanced, gun steady, her heart ice-cold. Viktor choked out a breath as his legs gave out. His jaw hung open as he took raspy breaths, his beady eyes wide in disbelief.

Zoe towered over his withering frame, satisfaction swelling inside her. "Who do you work for?"

Viktor's smirk flickered, just for a moment. Then he tipped his head back and laughed. "You'll find out soon."

Her eyes darkened. "This is for my mother."

Zoe drilled a bullet through his skull. He fell limp at her feet. His blood pooled around her boots. The spell broke. A strangled whimper escaped her throat and her knees knocked together.

Her chest heaved, adrenaline still racing through her as she turned back to Jeff. He was on the floor, blood pooling beneath him, his breathing ragged.

Zoe dropped beside him, pressing both hands over the wound. "Jeff, stay with me," she whispered, panic bleeding into her voice. Where the hell was her phone? Her frantic eyes searched the place, but her eyes were stinging with tears and everything was a mess.

He gave a weak chuckle, coughing. "Never thought I'd go down in this damn house."Zoe shook her head. "No, don't—don't do that, don't talk like that. I'll get help. Please hang on."

He gritted his teeth, his fingers curling weakly against hers. "Listen," he rasped. "Your mother... I loved her. Tell Gina about me. I know I wasn't there because I felt so g-guilty for betraying my family. I owed it to them to stay away b-but she was always on my mind."

Zoe swallowed past the lump in her throat, nodding. "I will. I'm so sorry."

"Don't be." He coughed, blood sputtering out of his mouth. "The man your mother worked for..." And then under the dwindling light of the day, Jeff went still.

All the air squeezed out of Zoe's lungs. She leaned back on her hands, taking in the carnage of the cabin.

Two dead men, and the name of the man behind it all had died with them.

FORTY-FIVE

PAST

Zoe stared at the door to her home. Her mind had been busy, her skin slick with sweat from the heat outside. Before opening the door, she checked her watch. Gina had to be picked up from her playdate in an hour. Would her mother go instead?

Her mother had been acting erratic these past few days. Paranoia had taken over her. She was always making sure the doors were locked and the curtains drawn. She rarely stepped out, mostly sending Zoe to run errands. Zoe would have chalked it up to the transition to a new house, a new city. They were always moving.

But it wasn't. She had found a stack of passports a few months ago in the attic. She knew marshals came every now and then. And she wasn't a kid anymore. She was fourteen years old. She knew exactly what was going on—her mother was hiding from someone.

They all were.

The key entered the lock. A twist and the door clicked open. Goosebumps sprouted all over Zoe's arms. A frigid feeling blossomed behind her chest. There was a draft. The window to the fire escape was open, the curtain billowing in the wind.

Rachel *never* left the window open. Especially not that one that had a staircase outside. Was Rachel out? No, she didn't go anywhere. Her shoes were still here. And then Zoe spotted something else—another tear in the fabric of normalcy. A chair in the living room had been knocked over.

"Mom!" Zoe shouted, her eyes searching the room. Why was it so quiet? She didn't know what to do, but before she could panic an open door caught her eye. The door to the washroom. She pushed it open.

Her knees turned soft and she slipped on the floor. Rachel was in the bathtub, blood leaking from a deep cut in her wrist. Her eyes were open, staring at the ceiling. Her lips slightly parted. Her body, still clothed, submerged in ankle-deep water.

Zoe somehow found the strength to rush forward, to get closer. But then she saw water marks on the bathroom floor. She couldn't think about what that meant just yet because everything inside her was splintering—her soul, her thoughts, the very fiber of her being. She cradled Rachel, forgetting how to breathe and for a moment forgetting how to live.

"No... no... no..." She wiped away her tears, but they kept gushing from her eyes. After what felt like forever, she stood up. Rachel's instructions echoed in her mind. And Zoe was a good daughter. She listened to her mother. It was her last wish. *Promise me you will forget about what happened to me. Promise me you will cover up everything. Tell them I killed myself.* With a cold, brutal efficiency, she grabbed a mop and cleared the water marks on the floor. Then she went to the living room and put the chair back in its position. Finally, she closed the window and locked it.

A last glance across the apartment to check she hadn't missed anything. Someone had been here. Someone had broken in and murdered Rachel, making it look like suicide. Zoe had done the first part and now came the second—to call the police.

But before she did, Zoe went to the bathroom and stared at her reflection.

What would happen now? Would she go into the foster system? Would they separate her and Gina? Oh, Gina... Zoe's head was spinning. A name kept trying to resurface, some faint memory trying to solidify like some part of her was trying to wake up, like her dreams and nightmares were morphing into reality. Zoe didn't understand what was going on. But she knew one thing—if there was one way to survive this horror, this total ruin of her innocence, this terrible knowledge of Rachel's murder, it was by honoring her mother's wishes.

She swore she would do as her mother had instructed: move on, forget. There was only one way to do that. She had to bury the truth, and all the feelings that came with it, deep inside her.

She had to split.

She opened her eyes.

The cabin in the woods was surrounded by glittering cop cars and ambulance lights. The crisp night air nipped at Zoe's skin. The forest around her felt vast, with towering trees standing like silent guards. She sat on a boulder, watching the paramedics carry out a body on a gurney, covered with a sheet. She didn't know if it was Jeff or Viktor.

She dug her elbows into her knees and stared at her hands. Flecks of dried blood were buried under her fingernails.

"Agent Storm?" a burly detective said. "We need to take your statement—"

"Not right now." Simon stormed out of a car, his coat swishing behind him and his eyes blazing. "This is FBI business."

The detective rolled his eyes but Simon pulled him aside and whispered something to him, showing his badge. The detective flattened his mouth and shook his head, walking away.

"What happened?" Simon was on his knees in front of her, his eyes searching hers. When she shivered, he draped a coat over her shoulders.

"Jeff was a federal prosecutor. He sent me that riddle about

Annabelle in Pineview Falls. But I guess Viktor Axenov followed me. He started shooting at us and the next thing I know..." She dropped her head in her hands. "Well, it was a shootout. He killed Jeff. I killed him."

"Viktor from Red Trigger?" He lowered his voice. "Z, why the hell is someone from Red Trigger following you?"

She shrugged. She hadn't thought this through. But now there would be an official investigation and inquiry and then a report. This was going to go on the books. An official record of her shooting Viktor dead.

Her scalp prickled. "Simon... this is a private matter."

"What the hell, Z?" he said, aghast. "You call me and tell me you're in a shootout and it involves a shadow organization and you expect me to just let it go?"

Her head was pounding. There was no time to think. She just wanted to get out of here without the detectives harassing her. An idea came to her. "It's related to that undercover assignment in Lakemore. I think Viktor was involved there and recognized me. He was following me. Developed a sick obsession. I have nothing to do with Red Trigger. Had no idea what it even was."

His eyes narrowed. "So he was just stalking you? A suspected hitman."

Not just a hitman. A hitman dispatched to kill Rachel—who, ironically, was also a hitman. Zoe didn't even know how to begin absorbing that information. "Yes. Hitmen can also develop an obsession with women. They have personal lives too, you know. Twisted fantasies. Bad dates." She rambled on.

He let out a chuckle. "Jesus, Zoe. Trust you to try to make light of a situation like this."

"Well, the thing is that because he's involved in Red Trigger, I'm worried if word gets out that I killed him—"

"They'll come after you," Simon whispered.

She nodded. "That's why I called you. I'm not asking you to cover this up but... I'm just worried."

His face hardened. "I'll take care of it. Are you okay, though? Killing somebody isn't easy. Even when it's someone who probably deserved it."

If only he knew just how easy Zoe had found killing Viktor. Power surged through her veins. A long-awaited satisfaction that made her blood sweeter. It felt surreal. She closed her eyes and relived that moment over and over again. The last bullet that went through his skull.

How his blood had sprayed like red mist behind his head. How his body had fallen to the floor with a thud. How his skull had cracked from the impact. Zoe wished she could forever hook herself into that moment and stay there. Keep breathing in Viktor's last breath.

She'd killed the man that had murdered her mother. The outcome she chased in fights, that pain she sought, her unfinished business, it had all culminated tonight.

Her phone rang. It was Lisa. "Hey."

"Agent Storm, are you coming to the station tonight?"

"Yes." She gestured Simon to give her a moment. "I was running some lead."

"Okay, because remember those shady transactions into Adam's account? I just found out where they're coming from."

FORTY-SEVEN

The biting chill of the evening air cut right through Zoe's sweater. The grand estate before them loomed in the dim glow of the garden lights, its towering columns and polished stone a testament to old money. She adjusted the folder in her grip, her fingers tightening around the crisp bank statements inside.

"Storm." Aiden climbed out of another car. His breath misted in the cold as he walked toward her. "Lisa told me to find you here. Where were you? I waited for you at the station and you didn't answer your phone."

Zoe struggled to find the words. "I... we'll talk about it later, okay?"

His gaze was suspicious. "You look... different. Is everything okay?"

"Yeah." Her teeth chattered in the wind.

"Here." He shrugged off his coat and draped it over her shoulders before she could protest. He frowned at his own action.

His scent enveloped Zoe and she wanted to close her eyes and slip into a dream where the day she just had never happened.

She rang the doorbell. The heavy oak door swung open. David Harrington stood dressed in a tailored charcoal suit, his sharp eyes flickering between the two.

"FBI," David greeted them warily. "To what do I owe this unexpected pleasure at this ungodly hour?"

Zoe stepped forward, leveling him with an even stare. "We need to talk, Mr. Harrington. Inside."

He hesitated for just a second, as a muscle in his jaw ticked. "Of course. Do come in."

The warmth of the house enveloped her after what had been a very long night. Simon had ordered her to resign from the case and suggested a replacement. But this case was personal now.

It was her mother's actions that had inadvertently led to Michael's death and the massacre. Her involvement had spurred a decades-long obsession in Jackie and the other killer, leading to two deaths and a disappearance. This "job" was Rachel's biggest regret. The one that had finally given her the courage to walk away from this life. Zoe's bond with Pineview Falls ran deeper. It was discovering a critical part of herself, uncovering her history. Now she needed to see it through to the end and finish the cycle started by Rachel.

The scent of aged whiskey and expensive cologne hovered in the air. David led them into his study. A lavish space lined with dark mahogany bookshelves and a roaring fireplace where Dawn had admitted not so long ago how, in order to save her company, she had created an immersive game based on a fire that had killed her daughter.

"Drink?" David offered casually, heading to the liquor cart.

Aiden shook his head. "No, thanks. This won't take long."

He smirked, pouring himself a glass of scotch anyway. "Somehow, I doubt that. My mother isn't here, by the way, in case it's her you've come to see."

Zoe dropped the folder onto the polished desk between them. "Let's talk about Adam Deader. Heard of him?"

The name hung in the air like an uninvited guest. David took a cautious sip of his drink before setting it down. "Adam? The reporter?" He tilted his head slightly. "Yes, I've seen him on television a lot lately. What about him?"

Zoe flipped open the folder, revealing a series of neatly printed bank statements. She slid them across the desk. "You've been making substantial payments to him over the last few weeks. Care to explain why?"

He barely glanced at the papers. "He did some work for me," he said smoothly. "Research. Writing. I pay for good information."

Aiden leaned forward. "Research on what exactly? Because from what we can tell, he wasn't writing anything official for you. Yet these payments suggest he was well compensated for something."

David's features tightened and he blinked rapidly. "I don't appreciate the insinuation, Dr. Wesley. Whatever Adam did for me is my private business. I'm under no obligation to discuss it with you."

"We're investigating two murders and a disappearance, Mr. Harrington," Zoe said. "I suggest you cooperate."

"You're wasting your time," he said finally, swirling the amber liquid in his glass. "Whatever business I have with Adam has nothing to do with the murders."

Zoe and Aiden exchanged a glance.

Aiden's voice dripped with threat, which made the hair on Zoe's arms stand on end. "Why don't we ask your mother? I'm sure Dawn would be able to shed some light on what business you have with Adam. I wouldn't be surprised if you're siphoning money from the company to pay him off."

David's nostrils flared. The fire crackled behind them, the

only sound in the thick silence. "This doesn't leave the room…" He glared at them. "Can you promise that?"

Zoe sat down and crossed her legs. "You don't get to negotiate here, David."

He sighed and slammed the glass down on the table. The remaining liquid splashed onto the marble top. "Our company has been reporting losses. Things have not been looking good for a while now. Way before this product was stolen."

"A product that you encouraged Jackie and Annabelle to steal," Zoe said.

Surprise registered in his eyes. "Yes. Mother hates me for the part I played in the incident. She'll never be able to forgive me. Which is why she relishes every opportunity to put me down, to not let me grow, to remind me how small I am." His teeth gritted. "I've fought with her several times to get me on the board, to give me some decision-making power but she's adamant. She claims she cares about nothing more than the company and still she won't give me a chance to save it. It's her way of having her revenge." His mirthless smile didn't reach his glassy eyes. "Over a month ago, a competitor approached me. They wanted to buy Harrington Group. We struck a deal. If I ensured that the stock price fell below a certain figure, low enough so that when the company is up for sale this competitor can swoop in and buy it at a very low price, they will make *me* the CEO."

"You're intentionally sabotaging your family company," Aiden stated. "That's why you planted the idea of the theft."

"It's not a family company." David scowled. "It's a one-woman show. If she cared, she would have given me a chance. Besides, doesn't it disgust you? A mother creating a game from something that killed her daughter and five other kids. I was negligent because I got distracted by some pretty woman, but Mother is just being a *bitch*." He spat out the last word with undisguised contempt.

Tears collected in the base of Zoe's throat. *Pretty woman.* She stared at David—a man who had also known her mother, albeit a different side to her. How was she when she wasn't just being Mom? When she was on the job? Did she walk differently? Did her voice change? Would she dress bolder? She couldn't ask him. She couldn't let anyone know about Rachel's involvement.

She had to protect her mother's dignity.

"So where does Adam fit in?" Aiden said.

"I've been paying Adam to create negative publicity about the company. Initially the plan was to run the story of the theft. But when Annabelle was found dead... everything changed. The stakes were higher. Adam sensed an opportunity. He began to strongly link the deaths and disappearances to the company."

"It was his idea?" Zoe raised an eyebrow.

"Of course it was," David snorted. "Have you not met the guy? He gets off on this. The story of a product theft is too dry for the likes of him. At the end of the day, I didn't care what the end result was. Whatever made the company look bad."

"That's convenient for you, isn't it?" Aiden pointed out. "Two employees of the company killed when you want the stock price to crash."

David's eyes widened. "I didn't have anything to do with this! That's preposterous."

An idea came to Zoe. She showed him a picture of the code found on Jackie that Adam's dog had consumed. "Does this mean anything to you?"

David took a long look at it. "No idea. What is it?"

Zoe didn't answer. But it didn't escape her how much of a coincidence it was that these women going missing and turning up dead was working out so perfectly for David.

"Isn't this convenient for him?" Zoe whispered as they were being ushered out of the house. "I'll get Lisa to check his alibi."

"The two people who could have testified against him are dead," Aiden agreed.

"Does he fit the profile?"

"From what I've seen of how much his mother belittles and controls him, yes. Maternal dominance leading to compensatory violence."

Zoe could imagine how this all worked out for David—a motive combined with a method that was justified in his broken mind. He had lost a sister to a fire that started because he hadn't paid attention. And then a heaviness settled inside her.

She glanced at David over her shoulder. He knew her mother, he knew Rachel *before* she was Rachel.

Her phone rang. It was Ethan. "Hey, how's it going?"

"Agent Storm, Lisa's busy working with the rangers looking for Amy, so I can't reach her, but remember the break-in at Annabelle Stevens's?"

A flicker. "Oh, yes, jeez, so much has happened since then I just assumed nothing came of it."

"We got a hit on CODIS. Ed Morgan."

"Ed Morgan?" Her eyes flashed to Aiden. "The detective who investigated the massacre."

FORTY-EIGHT

Zoe could taste salt in the back of her throat as she stepped out of the car.

The beach stretched long and narrow, hemmed in by jagged driftwood and dark, windswept pines that loomed just beyond the sand. Water slapped against the shore, churning up foam and seaweed. There was no sun, just flat, filtered daylight.

"Ugh, I don't even know what time it is." She scrunched up her nose at the sky, stepping out. "What's wrong with this state? Why is it always so dark?"

Aiden was next to her, his eyes closed and head tipped up, like he was savoring the wind through his hair and flicking over his skin. Zoe rarely saw him like this—relaxed, in the moment, and not busy dissecting anyone.

A smile spilled over the corners of his lips. "Quit staring, Storm."

"Shut up." She frowned. "So Ed is here?"

"Ethan said that Ed comes for a jog here."

"How did he find out?"

"Friend of a friend of a deputy knows Ed. Perks of a small town."

The wind came in restless bursts, cold and damp, whipping Zoe's hair into her face and sending her body slightly wayward from the force. Sand pricked her eyes. She was rubbing it off when Aiden's warm hand came to her face, gently brushing her hair away. She froze, her skin buzzing, and everything inside her became hot. When she opened her eyes, he was so focused on untangling her hair that she wondered what he had been like with his late wife, how he'd mourned her, how she'd died.

Just as quickly, he withdrew his hand and cleared his throat, looking around. "Luckily, the beach is practically empty. Oh! There he is!"

In the distance, Zoe saw Ed jogging toward them—in perfect shape, sweat coating his skin.

"Well, Ethan sent us his background check." Aiden said, reading from his phone. "Former Army. Served in a recon unit out of Fort Lewis. Marksman certification, high placement in advanced rifle courses. He was one of those guys who could hit a moving target at six hundred yards without blinking."

"Sounds like someone who would do just as well with darts. Could he be *Spector*? Any criminal history?"

"Got a dishonorable discharge in 2009. Something about disobeying orders. Two years later, he shoots a man outside a bar in Spokane. Claimed self-defense. Jury didn't buy it, but they gave him a light sentence—two years. Probably because of the PTSD angle."

"He was involved in the original massacre investigation." Zoe connected the dots, her eyes glued to Ed, who was doing laps in the distance. "That's how he and Jackie must have known each other. She was obsessed with it, probably reached out to him. And then when she and Annabelle planned the theft, Annabelle didn't know that her partner in crime was an obsessed psychopath who planned to hunt her down."

"His history is textbook: early conditioning in precision, control, high-stakes decision-making. All funneled into a military identity that collapsed when he was discharged under dishonorable terms." Aiden studied him. "Given his PTSD, Jackie's actions triggered him. And so he could have hunted her down."

"And enjoyed it so much that he took Amy, whom he would have known about through Jackie."

As they got closer, Ed noticed them and he slowed down. But something about their faces must have revealed their intention. Suddenly, he broke into a run and Zoe shot off after him.

The wind came at her sideways, slapping strands of wet hair across her cheek. Her soles slapped hard against the firm, damp sand, just inches from where the surf licked the shore.

Ahead of her, Ed stumbled. His knees buckled slightly—he was fit but older and already worn out from his jog.

"FBI! Ed! Stop!" she shouted through ragged breaths.

Ed didn't respond or slow down. Gulls screamed overhead.

Frustrated, Zoe ditched her boots, which were sinking in the dunes. She pushed herself harder, her thighs burning, her breath tearing at her lungs. From the corner of her eye she saw Aiden was trying to cut him off by heading in the other direction. But Aiden wasn't designed for fieldwork and he wasn't nearly as fast as she was.

Ed veered toward the rocks ahead. A jagged heap of barnacle-crusted stone that jutted from the beach like the ribs of a shipwreck.

"Shit," Zoe muttered.

He tried to climb. What an idiot, Zoe thought. His foot slipped, arms windmilled, and he dropped onto all fours. Zoe reached him just as he was trying to scramble up again.

She lunged at him.

He turned too late. Her shoulder slammed into his ribs and they went down hard onto the pebbles and wet sand.

Ed wheezed. Zoe rolled off him, panting, and then straddled his chest before he could move.

He flinched. "Please!"

"Why did you run, Ed? If you did nothing wrong?"

His mouth moved soundlessly. There was blood on his lower lip. Zoe grabbed his jacket collar and hauled him up enough to look directly into his face.

Aiden caught up, panting. "Jesus, how fast are you, Storm?"

"I'm actually not the fastest runner," she mumbled. "Ed, why did you run?"

His frantic eyes bounced between them. "Because I broke into Annabelle's house. When I was leaving, I cut myself on the window ledge. You got my DNA, didn't you?"

"You're smart," Aiden remarked. "Now tell us what the hell you were doing there."

"The massacre has haunted me," he admitted, a blush creeping up his face. "I saw in the news that woman was found dead but then you guys showed up and started asking questions about the massacre and the arson... I realized that it must be connected somehow. I always knew there was a cover-up. It wasn't an accident."

"You thought that someone wanted justice for what happened?" Aiden asked.

He shrugged, sweat plopping down his face. "Yeah, that's what I figured the connection was. Justice denied back then and some vigilante shit happening today. That's why I broke into that lady's house. I wanted to know if she had a connection to any of the victims or someone from the investigative team. On my way out, I was careless."

Zoe had been wondering the same thing—a connection forged from injustice years ago, how teenagers had died in a fire that stemmed from arson, not mechanical failure. She thought Jackie was pissed and was seeking revenge, which is why she'd sent Michael's hair to her. And whoever had killed Jackie had another motive—something to do with Harrington Group, the ones responsible for the conspiracy for hiding the truth about that night.

Ed wasn't entirely wrong.

"Why didn't you just come to us?" Zoe said. "It's a small town. We can always use volunteers."

He blew a frustrated breath. "Yeah, I know what kind of work volunteers do. Combing the woods, looking into anonymous tips. I wanted to help in a significant way. You don't understand, Agent Storm. That massacre is the identity of this town. Pineview Falls lives and breathes that tragedy. It would be an honor to contribute to that legacy."

Zoe rolled her eyes. Clearly Adam wasn't the only one willing to exploit pain—he did it for his career and Ed did it for his ego.

"Did you find anything?" Aiden cocked an eyebrow. "Annabelle's husband reported that the room was a mess."

He bit his lip, hesitating. "I might have..."

Zoe's spine straightened. "What?"

Ed pulled out a folded picture from the pocket of his shorts. Reluctantly, he handed it to them. "This was tucked in the back of the nightstand drawer. As if Annabelle didn't want anyone to find it."

Zoe unfolded it. Her fingers grazed the aged, weathered picture. Annabelle and a man standing in front of a waterfall. Their arms around each other, beaming at the camera. The ease, the intimacy, and the unsettling fact that this man was not her husband.

"Who is he?" she asked.

"I don't know. I've been trying to figure that out, but I don't have access to any databases or fancy technology."

"Storm, what do you want to do?" Aiden side-eyed Ed.

Zoe got in Ed's face. He wilted and for a second she felt bad for the man. "Thank you."

He blinked. "What?"

"This was very helpful. We appreciate it." She shook his hand. "But we have your DNA on file and you are under surveillance. You can go now, sir."

He swallowed hard and gave a jerky nod before jogging away.

"That was... kind of you." Aiden frowned. "So who is the guy in the picture?"

She pulled out her phone and began browsing. Something about this man rang a bell. A faint glimmer of recognition. She had spent a long time digging through Annabelle's social media —Jackie didn't have one and Amy's was essentially just LinkedIn. As she began scrolling, she found an old post, dated fifteen years ago of them holding hands.

Ian Monroe.

"Ex-boyfriend," Aiden declared. "She was hanging on to the picture of them. Hiding it in the drawer. That's telling."

"Something tells me this was the reason Annabelle and her husband were fighting."

FORTY-NINE

PAST

The wind tapped at the windowpane again.

Tap. Tap. Not like a knock, more like a solid whisper.

Rachel sat on the edge of the bed in her old gray sweater. The one that hung off one shoulder. "Ready?"

Zoe nodded, curling her knees up her chest, her toes chilly in her socks.

Rachel turned a page, though she never looked down at the words. "Once upon a time," she began, her voice low and dry, "there was a garden that grew in the middle of nowhere."

Zoe swallowed. "Was it a happy garden?"

Rachel's lips twitched, but she didn't smile. "It used to be. There were flowers and fruit and little bluebirds that sang until the sky turned pink at night. But one day, a viper slithered into the garden. Not loud. Not fast. Just... there."

Zoe pulled the blanket tighter.

"The viper was beautiful," Rachel said, her voice almost haunting. "Emerald scales. Eyes like gold. It didn't bite anyone, not at first. It just watched."

Zoe's throat ran dry. She decided then and there that she didn't like snakes. "Did they chase it away?"

"No, because they thought it was lonely. They thought maybe it needed love. But vipers don't want love. Vipers want silence. Vipers want obedience. Vipers want you to stop breathing."

Zoe's heart knocked against her ribs as she registered the almost wistful look on Rachel's face.

She looked at her then. Her eyes were dark, tired. So tired they looked like they were full of rain. "Zoe, do you know what vipers do to the people who get close to them?"

She shook her head slowly. Even though she didn't like being called Zoe. Her name was Emily. But Rachel had said she had a new name now. A better name.

"They wrap around them," Rachel said, sliding her hand over her own wrist, "and squeeze until the person can't tell if they're being held... or strangled." She turned the page, and Zoe noticed there was actually no writing. "There was a girl in the garden. She was quiet. Smart. Thought if she just stayed still, the viper wouldn't notice her. But vipers always notice."

Zoe looked down at her fingers, curled tight in the blanket. "Did the girl die?"

Rachel didn't reply. Not right away. "No... but she came close. And when she got away, no one believed there had ever been a viper. They said the garden was beautiful. That she must've dreamed the rest."

"That's mean," Zoe whispered.

"That's the world, baby," Rachel said, her lips a thin line. "It doesn't matter how loud you scream if no one wants to hear."

Outside, the wind pushed harder against the window. Somewhere down the hall, a floorboard creaked, slow and deliberate. Rachel strained to hear but Gina was still sleeping in her nursery down the hall.

"Sometimes," Rachel said, her voice colder. "A viper follows you home. It hides in the walls. It waits. But it still hisses in the dark."

Zoe didn't want to ask, but she had to. "Mom... is the viper real?"

Rachel turned to her, and her hand found Zoe's cheek. She brushed a lock of hair behind her ear. "Listen to me now, and don't ever forget what I tell you. If anything ever happens to me—anything at all—you tell them it was an accident. That I slipped. That I drowned. That I didn't mean it."

This again. Zoe blinked fast. "Why?"

"Because they won't believe you if you tell the truth. And worse, they'll make sure the viper hears it and the viper might come after you too... Do you promise, Zoe?"

It was the same routine every night. Every night after telling her a story, Rachel would make her promise the same thing. Zoe didn't like it. The first time she heard it, she'd burst into tears. But now the words were so engrained in her, the promise was a part of her blood.

"I promise."

FIFTY

The water scalded Zoe's skin, but she barely felt it. Not over the hum in her blood. That caffeine-buzzed, post-chaos electricity, still trapped in her limbs like a warning shot never fired. Her fingers twitched against the tiles, aching to do something, fix something, finish something.

It was the residual adrenaline still pounding from yesterday. Her phone had several messages from Simon wanting to talk about the shooting. He was delaying the inquiry until Amy had been found and she'd wrapped up this case.

An inquiry. Was she going to lie under oath about how she knew Viktor? Zoe hated lying. There was one lie she told the world and her sister—about Rachel. There was another lie about her dark thoughts and where she went to expel them. The lies kept piling up, making her queasy.

When she stepped out of the shower, she checked her phone. Gina had sent her a picture of her with the boys at the zoo.

Zoe gasped as she remembered Jeff's last words. How the hell was she going to tell Gina anything about this? She knew nothing about this, had no idea who her father was. But how could she deny a dying man his last request?

She cleaned the fogged mirror and stared at her reflection. Viktor was dead—the man whose hands had taken her mother's life. Surely now the hatred she carried around with her would finally disappear. The *Emily* that haunted her. But it wasn't over.

Viktor was just the muscle. He worked for someone; he had been sent by that person. The man who'd ordered the hit. Had Viktor given him the key to the safety deposit box? She had to find out more about Viktor. It was the only way this would end.

It was a sulky morning, the light barely leaking through the clouds, when Zoe walked into the station.

"Have we heard anything from the nearby police stations?" Zoe asked. "Any sightings? Any tips?"

Lisa chewed on the end of a pen and shook her head. "*Nada*. Ethan is leading a search party in the woods near the gas station where Amy was taken from. But—" Thunder clapped and instantly the heavens opened.

Zoe felt a flicker of annoyance. "How do you guys get anything done around here with this weather?"

Lisa shrugged. "It's all I've ever known." She gestured at the sheets of paper cluttering her desk. "I'm just going through Amy's cell phone records right now. Her last call was to work to let them know that she was running late."

Zoe dropped her shoulders. Her nerves were vibrating, an electric, jittery buzz crawling under her skin. Like the world was refusing to match the speed of her mind and will. She tapped a pen incessantly against her thigh.

"I just called the SEC." Aiden marched up to her.

"Huh?"

"About David's fraud to manipulate the stock price." He

paused. "What's going on with you? You hightailed it home yesterday."

If there was anything she knew about Aiden, it was that he was very good at breathing down her neck. "The federal prosecutor who sent me the letter died in a shootout. Because Viktor followed me."

His jaw hung open. "What the fu—?"

She grabbed him by the elbow and pulled him into a corner out of earshot. "I told you that Viktor was stalking me, right? I guess Darren gave him my message, so he decided to come after me himself."

"And where is Viktor now?" Zoe looked down at her feet, and Aiden understood. "Shit. Sorry, Storm."

"What do you mean?"

"The truth died with him, didn't it? You would have preferred him alive, so that you could interrogate him."

His words slammed into her with a force. She did need Viktor alive. And he could have been. But she had pulled the trigger anyway. It hadn't been instinct. It hadn't been necessity. It had been rage. Pure, blinding, volcanic rage. The kind that takes the wheel before you even realize you've let go. She could've aimed anywhere else. Could've dropped him without ending him. But she didn't.

She chose his head.

"What did that prosecutor say?" Aiden asked suddenly. "Why did he forward that riddle to *you*?"

"I... don't know." The lie filled her mouth with a sour taste. "I literally got there and the shooting started."

Aiden opened his mouth when there was an interruption.

"Is there anyone I can talk to?" a ragged, frustrated voice came out of nowhere. "I'm looking for someone," the man said, his voice tight. "Annabelle. I was told she's missing."

Zoe raised a hand. "Over here."

She didn't recognize the young man with curly, wet hair, his duffel still slung over one shoulder, a rumpled travel jacket hanging open. He looked like he hadn't slept in two days. His boots splish-splashed on the linoleum floor, leaving a trail of puddles that made Ethan pout.

Zoe stepped forward. "I'm Agent Zoe Storm and this is Dr. Aiden Wesley. We're from the FBI."

"I'm Ian Monroe. I'm Annabelle's..." He raised his eyebrows. "Friend."

"Why don't you sit down?" Zoe guided him to a chair. The man was lanky, all long limbs, someone who'd never quite grown out of his teenage slouch. "You just arrived in town?"

"Yeah." He dropped his duffel bag with a thud. "I took the first flight out from Houston after you guys called me and drove here from Seattle." His eyes welled with tears. "What happened?"

"I'm sorry, Mr. Monroe. But Annabelle was killed," Aiden said. "We're investigating her death."

"*What?*" He whimpered and covered his face with his hands. Zoe noticed that he didn't wear a wedding band. But Annabelle did. "What the hell happened? Was it her husband?" His eyes flashed with fury.

"Trevor? Why would you think that?" she said.

"They were fighting a lot."

"Did she tell you what they were fighting about?" Aiden asked.

"It was mostly work. Oh my God... Can I get some water?" He looked like he was in pain. Aiden slid a water in his direction. They watched him gulp it down. Zoe threw a glance at Aiden and he gave her a grim nod as if confirming that Ian's grief looked genuine.

"Thanks." He wiped his mouth. "Trevor was upset that she was working long hours, always on call, sometimes weekends too, when they had a young family. But the company was heading in a new direction. Announcing a video game. She kept telling him it was temporary but he shamed her for working."

The profile Aiden had put together was potentially of a man who felt threatened or small by successful women. Many thoughts flooded her at once—what if Trevor knew about Jackie through Annabelle? What if Trevor felt less like a man having to take care of the family while Annabelle was the breadwinner?

"I think it was disgusting," he added.

"So were you and Annabelle... having an affair?" Zoe asked.

"No, no." His cheeks flushed. "I'm her ex-boyfriend but we were just friends. We grew up together."

"Why did you break up?"

"I wanted to leave Pineview Falls." His face was somber. "The fire incident was suffocating. I don't know why she wanted to stay, so we eventually called it quits. But we stayed in touch here and there over the years."

"And when was the last time you saw her or spoke with her?" Zoe asked.

"Just two weeks ago." He sighed and ran a hand through his thick locks of hair. "We started talking a lot in the last couple of months actually. She was just going through this rough patch in her marriage and postpartum and this and that, so I was being there for her."

Aiden frowned. "You talked on the phone or email?"

"Facebook." No wonder Zoe hadn't found any correspondence between them. Social media records were notoriously difficult to obtain. After being stressed at home and work, perhaps Annabelle was seeking comfort in an old friend, maybe even old feelings were resurfacing. "Do you have any idea who could have done this?"

"We don't know, Mr. Monroe," Aiden said. "I was hoping you might have some useful information. Can you think of anyone who would want to hurt her?"

"No!" He sounded incredulous. "Everyone loved her at work. That's where we met.'

"You worked at Harrington Group?" Zoe leaned forward.

"Yeah, I used to. We worked in the same department. We built code to run logistics, warehouse tagging systems, optimization software for global warehouse systems, that kind of stuff. She switched out of geo-routing two years ago, I think, right around the time I changed jobs. But she's a trooper, eh? She stuck with that company and rose up the ranks."

"Code?" An idea sparked in her. She showed him a picture of the code INV-W7-D4-1553. "We found this at one of the crime scenes related to Annabelle's murder. Does this mean anything to you?"

He glanced at it, blinking hard. "It's been a while but it looks like internal warehouse codes. Except they don't actually exist. We used fake codes in testing so we wouldn't interfere with real shipments. Dummy values. The format matches, though."

Why would Jackie have this on her? "Can you decode it?" she asked desperately.

"Sure..." He frowned. "Normally, our codes would only go up to, say, W5 or D3. But here, it's W7 and D4? It doesn't match any actual warehouse. I think she repurposed our testing system to encode coordinates. We set a base value of 40 for latitude and 118 for longitude. Just to keep our test data separate from real-world numbers. So W7 means add 7 to 40, which gives you 47 degrees north. And D4 means add 4 to 118, landing you at 122 degrees west." He looked up suddenly. "When you combine that with the trailing numbers—1553—it refines the location to a very specific point."

Aiden was already looking up the coordinates. His eyes locked on Zoe. "It's an old storage facility."

FIFTY-ONE

The rain hadn't let up once since they'd crossed the state line. It came in sideways now, blown by a bitter wind, turning the car windows into a blur of cold water and streaked light. Zoe sat behind the wheel, her body strung tight as she drove slowly through the slick roads.

The world outside was like a dream. Headlights glowed like fireflies and storefronts were washed-out shapes. The colors were fluid, like a brush dragging through wet ink.

"When is your inquiry?" Aiden asked.

"Right." She averted her eyes. "I told Simon to hold off until we wrap up this case."

From the corner of her eye, she saw his fist clench. "It's too bad that you'll never know why that prosecutor sent that letter to you. The shooting started immediately, yeah?"

She swallowed hard. "Within a minute of me announcing who I was."

His eyes lingered on her. She felt it burn through her skin, through her lies. Did he know? She hid so much that she had no capacity for more secrets. "And Viktor just showed up and started shooting? I don't understand. He hired Darren to keep tabs on you to make sure you didn't go digging into your mother's death. You tell Darren to piss off. But why would Viktor show up out of nowhere and try to kill you?"

Blood crept up her neck and suddenly, it was stifling hot in the car. She couldn't tell Aiden—not about Rachel's involvement with Red Trigger. A hitman. Zoe herself had refused to let that information truly sink in. She held it at a distance, observing it through a thick sheet of glass, contemplating if this was something she could ever accept.

"Maybe my threat pissed him off. Maybe he realized that I wasn't going to stop."

"Maybe." He didn't sound convinced.

Her phone chirped and she quickly glanced at it. "Can you check this? I think it's from the cyber division. They were looking into Spector."

Aiden scrolled through the email. "They traced it to half a square mile in Pineview Falls but couldn't get the IP address."

"Seriously? Why not?"

"VPN's masking it. They'll need warrants to dig into the ISP and get any account info."

They reached the address and Zoe parked the car, sitting motionless as she stared at the building through the windshield like it might shift into something else if she just looked long enough.

Aiden exhaled in the passenger seat, fogging up the glass. "This is the place?"

She nodded, barely. "It matches the coordinates."

He leaned forward, squinting into the gray. "Looks like a building time forgot."

Ahead of them, the storage facility was half-swallowed by overgrown brush and chain-link fencing. Faded Harrington Group logos clung to concrete walls like bruises, cracked and worn by weather and time. The windows were either broken or boarded up. Nature had started reclaiming the structure. It didn't look like anyone had been here in years.

Zoe popped the door open and stepped out, the cold rain soaking her jeans in seconds. Aiden scrambled after her, holding a hand over his head.

"You're not even going to pretend that this doesn't feel like the beginning of a horror movie?" she said.

They kept walking. The wind stole his reply.

The gate was still partially standing, though the lock had long since rusted off. It swung open with a sound like metal coughing. They stepped through into the main yard, boots crunching on gravel and broken glass. The building loomed closer—its flat roof sagging slightly in the middle, ivy clinging to its seams.

Zoe stopped in front of the main door, a heavy metal slab with no sign, no warning. Just rust and silence. She looked at it, then at Aiden.

"You think this is still powered?" she asked.

"No."

She grabbed the handle and yanked. The door groaned open a few inches before sticking. Aiden stood beside her, and together they forced it open wide enough to slip through.

The air inside was still and stale, laced with the scent of wet concrete and rot. It was darker than it should have been, the only light filtering through broken skylights and thin gaps in the boards. Their footsteps and breaths echoed immediately.

"No one has been using this, that's for sure." Zoe wiped her grimy hands on her jeans. "David didn't recognize the code."

"I'm not entirely surprised. He's a high-level executive. I doubt he knows the product labels his warehouses are using."

She cupped her hands around her mouth and let out a "Helloooo!" Her voice bounced around before coming back to them. When Aiden raised an eyebrow at her, she shrugged. "I just wanted to get an idea of the acoustics."

Rows of storage units stretched out in both directions, numbered in faded white paint across dented metal doors. Some were open, filled with scattered junk. Others remained locked, untouched.

"Wow," Zoe muttered. "I don't know what I thought we'd find, but this isn't giving me warm and fuzzy vibes."

She pulled out her flashlight and started walking. "This place has been shut down for years. Why would Annabelle make a code of this?"

"And Jackie kept it. So it meant something." His eyes lit up. "What if this is where they planned to hide the game?"

"Possibly. The prototype is a VR headset. Maybe Jackie and Annabelle didn't want to hide it in their homes in case Dawn involved the authorities and there was an investigation."

"This place is huge." Aiden looked around and kicked a broken pipe out of his path, the clatter breaking the stillness like a gunshot. "But an ideal place to hide something."

The code was still folded in her jacket pocket, the paper damp but intact. INV-W7-D4-1553. The numbers had brought them this far—latitude, longitude—but the longer she looked at it, the more it didn't feel like just coordinates. That last sequence—1553—it kept repeating in her head like a metronome.

Maybe it meant more.

The numbers on the doors ticked upward slowly as they moved: 1507, 1508, 1509. "Aiden... do you think this 1553 could correspond to one of these units?"

She stopped in front of a rusted map pinned to the wall, barely legible. She wiped a gloved hand across it, revealing a crude layout. "Storage units 1500 to 1600. Back corridor," she read.

Aiden squinted. "Let me guess. We're going to 1553?"

She gave him a look, still not used to him trying to crack a joke or two.

The back corridor was narrower and darker, and the doors here were spaced closer together. As they walked, she watched each number rise—1544, 1545, 1546. Some of the units were open and empty. Others had doors sagging on hinges. But most were untouched.

And then she saw it.

1553.

The number was crisp. White paint, unchipped. The door itself was too clean and glossy, not collecting dust like the others. While the others were dulled by time, this one gleamed faintly in the flashlight's beam. It stood out.

It had a different lock, too: a matte black padlock, newer than anything else around it.

Zoe stared at it, her breath catching somewhere in her chest. "Why would anyone install a new lock in a unit here?"

"Fair enough," Aiden conceded. "What could the code be?"

Zoe stepped forward and ran her fingers over the number. The metal was cold beneath her gloves. She tried a bunch of numbers—Annabelle's birthday, 1553, the date of the massacre, but nothing worked.

"I really thought the massacre date would do it."

She smiled at him dryly and lifted the hem of her jeans. He blinked when she pulled out a crowbar.

"Seriously?"

"I'm always prepared."

"Yeah, but how did you even fit that thing in there?"

Zoe didn't answer. She was already working the lock. He sighed and stepped in to help, gripping the edge and pulling hard with her.

The lock groaned, resistant. It didn't want to break. Zoe braced her knee against the door. "One more pull," she said.

He nodded. "One, two..."

The lock broke free, the sound echoing down the hall like a starter's pistol. They both froze for a moment.

Then she reached out and gripped the door handle. For a second, she didn't move. And then—slowly, deliberately—she pulled the door open.

At first, she caught a whiff of sweat. It was the kind of air that was stale and empty, air that had been sitting too long trapped in a damp place. The room was shrouded in darkness for a few seconds before Zoe's fumbling hands found the switch.

Light flooded the room and Zoe felt her stomach drop.

In the center of the room, a woman sat slumped in a metal chair, limbs slack like a marionette with its strings cut, her clothes damp and dirty. Straps looped around her wrists and ankles, biting into pale skin. Her head tilted slightly to the side, chin to chest, hair matted and clinging to her face in damp strands. Her shoulders rising and falling.

She was alive, just.

She wore a headset—sleek, black, wired to something humming softly in the shadows behind her. The soft blue glow from the headset pulsed faintly.

"Amy!" Zoe took a step forward when Aiden's hand coiled around hers. "What?"

He put a finger to his lips, his eyes flickering to something on the floor. A shoeprint. Wet and brown. It was fresh.

And then there was a clang.

FIFTY-TWO

Zoe was already running.

Her boots pounded against the concrete and her breath tore at her lungs. The abandoned building groaned from rusted beams to hanging chains. And then she saw him—a hooded figure, turning around the corner.

Adrenaline pumped in her veins as she picked up speed. "FBI! Stop!"

The man hurried away. Corridors of forgotten junk towered around her. Filing cabinets, broken furniture, half-crushed boxes with numbers faded by time. It was dizzying—she couldn't work out where she was anymore, as she followed the faint echo of footsteps scattering away like mice.

A flash of movement ahead.

She pushed harder, dodging a tangle of hanging cables, ducking under a half-collapsed shelf. Her hand grazed something sharp but she didn't care.

A heavy thud. He'd slammed into something. A rusted metal cabinet, shoulder-first. She heard a sharp grunt, low and pained, but he didn't stop. The sound of his footsteps staggered for half a second but then he was sprinting again, clutching his shoulder.

Then—a sound.

The slam of a door. A bang. Silence. She skidded to a stop in a wide loading bay, straining her ears and eyes. There was only one exit—a side door swinging slowly shut.

Zoe stood there, her chest heaving, scanning every shadow, listening for the slightest hint of breath or movement. The facility backed onto a main street with a maze of alleys.

Nothing. Just the creak of metal. A drip of water. She glanced at her hand. A cut ran through the middle of her palm, scarlet red blood dribbling from it like dew drops. The burning sensation finally hit her. But nothing stung more than the fact that he was gone. He had gotten away.

"Are you up to date with your tetanus shot?" the nurse asked, wrapping Zoe's hand in a bandage.

"Yes." She had had to be after her regular injuries at the fight club.

While the nurse made quick work of securing her hand, she swung her legs back and forth as she looked around the cold, sterile hospital bathed in a pale, white light. Surrounded by tired eyes, half-read pamphlets, and machines that beeped in different rhythms, Zoe loved hospitals. The smell of bleach and latex mingled into something so distinct and comforting. She saw it as a place of hope.

"All done!" the nurse announced. "The woman you brought in is in room 302 on this floor. She should be good to talk now. She was dehydrated and exhausted but we gave her some fluids and broad-spectrum antibiotics. She's awake."

Zoe nodded. "Thanks." She hopped off the bed and found the room where a guard from the sheriff's office and Aiden sat. "Where's Lisa?"

"She's securing the crime scene and the game." Aiden stood up and fixed his tie and glasses. "Dawn got wind that the product has been found and wants it back but it's evidence."

"At least we found her." She finally said the words out loud. She stopped outside the door before going in.

"What is it?" Aiden asked behind her.

"I don't know..." The words died in her throat. Her surroundings rippled like she was part of a watercolor painting. She waited for the enormity of the events to hit her. She knew she felt relief that they'd found Amy; she knew that she felt vindicated after killing Viktor. But her body wasn't registering the intensity.

Was she even here?

A solid hand touched her shoulder, tethering her back to reality. "Zoe?"

He rarely called her by her first name. She blinked widely and then shook off his hand before opening the door.

Amy was draped on the hospital bed. Her hair fanned wildly around her face. Her body skinny as a whippet, having lost mass since Zoe last saw her. Her face had shallow bruises, and wires dug into her skin. But it was her eyes that haunted Zoe.

The bewildered, dazed eyes that saw things no one else did.

"Amy, you remember us?" Zoe perched at the foot of the bed while Aiden sat on a stool.

She nodded like it was a chore. "Agent Storm." Her voice came out rough and coarse. "Is this real?" She looked around, tears welling in her eyes. "I can't tell..." She began squirming and her pulse ticked faster. "This isn't real. This isn't..." She began thrashing her body, jerking against the restraints. Her fingers tore at the wires digging into her pallid skin. Monitors blared. A raw, guttural scream clawed its way out of her throat as if her body were rejecting the space around it. A group of nurses burst into the room, pushing Zoe and Aiden to the back.

Zoe watched in horror as they sedated her. "What was that?"

"A woman who doesn't know the difference between what's real and what isn't. That's what spending a long time playing that immersive game does."

Amy's body slackened. Her screams subsided and her breaths became deeper. The nurses left except for one—a middle-aged, no-nonsense one. "She needs to rest. Have you informed her family?"

"They're on their way. But we need to talk to her," Zoe said.

"She's been through severe psychological trauma," the nurse countered. "She's in no state to answer any questions."

"Look, in such cases the first few hours are critical," she explained. "There is a lot of information that is fresh in her brain because she still thinks she's in that environment. The more time she spends away from it in a safe place, the more her brain will start to forget the small details and begin the process of acclimatization by suppression. Whoever did this is still out there." He had been within reach and he had slipped away. Zoe wanted to punch herself. "He'll do it again."

The nurse looked unsure, then Aiden spoke up. "I'm a trained psychologist. I know how to handle this."

"All right. But if this happens again, then I'm kicking you out," she said before leaving the room.

"I'm impressed," Aiden said. "You've been reading up on your psychology?"

"I was just improvising. Can we get anything out of her?" She tipped her chin toward Amy, who was sleepy but alert. "She looks beat."

"It might work out for us. She's sedated, which means lower stress and fear. Though we'll have to talk to her again to get her signed statement."

"One shot is good enough for me," Zoe decided and softened her voice. "Amy, how are you feeling?"

"I'm okay," she whispered, her blinks lazy. "Where am I?"

"You're at the hospital. You're perfectly safe, okay?" Zoe clasped her frail hand in hers.

"Do you mind if we ask you a few questions?" Aiden said. "This will be hard but whatever you can tell us now will be very helpful."

She shuddered. "I don't know... I woke up in the woods and it was like I was being hunted." Her eyes were still glazed over, seeing images that were not real.

Zoe looked at Aiden, whose mouth was pursed tight. "Amy, I'm Dr. Wesley. I think you remember me. You were shown intense images and videos for hours on end. They weren't real."

"But they could have been... I felt it all."

"Do you remember what happened at the gas station?"

She closed her eyes. "I'd stopped to get gas. I stepped out but I don't remember anything after that. I think he came up from behind and put something over my mouth. I... I tried to fight him. I swear I did. But I couldn't. Everything went black."

"He probably used chloroform," Zoe said. "Did you ever see his face?"

"No. When I opened my eyes I was at Fun House. Lights were flickering, things were breaking, people screaming... it was awful. It just kept going on and on for so long. I would pass out and when I woke up, I'd be there again."

Zoe clicked her tongue and turned around, running her hands through her hair.

"Did you hear his voice or feel his touch?" Aiden's patience hadn't thinned.

"I don't know..." She groaned. "No... I think there was some grunting. Maybe a voice here or there. He kept apologizing to me."

"Apologizing?" Zoe chewed on the pad of her thumb. Her eyes flew to Aiden. Did the killer feel guilty or coerced? "Did he say why he was doing it?"

"No, it's all a blur now..."

"I know this is going to be hard, Amy, but I want you to focus," Aiden said. "When he took you, do you remember anything at all? The car, his scent?"

She shook her head. "It's all a blank. Trust me, I tried hard to fight the chloroform or whatever he used. But all I could sense was that it was a man. Though..." She squeezed her eyes. "I think he took me somewhere else first."

"Where? Do you remember anything?" Zoe said.

Aiden raised a hand to stop her talking. "We're going to do a light memory technique. You don't have to close your eyes unless you want to. Just... let yourself be back in that place again. Can you do that for me?"

She nodded sleepily.

"Let's start simple. The first time you gained consciousness. What did you feel? Describe it."

"There was... a chair. Metal. Cold. I was tied to it at first. It was bright. I could tell from the blindfold but it wasn't enough to see anything."

"Do you smell anything?"

"I... The woods. It smells fresh. Outdoorsy."

Zoe's breath trapped in her chest. They had located Amy in a storage locker—which meant that she had been moved.

"Did you hear anything?" Aiden pressed.

"I heard his boots when he walked in." The space between her eyebrows wrinkled. "I asked him why I was there. And he... mumbled something under his breath but I didn't quite catch it. I was about to pass out again but then I heard a foghorn."

Aiden frowned. "A foghorn?" She nodded, her eyes still closed. "Okay, just once?"

"I heard it again when he was loading me into the car. It was very clear, very distinct, which I thought was odd since I couldn't smell or hear the ocean." She opened her eyes, tears glistening. "And then I was in that new place that smelled like a basement. Who is he? Did you catch him?"

"Not yet..." Zoe said, remembering how she'd almost had him. "But the sheriff and her team are on site looking for any clues that might lead us to him. Did he say anything about putting that headset on you? Did he do that before in the woods too?"

"Only in the next place, not in the woods." Her voice was breathy. "But I know he wasn't comfortable in the woods. I could tell he was always pacing, mumbling. I don't know why." Her breathing began to even out as the sedative took over.

Aiden walked out of the room—too fast. Zoe excused herself and followed him outside into the hallway. His jaw was locked tight and eyes ablaze. "Aiden, what are you thinking?"

"Jackie killed Annabelle but this killer, maybe Spector, killed Jackie. And he hesitated with Amy."

"Maybe it was easier to kill Jackie because she was also a killer. Does that mean Spector didn't help Jackie kill Annabelle?"

"I don't know..." Aiden rubbed his forehead. "I would say he was more a passive participant or a witness. He was enticed by the violence."

Zoe shifted on her heels, impatience clawing at her when her phone rang. "Ethan, what's up? Find anything?"

"Agent Storm, have you heard from Lisa?" His voice was urgent and wavering.

"No... Isn't she at the scene with you?"

"Damn it!" he growled. "She never made it here. I've been trying her cell but it's turned off and she isn't at the station. But her car is still there. A deputy told me a letter arrived fifteen minutes ago."

Nerves rattled in Zoe's stomach. "What letter?" Aiden's eyes flew to Zoe.

"'Ticktock goes the clock. No more truths and no more lies. Only silence and goodbyes.'"

FIFTY-THREE

Zoe's heartbeats were tied in a strangling knot in her throat. She didn't realize Aiden had snatched the phone from her. She tipped backward, her back pressing into the cold wall, trying to catch her thoughts but they were spiraling into an incoherent mess.

"Storm." Aiden's strong, deep voice pulled her back and centered her. "This is good."

"He took Lisa, Aiden. How the hell is that good?" she yelled, not caring there were witnesses around.

"He's panicking." Aiden leaned closer in her face. "You almost caught him. We rescued Amy, and Ethan just told me that they found the prototype at the storage locker. Taking Lisa wasn't part of the plan. Hence the short poem too."

She patted her cheeks, her muscles spasming everywhere from the panic. "His poem doesn't contain a riddle this time. No puzzle for us to solve."

"He doesn't know what to do. He just fucked up big-time," Aiden said darkly. "Amy mentioned the foghorn."

"Yes. Amy was taken to the woods before he moved her to

the storage locker. She reported hearing a foghorn on two separate occasions. She said it was very clear," Zoe said.

"Foghorn?" Ethan said, and Zoe realized she'd had him on speakerphone the entire time. "There is a lighthouse on the bay. Whenever a ship passes by, it sounds off. It's a few miles from the forest, though. Did she hear it clearly? You sure?"

"She was certain. She heard it twice."

"Do you have a topographical map of the area?" Aiden asked, his eyes brightening with an idea.

"Yeah, back at the substation. I'll get someone to send you a picture right now. Hold up." He put them on hold.

"One of my brothers is an environmental scientist," Aiden explained to Zoe. "Over many holiday dinners, he talked about how sound loves long low clear paths. It travels poorly uphill or through dense uneven forests."

"So we can narrow down the region around the lighthouse," Zoe said. "She heard it distinctly twice. It couldn't have been a mistake."

Aiden's phone pinged just as Ethan's voice came through the phone. "You should have it now."

"I'm looking at it." Aiden zoomed in on the attachment. Zoe peeked over his shoulder at the map riddled with markings. "This is the lighthouse with the foghorn." He tapped a spot. "It has woods on the south, east, and north side. On the south side, there is a Forest Service road, here, these double dashed lines. The north is all uphill and dense, so it wouldn't have been there. But the east side also has dry stream." His finger circled a blue dashed line with a stream symbol. "If you're around there, you'd hear the horn echo down the whole valley like a gunshot."

"I don't know if I have enough resources to check both those sides." Ethan sighed. "I'll have to request help from other counties, unless the FBI can be faster."

"There has to be a way to narrow it down to at least one side," Zoe said. "We don't have time." She chewed on her thumb again—a habit she could tell annoyed Aiden. Lisa's image kept flashing in her mind. "Spector."

"What?" Aiden said.

"The Cyber Division had gotten back to us after tracking Spector's IP address down to a certain area." Zoe pulled up that email on her phone. "There has to be an overlap."

They huddled over their phones. Due to VPN masking, the net they had cast was too wide. But then Zoe compared it to the woods around the lighthouse. "It's the woods on the east."

The greenness was overwhelming. It filled her senses. She felt it everywhere inside her. Just damp, wet, green earth.

The tree line was a black wall against the deepening twilight. Towering Douglas firs and western red cedars crowded the trail, their trunks thick with moss and glistening with rain and their canopies blotting out most of the sky. The scent of wet pine and decaying leaves was rich enough to taste. She felt it coat her tongue.

"Are we close?" she asked Ethan, who seemed to navigate the tangled roots with more swiftness. It was still a big search area with mossy, feathery trees. Over six deputies had joined Zoe and Aiden to search through the woods. They had decided to divide and conquer.

"Just westward here." He gestured at the path that curved around the slope.

She squinted into the gloom ahead. The rain had come and gone earlier, leaving the forest drenched and silent. So silent that it pressed against her ears. There were no more tracks past this point, just slick underbrush and the uneasy stillness that set her teeth on edge. She couldn't imagine wandering these woods. The ever-present drizzle alone irritated her.

"I think I see something," she said.

The ground dipped into a narrow, winding trench where

the soil was pale. Exposed roots snaked from the banks like tendrils. Smooth stones and scattered branches. Moss clung to rocks in shaded pockets. Water once rushed through here.

"Do you copy?" Ethan said on his walkie-talkie but there was too much static. "Shit. I can't hear anyone."

"I'll stay here. You try to get someone."

Ethan disappeared behind her, still talking over his walkie-talkie. As Zoe continued scoping the area, she made a turn and noticed a cabin cloaked in fog. The roof was caved in on one side, the wood soft and gray. Ferns sprouted from the porch and the forest swallowed it whole.

Her hand hovered over her gun in the holster. She crouched low, eyes scanning the clearing. No movement. No sound. She edged closer, boots quiet on the soft ground.

Nothing.

The woods hushed as wind whooshed through. She peered around, searching in the dying light when she saw something.

Her heart kicked.

A few of the trees had a piece of cloth wrapped around the branches. Red cloth with a blue border like it was marking specific spots in the area.

There was something familiar about this. It was tucked somewhere in the folds of her memory. It came to her with a sudden force, every sense on fire.

The scarf Lisa had mentioned finding at home.

Jim Gray.

With a shaking hand, Zoe's hand went to her phone and then something hit the back of her neck. Sharp and pinching. A dart. An awareness whispered through her mind—she was being hunted.

FIFTY-FOUR

Eyes squeezed closed.

Ragged breathing.

Zoe tripped over a root. Her body fell like her bones were melting.

Her fingers found the dart buried in the back of her neck. She pulled it out and then felt three quick darts shoot into her upper back. "Ah!" A scream leaped out of her throat.

She rolled out of the way, curling her body under a root concealed by a bush. Something was happening to her. Her vision was sharpening and cracking. Her heart was thundering against her rib cage.

Adrenaline-laced darts.

Zoe peeked over the ledge and spotted Jim holding a rifle pointed in her direction. "Don't do this, Jim!"

Silence.

"You're only making things worse!" She breathed through the pain.

Instead, Jim floated toward her with the rifle.

Jim Gray. Forty-two. Software engineer. The sheriff's husband. Nerd, quirky, the kind of man that got on with everyone. She was met with stony silence for the longest time before he finally spoke, his voice throaty and deeper. "Finish the game."

As the adrenaline began to soak in, the pain began to dissipate. Zoe felt her identity was dissolving and someone else long dormant inside her was resurfacing.

Emily.

Emily shot up and ran through the woods just like she had many, many times in her dreams. Zoe didn't like the green, didn't like nature, it was too unpredictable, too obscure. But Emily had thrived in places Zoe hadn't.

Jim was right behind her, his footsteps loud, the rifle clicking and shooting. She ducked. It missed her, striking the tree next to her. Then another one. This dart hit the back of her knee and she lurched forward, crashing against another tree. It should have hurt but the pain was dulled by the fierce hormone pumping through her veins.

Everything was too fast, too bright, and too *big*. She was short of breath, and sweat matted her skin. A heaviness began pulling her chest inward.

He hadn't said, "Play the game." He'd said, "Finish the game".

The cabin. Lisa. Lisa was the key. She must be inside. The cabin was farther away now. She picked up a rock and threw it to the other side. A rabbit must have skittered across because the grass rustled. Through the bushes, she watched Jim head in the other direction. Seizing the opportunity, she sprinted toward the cabin.

Her heart thudded in her ears. She didn't mind the slippery ground with roots waiting to trap the unsuspecting walker, or the cobwebs of moss that brushed her face. She blended in with her surroundings, ducked low, crawling to the cabin on her elbows and knees.

A shot rang out. Loud. Making everything shake.

In the haze of the stress, she realized it was a gun. Not a rifle shooting hunting darts. She patted her body. Relief surged through her feeling her gun was in her holster. Where did Jim get a gun? And why was her skin thrumming so hard?

Shit. Shit. Shit.

If Jim was shooting a gun, he was desperate. She finally reached the cabin. It was dark and damp and cold inside. An unconscious Lisa was splayed on the ground, a trail of blood running down the side of her face.

"Lisa!" Zoe ran to her and felt her thready pulse. She was alive. But she had been hit on the head. Zoe grabbed her phone, but there was no signal. Lisa's gun was missing—that was likely what Jim had fired.

What was going to happen now? There was only one way to finish the game. It was too harsh, though. Zoe would have never done it.

But Emily could. Emily could do everything Zoe couldn't.

With a grunt, she hauled Lisa's body up, transferring her weight onto her, and limped outside the cabin.

"Jim," she yelled, her voice echoing through the woods. The skin on her back with the buried darts began to throb. "Show yourself or I'll kill her!" She pressed the gun against the neck of Lisa, who was still passed out and like a deadweight on her.

Jim appeared from in between the trees with his blank, startled stare. With a trembling hand he pointed a gun at her. His rifle hung over his shoulder.

"Game over, Jim." She bared her teeth. She was angry, *furious*. How dare he hunt her? How dare he treat her like an animal?

Seeing Lisa, his attitude changed. "Don't hurt her," he said softly.

"Then put the gun down."

He exploded. Hair wild, face pale and streaked with dirt and tears. He marched up to them with a frantic energy that would have normally unnerved Zoe. "I can't be here, Agent Storm. You don't understand, do you? It's one foot in this world and one foot in the other. I can't promise that I won't do it again. I can't help myself."

She swallowed hard, her breaths choppy and seething. "I don't care about your excuses. You don't get to hunt me or anyone else anymore. Put the gun down or watch your wife die."

"But how do you know this is real?" he asked hysterically. "What if tomorrow you woke up and someone removed the headset and told you that Zoe Storm was just a character you were playing? That *this* is what wasn't real?"

If only Jim knew the irony of the moment. If only he knew he wasn't dealing with Zoe Storm right now. "Do you love her?"

"Of course I love her! She's the one, my true love. What did I do? I just wanted to play..." His eyes bounced around, unable to focus on anything. She could see the madness seeping out of him, the chaos unspooling. He was trying to get a grip on in his surroundings. But the dissociation was too strong and jarring.

"Are you going to put the gun down or what?" She pulled Lisa harder against her. She'd begun to twitch, like she was about to wake up. "She's going to die knowing you did nothing to protect her."

His breathing sped up. His mouth fell open. A sob caught in his throat. "No."

"For Lisa."

"*Who?*" he asked.

Then his eyes locked onto hers. And something shifted. The distressed confusion and agony dissolved into blankness. There was a clarity in his eyes. His mind had decided what was real and what wasn't. She knew what was coming. She aimed the gun at him but he was quicker.

The sound was deafening and sliced through the thick white noise of the forest, scattering birds into the sky.

The world folded.

She staggered back, winded. Pain bloomed like fire beneath her ribs, ricocheting through her body. She buckled to the ground, the trees a blur spinning out of focus. As her eyes started to close, she slipped into darkness, waiting for Zoe to save Emily again, but instead she heard Aiden's faint voice.

FIFTY-FIVE

The first thing Zoe felt was the weight.

Not pain but heaviness. Like someone had poured concrete into her body.

Then came the light, sterile and sharp, penetrating closed eyelids. She turned her head instinctively, but even that small movement sent a ripple of nausea through her. Something tugged at her arm—an IV. Her throat was dry, raw, and incredibly painful, like she'd swallowed glass.

A distant beeping rose in the background. Her thoughts were wispy, floating in the air like smoke. The memories started to trickle back. She remembered a broken bridge, a stream of river with churning water, and skeletal trees twisting in odd shapes, poking the sky.

And then she remembered her body caving in, her stomach folding, her back smacking against a rock, her hand drenched in sticky, gushing blood.

She blinked. The world swam into shape.

White ceiling tiles. The faint smell of antiseptic. Machines she couldn't name blinking softly around her. A curtain pulled halfway around her bed.

Hospital. *Thank God.* She wasn't dead.

The ache in her side was deep and dull, but alive. Like something had burrowed its way in there and gone to sleep. She tried to move her hand. It responded, barely. Her fingertips felt like they were wrapped in cotton.

A moment later, the curtain was drawn back.

A nurse in soft blue scrubs smiled down at her. "You're awake," she said gently. "Take it easy. You've been through a lot."

Zoe blinked up at her, her mouth dry, her mind full of holes. "What..." she managed to rasp. It burned. "What happened?"

The nurse reached for a cup of water with a bendable straw and held it out. Zoe sipped greedily, coughing once, then drank more. "You're in hospital," the nurse said. "You came out of surgery a few hours ago. How do you feel right now?"

"Like I've been run over by a truck," she grumbled weakly.

The nurse chuckled. "The bullet went through your lower left side. Nicked a rib but missed anything vital. You were very lucky." Zoe resisted the urge to roll her eyes at the word *lucky*. "Your vitals look good. The doctor will come see you soon. He's wrapping up another surgery right now."

"How did I get here?"

"You have resourceful friends," the nurse said vaguely before leaving. Zoe searched for her phone when the curtain was drawn back again and two figures approached.

Aiden and Simon. Both tall, wearing black coats, a grim expression on their faces.

"Either you're here to abduct me or you're male strippers. I can't tell," Zoe said.

"What's wrong with you?" Simon pinched the bridge of his nose while Aiden's mouth twitched, holding back a smile.

"Many things. Why do you think I took my sweet time with that psych evaluation?" Aiden said and then turned to Zoe. "How do you feel?" His body was wired and stiff.

"Peachy. Wait, you were there. You brought me here."

Aiden nodded. "It wasn't long after we heard the gunshot that we found you."

"What happened to Lisa and Jim?" she asked.

"Lisa's fine. Just minor injuries. Jim is in custody." Zoe didn't miss Aiden's hardened stare.

Zoe glared at Simon, the question burning in her eyes—why was he here? She knew why. All three of them did. The dull pain in her abdomen was nothing compared to the awkwardness that hung low in the room like smoke.

"I don't think you're allowed more than one visitor at a time here, so I'll wait outside." Aiden rubbed the back of his neck. "I'll see you in a bit."

Once Aiden had left, Simon relaxed and sat on a chair next to her. His hand reached out to hold hers, but she pulled it back. "Simon... you didn't have to come all the way."

He looked crushed. "I get a call from Aiden that you were shot and you think I wouldn't come."

The memory came back in fragments. Was someone else there too? She almost had it but Simon distracted her. "Z, I'm sorry. I shouldn't have sent you on this case."

"You didn't send me. The riddle was addressed to me, remember?"

"I suppose." He looked like he wanted to say something else but held back. "So you and Aiden, huh? Is that why you haven't been returning my calls?"

"Me and Aiden?" she squeaked. "What?"

"Oh." He frowned. "He's been worried sick about you. I figured..."

A warm feeling rose in her chest as she shook her head. "Nothing is going on."

"Good." The edges of his face softened.

But why did the denial feel like a lie?

. . .

"Are you insane, Storm?" Aiden's eyes were wide as Zoe dragged herself into work next morning.

"Yeah, have you met me?" she quipped, suppressing a wince.

There was one part of the job that Zoe despised almost as much as breaking the news to someone that their loved one had been killed. It was the part that nobody thought much about. When she would single-handedly tell someone that their loved one had killed someone.

Ironically, the weather had turned bright and sunny. The first day Zoe had seen the sun in Pineview Falls. A day with blue sky with cotton-like clouds, dappling shadows on sidewalks, and scent of spring.

Zoe watched Ethan remove the missing person poster of Amy from the bulletin board with a satisfied smile on his face.

Since Amy had been found alive, the tension that had held the substation in a perpetual chokehold had dispersed. The deputies' smiles and shoulders were more relaxed, conversations were less somber. Pineview Falls had been stuck in a stress position for almost two weeks and was finally uncoiling, unwinding, and finding its flow again.

A smile cracked on her face. But then she saw Lisa coming out of the washroom, looking pale. When they locked eyes, Lisa's face fell.

"How's she taking it?" she asked Aiden, who was absorbed in some report.

"She's in denial. Nonreactive. Classic first response." He didn't look up.

"They're bringing Jim up from holding. Apparently, Ethan tried to talk to him yesterday but he didn't get anything out of him."

"Did you try?"

"No, I spent the night at the hospital," he said fleetingly. "Hmmm." He frowned, distracted.

"What is it?"

"I'm just going through the reports, making sure everything is airtight for when we hand over the evidence to the DA's office. When did you say Viktor showed up at Jeff Gold's house?"

Zoe's stomach folded. "Why is that important right now?"

"Because the cases are connected. Jeff Gold sent you Jackie's letter, so whatever happened there has to go in here." He flipped through the pages. "The timeline doesn't make sense."

Shit. The alarm in Zoe's head went off like a siren. She scrambled to come up with an excuse as Aiden kept connecting the dots.

"You said he was there in less than five minutes after you, but the report says the shooting started fifteen minutes after you said. So you must have had a chance to talk to him." He stared at her. "Storm, what's going on?"

Her face was too hot. She felt her cheeks redden. "Can we talk about this later?"

The next thing she knew she was being dragged away by him.

"You're lying!" Aiden snapped.

"I'm not!" Zoe said, her breaths choppy, her chest heaving. She met his fierce, burning gaze with determination. Seconds ticked by, stretching to infinity as Zoe focused on steadying her breathing and keeping her facial muscles still.

She was skilled at deception but Aiden was better at spotting it.

Strips of flickering white light lit the narrow hallway, which smelled of cleaning product and sawdust. Some people turned around the corner, chuckling and chatting, but they froze when they saw Zoe and Aiden.

Zoe swallowed hard, feeling eyes on them when Aiden

grabbed her by the elbow and pulled her through a door into the empty staircase in the back of the building. "Watch it!"

Aiden let go of her and put his hands on his waist, breathing hard. "Storm, the timeline doesn't make sense. There is a discrepancy in the reports."

Damn it. "Maybe it's a mistake. I must be misremembering." Behind his glasses, his eyes narrowed. She pressed her back into the cold wall. The heating didn't permeate this section of the building, where her breaths seemed to bounce around the concrete walls. She desperately tried to think of an excuse, an explanation, a believable lie.

She drew a blank. "Have you told anyone?"

"No one." He seemed offended. "Storm, you know something, don't you? What are you hiding? You aren't *misremembering* anything. It's obvious by your face."

Zoe knew things—her mother's connection to the case, Jeff Gold being Gina's father and the fact that she didn't *have* to shoot her mother's killer, Victor, dead. It had unsettled her, unnerved her. "I need time."

He was puzzled. "Time for *what*?"

"To think and... just give me time. I need to figure something out." Her tongue lay heavy in her mouth. The words were on the verge of spilling out. Aiden's eyes bore into hers. "Please, Aiden. Just trust me."

The corner of his mouth twitched as he scoffed. "I didn't expect dishonesty from you, Storm."

Zoe felt the full force of his words. He left her standing on the staircase. The sound of the door slamming shut bounced around and the air whooshed. When she was alone, heaviness made her chest sink closer to her spine.

A scream was knotted in her throat. She clutched it tight and breathed through it. She had tampered with evidence to protect the memory of her mother.

She went back out at the sound of a mild disturbance. Jim

had clomped in, wearing a hoodie that looked too familiar, his shoulders hunched and his eyes lined with shadows. His hands were cuffed and a uniform was with him. His disoriented gaze was taking in the station when they latched on to Zoe's. Instinctively, his hand touched the shoulder he'd injured in the chase.

Zoe tried to stay composed. She didn't want to give away how affected she was. Jim had seen a different side of her, a different her. Someone who rarely surfaced. But she was too shaken by Aiden's outburst.

Zoe and Aiden were heading toward the interrogation room when Lisa blocked their way, frenzied. "Let me talk to him."

"Lisa... I know this must be unimaginably hard," Aiden said.

She glared at him. "Yes. You can't imagine it."

"He was the one who lured you and abducted you, Lisa," Zoe said. "I confronted him. He struck me with the darts and then shot me."

"There must be some misunderstanding! I bet you cornered him and that was just his reaction to being wrongly accused. This is a man who struggles to shoot a deer!" Angry tears bubbled in her eyes. "Listen," she wagged her finger at them, "I get you're the suits and I know I'm still a small-town sheriff with a cheating husband, but you're not putting this on him so that you can win some medal. He's innocent. The person who did this is out there and will do it again."

"Jim is wearing the same hoodie as the man I chased at the storage facility—"

"A lot of people own a hoodie like that."

"I can tell his left shoulder is injured, which is the same as the killer's injur—"

"He might be feeling stiff," she volleyed back defiantly. "What else you got?"

"The scarf, Lisa," Zoe said softly. "That scarf you found at your place. It was used to mark the area. And we are getting his devices to confirm he's Spector."

Aiden spoke in a low voice. "Individually, these are coincidences. Together, it's a smoking gun. Let's just talk to him for a minute, okay?"

"I want to be there."

"If you feel we aren't approaching him the right way, then step in at any time. Agent Storm and I won't stop you."

Lisa's eyes dropped, her lips quivered. She thought about it and then gave a slight nod.

With a sigh of mild relief, Zoe followed Aiden into the room. She didn't know what was worse, Lisa's grief or the waves of anger unfurling from Aiden directed at her. He wouldn't even look at her, his face hard. It left her cold.

Jim sat nervously at the table in the middle of the room. His disheveled hair made him look younger. He looked so harmless, not at all foolhardy. A man with an abundance of aimless intelligence was a dangerous man.

"The FBI is getting your computer from your place and CSU is combing through the crime scene at the storage facility where Amy Andrews was discovered," Zoe said. "Are we going to find your DNA there? Are you Spector?"

Jim flinched. His eyes turned red like the tip of his nose. "Where's Lisa?"

"She's taking a moment to herself," Aiden said. "Amy will identify your voice. You talked to her."

It was written all over his face. The guilt. The shame. The fierce denial. He swallowed hard and flared his nostrils. "Lisa doesn't want to talk to me, does she?"

"She will. I know much she matters to you." Aiden played him like a fiddle. "She's the only one that tethers you to this world."

Jim's jaw ticked.

"You've been living inside something. And sometimes... that kind of world gets its hooks into you. Blurs the line," Aiden continued. "It splits your identity into two. There's a Jim in this world, the real world, and there's a Jim online."

He exhaled sharply. "You think I'm crazy."

"No," Zoe blurted and took a staggering breath. He had seen her duality, just like she had seen his. In a way, it wasn't Zoe and Jim who had had that violent confrontation in the woods.

"I think you're wired differently. I think reality stopped giving you what you needed, and something else did. Something artificial," Aiden said.

"What was it, Jim?" Zoe asked. "What happened to you?"

"My father tried so hard to turn me into a hunter." His eyes were far off. "I was only thirteen when he gave me a gun. But damn me, I could never go for the kill. Even when I went hunting with Lisa. She always pulled the trigger but I couldn't."

"Why?" Zoe asked.

He shrugged. "I guess I always knew I wasn't good enough. I sat there watching the world go by, people grow and expand and make progress in their careers, and I just kept going back to that same memory with my father when he was disappointed in me for not being able to hunt, for not being able to be a man."

"That memory was the ignition point," Aiden said.

"It was. It all started from there. And this world continued making me feel smaller. The only time I felt good about myself was when I was playing video games. It gave me purpose," he said. Zoe frowned but waited for him to continue. "It just grows on you. In the beginning, you play for an hour every day. You think it's a hobby. You're just passing the time and taking a break. Then it becomes several hours a day, and before long it starts breaking something inside you. Hesitance. In that world, I could hunt. I could be a real man. I could shoot and kill people... I couldn't do that even to a deer in the real world."

There it was. Aiden had loosened the knob and his madness came rushing out in torrents.

"But even that gets old, doesn't it?" Aiden said gently. "Being a man in the virtual world wasn't enough."

"It was something I had to prove to myself. That itch. That obsession." He shook his head. "My father would be so proud that I finally embraced the violence, embraced the true nature of being a man. Because a real man hunts and provides." A delirious look crossed his face. "I even started to enjoy it. You feel the recoil, the tension, the wind... and then it became easy to lie to myself that it was all a game. That this was also a game." His eyes widened like he had a eureka moment. "What tells you that this place is real?" He looked around. "Because you are *in* it. You feel this desk and chair, you hear those guys talking outside, you can feel the draft from that vent. That's how you know it's real. So that place in the game is real too. The only difference is that you can slip in and out of that world."

"And Jackie understood this?" Zoe said.

"She was the only one who did. Those dates we went on... that's why we connected. We met online, talking about the latest video games." A shadow crossed his face. "She said she and her friend stole some crazy prototype of a game based on the massacre. And I saw an opportunity to get a taste of that violence my father wanted me to know intimately. He told me I had to *earn* my right to be a man."

Zoe suppressed the urge to roll her eyes. But Aiden was fascinated. "And what led to the escalation? Why involve Annabelle?"

"I don't know." He yanked at his messy hair. "It was Jackie's idea. She was addicted. She wanted the real thing. She said Annabelle was just playing the role of the victim. I didn't know, I wasn't there for any of it. She told me later."

"The stress killed Annabelle from the hunting darts," Zoe said, unable to keep the bite out of her tone. She saw Aiden shoot her a warning look. "She has two children, Jim. How does that make you feel?"

"Of course, that wasn't your intention," Aiden said. "You didn't lay a finger on Annabelle, did you?"

"Exactly. Jackie said she'd take care of the body but then she started talking about getting someone else. But I wanted to give it a try." He was high on the memory, headiness glistening in his eyes. "I couldn't believe I did it. What I wasn't able to achieve with a deer, I was able to do with Jackie."

"Why did you hunt Jackie if you were a team?" he asked.

"I guess somewhere deep down I was angry and shocked at what she'd done. Here I was, unable to hunt a deer, and this woman had hunted a human being." He bared his teeth, self-loathing shimmering in his eyes. "I was also disgusted at her and myself and I just... didn't plan any of this; I didn't even use the contraption on her. But when I started shooting, I finally felt that thrill, that power my father felt. Lisa feels... I just kept going and going. She morphed into something else altogether. When it was over, I left her at Fun House because that's what she would have wanted her final resting place to be, considering her obsession."

"Then why did you send us a letter?" Aiden asked. "If you didn't plan this."

"Because then everything became this... game!" His eyes were ablaze. "Don't you get it? There is no distinction anymore. It all merges into one." His teeth dug into his lips. The frustration poured out of him. "I continued what Jackie started. I was so afraid that I wouldn't be able to do it again. Be a true man. Hunt. Be a predator. This town constantly talks about the massacre as if it's a thing of the past but it's not. It's happening. Right now! Do you see it?"

"Why did you take Amy?" Zoe asked.

"I knew about her through Jackie... She always talked about how accomplished her step-sister was. I looked her up and she was head of R&D of a gaming company. Ironically, I'd applied for a job in her department but didn't even get an interview.

Can you believe that? I went to a better university. I have plenty of experience. And this woman decided my résumé wasn't good enough for an interview. I thought about how it would feel to hunt someone like her. If Jackie made me feel like a man... then..." He closed his eyes, wincing.

"You couldn't do it," she finished for him.

He shook his head slowly. "First, I took her to the woods where Annabelle and Jackie were killed. But I just... something stopped me. I thought a change of location would do, so I took her to the storage locker where the prototype was stored. I put a headset on her because I needed time to find the guts to do it. But I..." He played with his fingers. "I lost it again, didn't I? That feeling, that rush, that power."

Coldness seeped into Zoe's chest. Suddenly, the door to the room flew open, banging against the wall. Lisa whirled past them and flew at Jim. His chair fell with him and both were on the floor.

"How could you?" she cried, throwing punches at him as he held his hands up to shield his face.

"Lisa!" Zoe wrapped her arms around her middle to try to pull her away but the sheriff was writhing and convulsing.

"You ruined my life!" Lisa screamed at the top of her voice. "You've taken everything from me!"

"I'm sorry," Jim sobbed, curling into a ball on the floor. "I'm so sorry."

Seconds later, the room was filled by deputies. Two of them took Jim away while Ethan put his arm around Lisa trying to calm her down.

"Well, we got a confession," Zoe said to Aiden. "He'll plead insanity."

"He should. You saw how his sense of reality is totally distorted."

It had started off so simply. A bad economy led to a job termination. A brief affair, a detour in a complicated marriage.

A man who immersed himself in video games to kill time. And then it went from that to being fun, and from fun to an addiction, and after addiction came disillusionment.

"It's not simply disillusionment. What we're seeing is a classic case of unresolved identity conflict. He internalized a hypermasculine ideal. Domination, control, predation, all reinforced by early family dynamics. Likely socialized to believe that power equals worth, especially in relation to women. As his external success grew, so did his internal fracture: he felt repressed, emasculated, possibly by the shifting power dynamics around him. When he could no longer assert control in socially acceptable ways, the aggression turned inward and then outward again. What he couldn't do with animals, he redirected. It's a displacement of primal instinct layered over decades of feeling inferior."

Silence hung between them. Zoe lifted her eyes to him. Was he still mad at her? He wasn't volatile but there was a sudden distance between them she couldn't breach.

FIFTY-SIX

Lisa was shaking uncontrollably.

Zoe wrapped a blanket around her and handed her a cool glass of lemonade. She lowered herself to her level, and looked her in the eye. "Lisa..."

"I didn't know." She sputtered out the words, her face frozen in uncanny horror. "I swear... I... Oh my God, how could this have happened? Who is he?" Her red, teary eyes stared up at Aiden. "Who is he?"

Zoe couldn't answer. The duality inside Jim was so stark, like an inner fault line that had finally caused a crack too deep that it swallowed everyone around him. It was too close to home. As she watched Lisa, she wondered if this was the fate that awaited Gina too. If one day Zoe would snap and be consumed by that rage preserved for organized fights and do something so catastrophic.

Perhaps it was a good thing that Aiden was mad at her. He didn't need to get close. No one should.

A tall, imposing woman with flaming red hair and harsh but striking features arrived around the corner—Mackenzie Price.

"Detective Price?" Zoe blinked in confusion and the memory hit her. "Oh my God, you were there!"

"I need your assistance on a case, so I came to Pineview Falls." She folded her arms. "I found out at the sheriff's department where you were. When I got there, you had already been shot and Dr. Wesley was standing over you. For a second, I thought he was the one that shot you."

"I don't like guns." Aiden shook his head.

"That's it? Not, 'Why would I shoot Zoe?' You're the one who needs a psych evaluation. Ow!" A string of pain pulsed down her side when she shifted slightly. This was going to be a long recovery.

Aiden's lips twitched. She bit her tongue, remembering their earlier hostile exchange.

"She was the one who shot Jim in the knee," Aiden said.

"And that's why I was in hot water for getting involved in a face-off in a federal case. Sorry, I couldn't visit you in hospital. I was busy giving my statement and apologizing to the higher-ups."

"Thank you." She smiled weakly at Mackenzie and glanced at the shining ring on her finger. "How's Nick doing?"

"He's a bit of a hard-ass as the sergeant." When her phone chirped, she frowned. "I'll be back in a minute."

"I'm sorry, Storm," Aiden said softly, his face haggard. "I shouldn't have reacted the way I did."

"I get it." She played with a loosening thread on her sweater. "I don't know what I was thinking." She took a hitching breath, her body tensing. "I was protecting my mother, Aiden."

He was taken aback. "Your mother? What does that have to do with any of this?"

"She was the woman who distracted David while Viktor sabotaged the haunted house. This was Red Trigger business."

"They wanted a bunch of teenagers dead?"

"Just one. Michael. The son of some developer who was

interfering with their operations. They needed to send him a message, and the rest of the kids were collateral damage."

"Your mother worked for them?"

It was the hardest confession of Zoe's life. But she couldn't bring herself to share with anyone that Rachel was a hitman for the organization. She had taken lives.

"I still don't know entirely what her role was but I guess I just wanted to protect her memory."

"I understand now."

"Thanks. Please tell me you didn't call my sister." She threw her head back.

He laughed. "I told them not to. I figured I should ask you first."

"Good. Gina doesn't handle bad stuff very well." She bit her lip, a heavy weight sitting on her chest. There was that message from Jeff that she was supposed to convey to Gina. How was she going to do that? Where on earth would she begin?

"Storm..." Aiden fumbled to find the right words, sounding unsure. He never did that. He was always certain and calibrated in his responses. "About Red Trigger, I was—"

Mackenzie returned. "Sorry, that was Nick. He was just checking up on me."

"I never asked you, what case did you need my help with?" When Mackenzie's eyes flickered to Aiden, Zoe assured her. "I trust him. It's okay."

Mackenzie's face turned serious. "Nick and I have been looking into a cold case from about a decade ago. A homicide. With the new DNA ancestry technology, we sent an old sample for retesting." She paused and took a shuddering breath, like she was almost second-guessing herself. "There was a fifty percent match... to you."

"What?" Zoe said. She felt everything tilt and go out of focus. "What does that mean?"

"It's a sibling match," Mackenzie continued slowly, gauging

her reaction. "I know you have a sister who lives on the East Coast. But this DNA is male. Do you have a half-brother?"

Zoe had no idea. She couldn't breathe. Her pulse was skyrocketing. A cold, brutal sensation coated her bones. Aiden was at her side, telling her to calm down. "No, I had no idea."

Mackenzie looked down, biting her lip. "I had a feeling you didn't, which is why I wanted to break the news to you in person."

Zoe didn't know how many more secrets there were for her to unearth. But she knew deep down that this could finally lead her to the mastermind behind her mother's death.

She was going back to Lakemore.

EPILOGUE

The drone of the sheriff's station was comfortingly dull. The sound of computers buzzing, phones chirping now and then, and the low murmur of conversation. Lisa Gray sat at her desk, halfway through a stale cup of coffee, pretending to care about the number of unopened emails on her screen.

There was a comfort in slipping back into what was familiar. She decided that she liked predictability—she knew the sound her chair made when she swiveled, how lukewarm the coffee that dribbled out of the machine was, and how the receptionist—an old lady civilian volunteer—would hum the same tune every morning.

Like a warm blanket after a storm.

But something was different. The picture of her and Jim she kept on her desk was missing. Her entire being was fragmented. There was the Lisa who was the wife of a murderer, and there was the Lisa who showed up at work.

The first day she'd arrived all eyes had been drawn in her direction, their gazes sticky and stinging. She'd left early with tears bubbling in the back of her throat. But the next day, she showed up again. It was the only life she knew.

These boring brown walls, the slow Internet, and sullen, gray skies.

Across from her, Deputy Toby cracked sunflower seeds between his teeth and let the husks fall into a paper cup.

"You see that raccoon video I sent you?" he asked, not looking up.

Lisa didn't even pause in her typing. "The one where it steals the pizza?"

"Yeah. Clever little bastard."

"They're getting bolder," she said, sipping her coffee. "Next thing you know, they're gonna want our badges."

Toby chuckled, feet up on his desk. "Why are you still here, Lisa?"

"What do you mean?"

His chipper demeanor dimmed. "You helped crack open a big case with the FBI. And this county won't let you forget the scandal. We're small-town people."

She smiled faintly, but it didn't reach her eyes. "I'm fine, Toby. This is my home. Why should I uproot everything when I did nothing wrong?"

The revelation had clogged her senses. She was cloudy and distracted. Maybe she was making a mistake by staying. Maybe she wasn't thinking straight anymore. These past few days in particular, Jim's betrayal was sitting inside her stomach like a ball of gunk. She would wake up in the middle of the night, sweating and nauseated.

But this morning, her mind whispered something to her.

Her hand drifted to her stomach in a quick, unconscious motion before she stood.

"Back in a sec," she said, grabbing her phone and heading down the hall.

The bathroom was cold, the kind of cold only bad lighting and old tile could make worse. She locked the stall and pulled the small pharmacy bag from inside her jacket.

Her fingers moved quickly. The box crinkled open and the test unwrapped. She stared at it for a second longer than she needed to—then did what she came to do.

Time stretched while she waited and exited the stall. She leaned against the sink, arms crossed, watching the second hand of her watch tick by.

Finally, she looked down.

Two lines.

Her breath caught, stuck somewhere between her chest and throat. For a second, everything stopped moving, like the world had been wrapped in glass. A single breath and everything would come crashing down.

She turned to the mirror.

Her reflection stared back, stunned and pale. Awkwardness flared, steeling into full-blown panic. She turned on the tap and splashed cold water over her face.

The one thing she'd wanted for years and now she had it. Did she even want this anymore? What the hell was she supposed to do now?

A knock sounded at the door.

"You fall in or what?" Toby joked.

She closed her eyes for a beat. Her voice cracked. "I don't know."

* * *

The crystal-clear clarity came to Dawn one rainy morning.

It was a soft, persistent patter against the windows. Outside in the gardens, she could see her daughter's grave. The house had been built in such a way that it was visible from every window. She had spent years drowning in the grief of living without her daughter. That's why she had never moved, why she had kept the view of her grave. She wanted to stare her pain right in the face to defeat it. But over the years, she had been buried deep under it.

When David walked into the kitchen, she was nursing a hot tea. "She was always jealous of you."

David froze in his tracks. Dawn had never talked about her to him. It was a poisonous subject that percolated between them. "Why?"

"Because I gave you more attention. You were my firstborn. That's the thing about that first child. Love is equal, but the impact isn't. Your first child changes you and the rest just grow from what you've already become." She looked up at him. Her eyes were red-rimmed, exhausted. "And then losing your child destroys you."

He winced like she'd slapped him. "Mother, you have *no* idea the guilt I carry—"

"I know, my sweet child." He almost reeled from her softness. It was a side to her that he hadn't seen in decades. "I used to only think about you and your future, and I neglected her and minimized her achievements. And now I've lived the majority of my life only thinking about her and trying to find my way back to who I was. But I never will. I have accepted that."

A long silence hung between them. Thunder rolled in the distance.

"I didn't just lose a sister that day. I lost a mother too." David sat next to her, staring out the window.

"When did we start hating each other so much, David?"

He scoffed. "We don't hate each other, Mother. We're just angry. All the time."

Dawn placed the bottle of her pills silently on the counter between them. She didn't look at David but heard his breath hitch.

Another silence stretched—this time it made her skin crawl, like something ancient was shifting between them.

"I've hated you," she admitted at last. "Every goddamn day. But not because you failed her. I hated you because you reminded me that I failed her too."

"You've put me down. Every single opportunity you reminded me that I wasn't good enough and that the purpose of my life was to bear your wrath and be punished for being negligent that one night."

"And so you decided to slowly kill your own mother." Her voice cracked and her eyes stung with tears.

His nose turned red as he sniffled, tears running down unchecked. "I... I don't know, Mother. I'm sorry. I didn't know what I was thinking. I didn't know anything anymore."

She reached across the table, her fingers brushing against his hand. For a second, the years melted away, and she was just a mother holding on to her boy. "We've forgotten the love we had, David. We have felt nothing but pain," she said, softly, "but I can't carry it anymore. I'm tired of the weight."

David's shoulders shook. He bit back a sob and covered his face with one hand. She let him wallow in it. She let both of them wallow in it. She was tired of blotting it out. Somewhere she was still holding on to David, that's why she was punishing him by trying to control him.

She could either forgive him or she had to let him go. There was no other way to overcome the pain that haunted her.

Slowly, she pulled her hand away. Her voice came out cold and sharp. "I've accepted I can't forgive you, David. I never will."

He looked up, confused. "What?"

She stood up. Her small frame seemed to fill the room now. "I know what you've been doing. Adam reached out to me and made a deal. Inside scoop on our monumentally messed-up family in exchange for not helping you bring down my company."

His eyes grew large and his body went rigid. "Mother..."

A throng of men in suits and jackets blasted inside the room. The man leading the charge walked straight up to David. "David Harrington, you're under arrest for your involvement in a scheme to manipulate the stock price of a publicly traded company. You are being charged with market manipulation, securities fraud, and conspiracy to commit fraud in violation of federal law."

Dawn tuned out the FBI agent as he recited David his Miranda rights. She turned her back on her son as he was dragged away and out of her life for good.

Now it was just her and her daughter.

* * *

It wasn't often that Zoe visited Rachel's grave. In true Rachel fashion, her mother had wanted to be buried somewhere where it rained and stormed often. Zoe knew her mother had roots in Washington State. She also wondered how the hell they were related when they had nothing in common—except for their patience for tolerating Gina.

The sky hung low and heavy, a thick sheet of gray that pressed down like a weight. Water pooled in uneven patches along the winding cemetery path, reflecting the bare trees that stood like brittle skeletons brushing against the dull afternoon light.

She wrapped her coat around her, moving deliberately through the rows of headstones.

Her boots sank slightly into the wet soil. Her stomach was still tender. The stitches that held together her skin throbbed and stretched with every step she took. In Zoe's time with the FBI, she had never once been shot. Now that a hole that been drilled through her stomach, she felt like a part of her was gone forever.

A roll of thunder and it started to drizzle. Names, dates,

etched words of remembrance blurred under the streaks of water running down the marble like old tears. When she reached a small, plain headstone wedged between two more elaborate stones, her feet stopped moving.

Her breath stuck in her throat. Her eyes fixed on a bouquet of yellow roses resting against Rachel's headstone.

Who was here?

She looked around, but the cemetery was empty. Just rows and rows of stone on a green carpet, not a single shadow in sight on this rainy day. Yellow roses were Rachel's favorite flower. Who would visit Rachel? Gina was back in Vermont and Rachel didn't have any other family or friends—certainly no one who knew she was buried in Lakemore.

"Who's there?" she called out, her voice bouncing back to her. The only reply was the wind, shifting, moving, whispering through the empty spaces.

Her breath fogged as she bent down to pick up the bouquet; the flowers were now soaked in rainwater. There was no card. But there was something else.

Origami. A yellow paper folded into the shape of a dove, inconspicuous and blending with the roses.

She pulled it out and opened it.

Her heart thundered inside her chest.

Viper is coming for you.

A LETTER FROM RUHI

Dear reader,

I want to say a huge thank you for choosing to read *Run for Her Life*. If you enjoyed it, and want to keep up to date with all my latest releases, just sign up at the following link. Your email address will never be shared and you can unsubscribe at any time.

www.bookouture.com/ruhi-choudhary

I would be very grateful if you could write a review. I'd love to hear what you think, and it makes such a difference helping new readers to discover one of my books for the first time.

I love hearing from my readers—you can get in touch through X or Goodreads.

Thanks,

Ruhi

ACKNOWLEDGMENTS

Writing is a lonely job, but publishing is all about teamwork. I'm extremely grateful to my editor Nina Winters for her passion, hard work, and commitment. I thoroughly enjoy developing stories with her.

Big thanks to editors Anna Paterson and Ian Hodder, cover designer David Grogan at Head Design, narrator Stephanie Cannon, and my publicist, Noelle Holten, for their commitment and brilliance. The entire team at Bookouture has been very kind and supportive.

My husband, Aditya, for always encouraging me and being my pillar. My son, Krish, the light in my life. My parents for their love. My sister and friend Dhriti, for always being in our hearts and looking after us. Sasha for always inspiring me. All my friends, especially Rachel Drisdelle, Michelle Feigis, Dafni Giannari, Scott Proulx, Kaushik Raj, and Sheida Stephens for their excitement, sense of humor, and support.

Most of all, I'm grateful to the readers. Thank you so much for taking the time! I appreciate each and every one of you and would love to hear what you thought of the book.

PUBLISHING TEAM

Turning a manuscript into a book requires the efforts of many people. The publishing team at Bookouture would like to acknowledge everyone who contributed to this publication.

Audio
Alba Proko
Sinead O'Connor
Melissa Tran

Commercial
Lauren Morrissette
Hannah Richmond
Imogen Allport

Cover design
Head Design Ltd

Data and analysis
Mark Alder
Mohamed Bussuri

Editorial
Nina Winters
Sinead O'Connor

Copyeditor
Anna Paterson

Proofreader
Ian Hodder

Marketing
Alex Crow
Melanie Price
Occy Carr
Cíara Rosney
Martyna Młynarska

Operations and distribution
Marina Valles
Stephanie Straub
Joe Morris

Production
Hannah Snetsinger
Mandy Kullar
Ria Clare
Nadia Michael

Publicity
Kim Nash
Noelle Holten
Jess Readett
Sarah Hardy

Rights and contracts
Peta Nightingale
Richard King
Saidah Graham

Dear Reader,

We'd love your attention for one more page to tell you about the crisis in children's reading, and what we can all do.

Studies have shown that reading for fun is the **single biggest predictor of a child's future life chances** – more than family circumstance, parents' educational background or income. It improves academic results, mental health, wealth, communication skills, ambition and happiness.

The number of children reading for fun is in rapid decline. Young people have a lot of competition for their time, and a worryingly high number do not have a single book at home.

Hachette works extensively with schools, libraries and literacy charities, but here are some ways we can all raise more readers:

- Reading to children for just 10 minutes a day makes a difference
- Don't give up if children aren't regular readers – there will be books for them!

- Visit bookshops and libraries to get recommendations
- Encourage them to listen to audiobooks
- Support school libraries
- Give books as gifts

There's a lot more information about how to encourage children to read on our websites: **www.RaisingReaders.co.uk** and **www.JoinRaisingReaders.com**.

Thank you for reading.